William Hepworth Dixon

History of Two Queens

I. Catharine D'Aragon. II. Anne Boleyn.

William Hepworth Dixon

History of Two Queens
I. Catharine D'Aragon. II. Anne Boleyn.

ISBN/EAN: 9783741167881

Manufactured in Europe, USA, Canada, Australia, Japa

Cover: Foto ©Andreas Hilbeck / pixelio.de

Manufactured and distributed by brebook publishing software
(www.brebook.com)

William Hepworth Dixon

History of Two Queens

COLLECTION

OF

BRITISH AUTHORS

TAUCHNITZ EDITION.

VOL. 1320.

HISTORY OF TWO QUEENS BY W. H. DIXON.

VOL. I.

HISTORY

OF

TWO QUEENS.

I. CATHARINE OF ARAGON.

II. ANNE BOLEYN.

BY

WILLIAM HEPWORTH DIXON.

COPYRIGHT EDITION.

VOL. I.

LEIPZIG

BERNHARD TAUCHNITZ

1873.

TO

THE DUKE AND DUCHESS

OF

MANCHESTER

THIS

HISTORY OF TWO QUEENS

(COMMENCED AT KIMBOLTON CASTLE MANY YEARS AGO)

IS

GRATEFULLY INSCRIBED.

PREFACE.

To group around the figures of two crowned and starless women the events of which they were the leading types and memorable victims is the purpose of this work. To understand the passion of their lives we must stand amidst the conflicts out of which they came and into which they merged. Each is accepted as a type of what was best and worst in the revolt from Rome and the unfurling of a separate national flag. Each queen became a heroine of her party, and her human nature is forgotten in the cause for which she stood. In fact, we see these women through their children, and we judge of them by what took place in after times. It is through Mary that we guess at Catharine; through Elizabeth that we guess at Anne.

While collecting my materials, I have visited all the places in which my story lies. Many years ago I first went to the Alhambra; and in after years I have visited every other town in which Catharine

lived. The Notes and Documents show the sources
of my information, most of which lies in manu-
scripts; and I have printed in the originals such
passages as support the views most likely, from
their startling nature, to be challenged by those
who know Spain only from books published under
authority of Inquisitors.

My obligations to archivists are endless, and I
will but mention those of Simancas, Alcala, and
Venice. To Sir Thomas D. Hardy, Deputy Keeper
of the Records, my literary debts are very great;
and Don Pascual de Gyangos, Mr. Rawdon Brown,
and Mr. Joseph Stevenson, have rendered me assistance in Spain, Venice, and Rome respectively, for
which my thanks are but a poor return.

> 6 ST. JAMES'S TERRACE,
>   REGENT'S PARK,
>   *March*, 17, 1873.

CONTENTS

OF VOLUME I.

———

BOOK THE FIRST.

BIRTH OF CATHARINE.

BOOK THE SECOND.

CATHARINE'S CHILDHOOD.

BOOK THE THIRD.
ENGLAND.

BOOK THE FOURTH.
BRETON WAR.

BOOK THE FIFTH.
CATHARINE AT GRANADA.

BOOK THE FIRST.

BIRTH OF CATHARINE.

CHAPTER I.

Friends of Light.

1485.

1. FERNANDO was afield against the Moors in what he called a holy war, and Isabel, his consort, was at Cordova, among her children and inquisitors, while a crime that was to ring through earth and heaven was being prepared in Aragon; a crime that was to shake their throne, to draw them up into the north of Spain, to give the Queen a violent shock, to cause the birth of a princess some weeks before her time, to stamp the policy of King and Queen through all their future years.

2. The King was fighting hard, and something had been won. Cartama had been carried at a rush, and Ronda had been taken by surprise. But Loja had defied his arms; the Vega of Granada had been closed against his raids; and Cabra's capture of the Caliph Abd-allah had been avenged by Az-zaghal, that Caliph's uncle, who had routed Cabra in a splendid night attack. The Queen was

caring for her health, for she was near a time when
every one who wished her well was praying that her
saints would bless her with a second son.   Her
only boy, Don Juan, was a feeble child; as comely
as an angel, and as little likely to remain on earth.
All Spain was asking from her house a king, a
warrior, and a man.   But she was mainly busy with
that "new and holy Office," over which her ghostly
father, Tomas de Torquemada, had been called to
reign.

The crime that was to stay the clang of war
was caused by an attempt to plant this Office in
the soil of Aragon, and was concocted by a band
of counts and knights, of advocates and doctors,
who were known as Friends of Light.

3. These Friends of Light were found in every
part of Spain, but chiefly in those ports and districts
which enjoyed some intercourse with Italy — the
land of light.   They were the pupils of Lebrija and
Barbosa; children of the great revival; readers of
the classics; patrons of the printing-press.   At
Seville, Alcala, and Salamanca, many of those
youths who heard the pupils of Landino and Poli-
ticiano lecture on the Greeks, had learned to feel
that Homer and Thucydides might yield them richer
nutriment than any of their Lives of Saints.   These
youths were called Amantes de las Luces, and they
loved a teacher better than they loved a monk.   As
learning was the light of heaven, a man who bore
some portion of that radiance seemed to them a
messenger of heaven.   A man could teach; who
cared to ask if he were Goth or Moor?   To them

he was a master of the liberal arts.   His lore was
precious, and they prized him for that lore.   A
scholar like Antonio de Lebrija, or like Ayres de
Barbosa, found a host of followers in the higher
ranks, and most of all among those noble families
in which the blood was mixed.   Tudela and Lerida
were schools of light.   But the Dominican fathers—
and especially those of Santa Cruz in old Castille—
were up in arms against this pagan learning.   Paul
the Second had declared that he who reads Homer
in his youth, is likely to worship Jupiter in his
middle age.   Supported by this papal verdict, the
Dominican preachers told their hearers that the use
of reading is to learn their duty to the Church,
and that a Christian cannot learn that duty from a
poet who had never heard of Christ.   This pagan
learning was a snare for souls, and he who fell into
the trap was lost to God.

4. In contrast to these ignorant fathers, the sup-
porters of a Greek revival took this name of Friends
of Light.   Though they were scattered up and
down the country, they were strongest in those
provinces and cities where the people had preserved
their ancient rights.   They lay entrenched along
the Ebro, from Tortosa to the Pyrenees.   In every
part of Aragon, the cities had their fundamental
pacts, their local parliaments, their communal laws.
In every part of Aragon the Friends of Light were
many and of high repute.   A mayor was usually a
Friend of Light; a judge was usually a Friend of
Light.   Luis Gonzales, Secretary of State, was ranked
among the Friends of Light.   Gabriel Sanchez, Lord

Treasurer, and his brother Fernando Sanchez, Paymaster General, were considered Friends of Light.
Felipe de Clemente, Protonotary of Aragon, was a
Friend of Light. Alonzo de la Cavalleria, Vice-
Chancellor of Aragon, was a Friend of Light. Pedro
Cerdan, Miguel Coscon, and Martinez Gotor, three
of the leading men in parliament, were Friends of
Light. In truth, the Casa Blanca, where the Cortes
sat in Zaragoza, then a bright and semi-Oriental
palace, standing near the grim cathedral of La Seo,
might be ranked, alike in outward beauty and in
moral purpose, as a House of Light.

5. Among the deputies were many who had
sprung from Oriental roots. Their fathers had submitted to the Cross and suffered baptism by the
Church; but they were thought to nurse a secret
fondness for their ancient faith. They kept their
bodies and their houses clean; no smoke ascended
from their hearths on Friday after sunset; they were
learned, liberal, and alert; they watched the stars,
and understood the course of trade. To fathers
who were hot in zeal and dark in vision, these were
signs of an imperfect faith. Nay, who could tell,
if in their private thoughts these Hebrews never
turned from saints·like Dominic and Francis to
Jehovah? But the men were high in place and
strong in wealth. Fernando's household swarmed
with Jews. When seeking servants who could do
his work, that sovereign never stopped to ask a man
of genius whence he came. His ablest servants
were of Oriental race. Gonzales was of Hebrew
stock. Sanchez, Cavalleria, and Clemente, though

of ancient lineage, had a "taint" of Hebrew blood. Clemente's father had been recently accused by ignorant monks of heresy. Gotor was a Jew in race; Cerdan was a Jew in race. A man who held no public office, yet of higher credit in Fernando's tent than either Sanchez or Gonzales, was Isaac Abravanel, a prince among the Friends of Light. Abravanel was no less eminent for his wealth and learning than for his illustrious birth. Don Isaac, as his people called him, was descended from the House of David, and his family had dwelt in Spain, the second Israel, from the times in which the Temple on Moriah was destroyed. A minister of Affonzo, King of Portugal, he had quitted Lisbon on that ruler's death, and coming to Castille had founded banks, and helped Fernando by his knowledge of the world. Such men as Sanchez and Abravanel mixed easily with the highest class; and families who traced their lineage to the days of Cæsar, and affected to derive their names from those of Hercules, had run their azure blood into these brighter currents of the East. But if these men of liberal mood were strong at court, they were yet stronger in the Casa Blanca. In the court they found some rivals in the knights of Santiago and Calatrava, in the brethren of St. Francis and St. Dominic, in the warlike bishops, cardinals, and monks; but in a free and popular assembly, jealous of their ancient charters and their local laws, these military and religious zealots held no place. Tact, knowledge, eloquence, were required to sway the Cortes. He who knew the history of Rome and

Athens, could display his reading with effect in
Zaragoza and Lerida, where the forms of public
life bore some resemblance to the systems followed
in those ancient states. This knowledge was a
property of the Friends of Light. Nor were these
liberals less renowned in science than in statesman-
ship. Zacuto, the most learned man in Zaragoza,
was a Jew. He filled the chair of mathematics and
astronomy, and his lectures were the chief attraction
of the University. All lay professors in the University were Friends of Light.

6. Among the highest nobles of the realm stood
Blasco de Alagon, Señor of Sastago, and Juan de
Urrea, Señor of Aranda. Blasco de Alagon, owner
of one of the widest lordships in the kingdom, one
of the gayest palaces in the capital, was a scholar
and a friend of scholars. Juan de Urrea, lord of a
princely sweep of mountain frontier, was the chief
of a distinguished race; a race of poets, statesmen,
and divines, who rank among the great celebrities
of Spain. He was a scholar, and a friend of
scholars. Hardly less conspicuous for his birth
and wealth than these great nobles, was their neighbour Juan de Abadia. All were Friends of Light.
Abadia was not free from "taint;" an ancestor
having taken to himself a Jewish wife; but Alagon
and Urrea might have boasted of the bluest blood
in Spain. These magnates were connexions of
Martinez Gotor and Pedro Cerdan. Gotor, a soldier,
was lieutenant of Zaragoza; Cerdan, a civilian,
was an orator of the Casa Blanca. Like their race
and class, these noblemen were Friends of Light.

7. But if the Friends of Light were strong in court and Cortes, country-house and college-close, their enemies, the monks and friars, were stronger in the streets and alleys, by the city gates and on the Ebro banks. The rabble of the town were with the monks; for Zaragoza was a sacred city, blessed by two miraculous virgins, each with a cathedral for her shrine; La Seo, where an image of the Virgin had been heard to speak; Del Pilar, where a. second image of the Virgin had been seen to sit; to each of which a crowd of pilgrims flocked from far and near, who filled the alleys with their fervour, and enriched the craftsmen with their gold. These pilgrims brought with them the savings of their lives. No little of these savings dropped into the sacks of monk and priest; the Lady of the Pillar being a public mendicant, and every one who knelt beside her shrine being told to lay a copper at her feet. All day there was a chink and roll of coin along the marble floor. But every one had part and profit in the pilgrim's purse. A trade was driven in candles, crosses, pictures, rosaries, and charms. A crowd of lepers, slaves, and prisoners, hung about the sacred porch. A thousand smiths and dealers lived by chasing and supplying images of the goddess on her jasper shaft. The shops and inns were fed by these great swarms, not one of whom trudged home from Zaragoza till his final piece was spent. Each citizen, according to his craft, had cause to shout, "Long live our Lady of the Pillar—Santa, Santissima!" Between the fathers who had charge of these cathedrals, and the rabble

who existed on the pilgrims, there were bonds
arising from a common interest and a common
creed. The Friends of Light had no specific ties.
They had no seat, no fund, no general. They were
not an order, and still less a church. For two
things, and for two things only, they had worked
together; in supporting the lectures of men like
Antonio de Lebrija, and in baffling the designs of
men like Tomas de Torquemada.

———————

CHAPTER II.

Order of St. Dominic.

1485.

1. THE Dominican friar, to whom the Queen, while she was still a girl, and living in the convent of Arevalo, had pledged her word that, if she ever came to reign, her task should be to root up heresy from the soil of Spain, had held her sternly to that pledge. No sooner had she seized the crown than she was called upon to yield the first-fruits of her victory to God, by founding in her states a new tribunal of the Church, and giving to the judge of that tribunal an unlimited rule of life and death. A model for the Holy Office, which was Spanish— and not Catholic—in its genius, lay at hand.

2. Domingo de Gusman, a Castillian who is known to later ages as St. Dominic, had founded in the thirteenth century an Order of Preachers, after- wards called Dominicans in honour of their master, with a view to curbing heresy by word of mouth instead of by the civil arm. Domingo heard of men being stabbed and hung for lapse of faith who might have been recovered to the fold by gentler means. He thought it might be well to trust in truth; to wrestle with erroneous doctrine; to rely on reason, eloquence, and art. What sinner could

2*

resist good books, grave sermons, and the precepts
of a holy life? His pupils had been preachers,
teachers, and examples of the faith. They had to
study much, to labour hard, to hold a sober course.
Their only arms being wit and skill, they had to
master many sciences, to gain proficiency in many
arts. Whatever told upon the ear they had to learn,
whatever told upon the eye they had to do. The
ardent spirit of their master lay upon them, and
they touched that spirit with a yet more sacred and
refining fire.

3. The school of Dominic had given the world
such patterns of a Christian life as Walter Mauclerk
of London and Saint Ambrose of Siena; such lights
of learning as Thomas Aquinas and Raymond de
Pegnafort; such eminent writers as Nicolas Trivet
and Pietro Martire; such splendid architects as Sisto
and Ristoro; and such perfect painters as Angelico
and Bartolommeo. Dominic had found his aptest
scholars in Italian cloisters, and in Italy his Order
held a higher rank than it acquired in Spain. At
Florence men were drawn to church by moral force
—the preacher's fervour and the painter's art; at
Seville they were driven to church by bodily fear—
the sight of dark familiars and the smell of burning
flesh. Each country had a method, and a man in
whom that method took a living shape. In Italy,
the chief Dominican was Fra Girolamo Savonarola;
in Spain, the chief Dominican was Fray Tomas de
Torquemada. Fra Girolamo was a man of learning,
an enthusiast for freedom, and a true reformer of
his age. Fray Tomas was a dull and coarse fanatic,

voiceless in the pulpit, ignorant of the arts.   While
Fra Girolamo was listening at the feet of Mirandola,
Fray Tomas was roasting the disciples of Mirandola
in Seville, Cordova, and Jaen.   When Fra Girolamo
became a leader of the liberal ranks in Florence,
Fray Tomas was employed in hunting down the
liberal ranks in Zaragoza.   Fra Girolamo was a
Friend of Light.

4. The Spanish father was a man of sixty-five.
Of noble birth, he chose the hood in preference to
the plume and sword.   A born ascetic, he could
shut his lips on tempting food, and turn his back
on rank and fame.   He loved to hide and shiver in
his cloister at Santa Cruz, which he had got the
Queen to repair for him at Segovia.   He liked to
pierce and tear his flesh, and come into a church
with clots of gore upon his face.   For sixty years
he had done little to excite the wonder of mankind.
As Isabel's confessor, he had won from her that
pledge to root up heresy from the soil of Spain;
but no one knew what use he was to make of the
Infanta's vow; and had he died at sixty years of
age, he might have left behind him an obscure and
blameless note, instead of that red light, which, like
his name, is evermore in human memory a "burning tower."

5. There being an "office of inquiry" in many
cities, the Dominicans of Santa Cruz had asked of
Isabel such a league between their order and the
crown, as would revive this office of inquiry; so
that they might be the judges of opinion, and the
Queen be forced to execute their sentences of death.

The natural seat for such an office was Toledo; but the Queen had shrunk from setting up these brethren in her capital. Toledo was the stronghold of a country ruled by ancient laws and popular magistrates.   The Cortes would protest against illegal fines; the judges might protect their fellow-citizens from arrest.   Carillo, the Archbishop, was at Alcala in bitter mood, disgusted with the court of Isabel, and anxious to restore his lawful Queen. She could not think of asking his consent. Nor would the brethren of St. Francis, jealous as they were of the Dominicans, endure to see them in the capital. Toledo was the city of St. Francis.   Isabel was a Franciscan in the third degree.   The royal children were Franciscans, in accordance with their age and sex. The Cardinal of Spain was a Franciscan. Almost every one at court was either a lay brother or a lay sister of their order.   In Toledo Isabel was building that Franciscan convent of San Juan de los Reyes, which her architects were told to make the grandest edifice in Spain. To fix her holy office in Toledo would have been to plant it in the midst of powerful and vindictive foes.   This office, therefore, had to be established in a city where the crown was not restrained by charters, primates, and religious orders. Seville was a crown estate.   In Seville an inquisitor would have no ancient pact, no modern bishop, and no popular magistrate to fear. The province, as a conquest, was an appanage of the crown.   Mendoza was Archbishop, and the people, who were mostly slaves and villagers, had no rights which they could plead in bar. A colony of Jews had settled in the town; these Jews were rich in gold and jewels; so that wealthy victims could be found at once; and wealthy heretics, whose money might be poured into the royal coffers, were the surest means of proving to Fernando that his consort's holy office was a good and useful court.

6. A Moorish castle, standing on the farther bank, in the rough suburb of Triana, had been offered to the fathers as their seat and jail. This home had suited them. A dark and rambling edifice, it lowered along the Guadalquiver, with a range of vaults below the water line. The gates were covered by a park of guns. Before these gateways spread a net of streets and lanes, in which lay reeking nearly all the filth and refuse of a populous city; gipsies, smugglers, bandits, coiners, runaway monks, and slaves. Some potteries, knackers' yards, and soap-works lay about. All foul, unwholesome trades were banished to Triana; and in this low suburb, where a dozen silver marks would either hire a bravo's knife or buy a gipsy dance, the Dominican fathers held their court of death.

7. Fray Tomas had not been the first inquisitor. When Isabel sent for bulls empowering her Dominicans to judge and punish heretics, a cautious pope had tried to put her off; but she had pressed her suit from day to day; and Rome, not yet aware how far her powers might be abused, had yielded to her wishes. But the church in Spain had been as hard to conquer as the church in Rome. Carillo had withheld his blessing from the work. Talarera had opposed them in the closet and confessional.

Mendoza, though a courtier, had refused to let them labour in his diocese. A scholar, with a scholar's feeling for the power of argument, and a Franciscan's scorn for the Dominicans, he had tried if tracts and books might not achieve the ends expected from the rack and brand. Some months had passed in scattering sheets among the Jews and Moors, until a Jew of Seville, who had read these missives as a challenge, had been bold enough to answer them in print. At once the Order got a license to begin. A Jew who answered for his faith was not to be endured; and in a week the rabble had been treated to an Act of Faith; a pastime more exciting than a bull-fight, even when a matador was gored to death.

The fathers had not laboured long before the King, surprised by the abundant stream of gold which flowed into his coffers, had expressed his warm approval of his consort's Holy Office. But the Roman court had seen less reason to rejoice. The powers conferred by Sixtus had been grossly used, and rather for political than religious ends. His bulls had given the fathers power to bring in such as wandered from the fold; but they had turned these powers against the Jews, who, never having been baptized, could not have wandered from the Catholic fold. In almost every case the motive had been greed of money rather than concern for truth. The fathers, too, had proved themselves unfit to occupy the judgment-seat. They had condemned the innocent; they had violated graves. All honest men were outraged by their deeds; and when the pontiff heard that in a single year two thousand human beings had been burnt in Seville, he was tempted to revoke his breves, though he might have to mortify the Queen. But Isabel told the Pope that things had gone a little wrong through want of caution, but that all would soon be put in order if some aged man, like Fray Tomas, her confessor, were included in the papal patents. Sixtus, willing to believe and to atone, had put the name of Torquemada in his bulls.

8. In no long time Fray Tomas had subdued his colleagues. His relations with the Queen conferred on him a voice which no Dominican brother could resist. If the Dominicans were growing in repute, Fray Tomas was the author of their rise. His pupil, Fray Diego de Deza, had been named preceptor to Don Juan. His colleague, Fra Pietro Martire, was a private secretary to the Queen and general tutor to the prince. The Blacks were gaining on the Greys. Although the Greys stood first, they were no longer all in all. While Isabel was building her magnificent convent at Toledo for the brethren of St. Francis, she was led to found a splendid convent at Avila for the brethren of St. Dominic. If the cloister of San Juan at Toledo was to celebrate her closing of the civil war, the cloister of Santo Tomas at Avila was to celebrate her planting of the Holy Office in Castille. If the Franciscan convent was to bear the name of Isabel's patron saint, the Dominican convent was to bear the name of Torquemada's patron saint. To gratify the brethren of St. Dominic, this convent of Santo Tomas of Avila was built with money snatched from Jews whom

they had put to death. If envy had not been a sin,
the proudest brother of St. Francis might have envied Torquemada as he rode along the streets of
Seville with his forty mounted guards in front, and
his two hundred men on foot behind.

From Seville he had thrown his feelers into
other of the crown estates.   A branch was fixed at
Cordova, where the Queen was keeping court.   A
second branch was opened at Villa Real; a third at
Jaen; and other branches were established in the
conquered Caliphates.   But Torquemada was a daring man.   From Villa Real he advanced on Leon,
and the city of Valladolid became the seat of an
inquisitor.   No sooner was Carillo dead, than Isabel
allowed Fray Tomas to erect an office in Avila and
Toledo.   When the Pope sent out to Torquemada
on the Queen's demand a patent as Inquisitor-
general of Castille, he only gave effect in writing to
a living fact.

Castille and her dependent states were yielding
slowly, sullenly to the Queen, with protest here and
there, stamped down and punished with unsparing
heel.   The cities of Castille invoked the aid of
Zaragoza, Barcelona, and Valencia; but the men of
Aragon stood aloof, as free-born mountaineers are
apt to stand aloof when neighbours in the plain are
calling out for help.   They never dreamt that an
inquisitor would show his face in Zaragoza.   Had
they not their Casa Blanca and their fundamental
pact?

CHAPTER III.

Inquisition in Aragon.

1485.

1. ALOOF and proud, these men of Aragon had joked and laughed at their submissive brethren in the plains; but now the time had come for them to feel the yoke, and find how little could be done by prayers and protests, even when they called upon their Cortes, and produced their fundamental laws.

In April of the previous year, Fernando had convened a council in the town of Tarazona, on the frontier of his kingdom, where, on the advice of Andreas Sart, a doctor of the canon law, and the assent of Alonzo de la Cavalleria, Vice-Chancellor of Aragon, he had "decreed" the introduction into Aragon of his consort's "great reform." The King was poor, and many of his counts and citizens were rich:—the brethren of St. Dominic had shown him how to fill his chests. The King was troubled by his Parliament, many of whom were Jews:—the brethren of St. Dominic had shown him how these liberal orators might be crushed. An Inquisition was decreed.

2. A loud and strenuous opposition to this edict rose on every side; in town, in castle, nay, in

cloister; for the brethren of St. Francis and the
fathers of St. Benedict were as much opposed to
the Dominicans as were the Friends of Light. The
thing was new, and they were steadfast to their
ancient ways. No Cortes could have introduced the
Inquisition; for this new and terrible court was contrary to the fundamental pact. "No inquisition
shall be held in Aragon," their charter said. An
"office" of inquiry had existed many years in Zaragoza; but this "office" of inquiry had no visible
home, no special treasury, and no separate chief.
Alonzo, the Archbishop, was inquisitor; Juan de
Gomedes, vicar-general, was his adjutant; but they
had other duties than inquiry after such as went
astray. They lived in the great palace under the
cathedral tower; but no one thought of calling them
inquisitors, and their house an inquisition. Don
Alonzo, the Archbishop, was a lad of fifteen years;
a natural son of King Fernando, and a madcap
darling of the Ebro watermen and city mobs. Gomedes was a sober priest, who liked to steal from
palace to cathedral, in the sombre aisles of which
he said his office, and to glide across the plaza to
his dinner and repose. Residing under the Archbishop's roof, and close to the cathedral of La Seo,
where his duty lay, he had no wish to stir up strife
and fill the street below with tumult. For the mobs
of Zaragoza were no feeble folk. Loud, fierce, and
superstitious, they were easy to excite and difficult
to restrain. The Ebro roaring past their walls was
not so rough, so reckless, and so swift in wrath.
They knelt in terrible fear and joy before the image

of their patroness and guest. The Virgin was supposed to love their city, and to quit betimes her
throne in heaven to sit and listen to their nones
and vespers on her jasper shaft. Around that pillar
knelt by night and day a throng of pilgrims; rude
and ignorant rustics from the fields, and no less
rude and ignorant rabble from the towns. To stir
these throngs was easy; but Gomedes had no wish
to kindle sparks of fire beneath his roof. He would
have shrunk from stirring up their blood by acts of
faith; solemnities which woke the passions of a
Spaniard like a bull-fight. Nor was Juan de Gomedes eager to inquire. He owned no separate
fund; he could not force the mayor to act for him;
he had no power to seize a heretic's goods. In
brief, this meek inquisitor held an unseen court, inflicted shadowy censures, and relied for discipline
on moral means.

3. Fernando's edict was to sweep away this old
tribunal of inquiry, and replace it by a new and
vigorous court. He wanted such a court in Zaragoza as his wife had fixed in Seville and Valladolid; a court that could arrest his wealthy subjects in the name of holy Church, and having
found them wanting in some article of faith, might
give their bodies to the flames, their monies to the
Crown.

4. Fray Tomas had been fully armed. He was
empowered to fix his seat in any place; to frame
his codes and rules; to name his deputies and familiars. Every officer in Aragon, from the Mayor of
Zaragoza to the Grand Justiciary of the kingdom,

was to aid his deputies in their quest. He was to
seize suspected men, to hold them in his ward, and
judge their lapse from Catholic truth. He might
proceed against them in the dark; refusing to con-
front them with his witnesses, or let them know
the scope and nature of his charge. He might
compel them, by the use of screw and jack, of cord
and wheel, to open out their secret crimes. If he
believed them guilty of backsliding, he was autho-
rised to send their bodies to the stake, and give
their chattels to the King.

A cry of rage had risen from every town in
Aragon and her dependent states. The upper
classes would not read, much less accept, this royal
edict, for a court with such exceptional duties was
against their charter. Were they conquered Moors?
The King had sworn to guard their charter, as his
title to the throne. They saw in his decree a temporal measure, and opposed it on a temporal ground.
They stood upon their ancient laws. Valentia, Cataluña, and Sardinia, the outlying states of Aragon,
approved this protest. Rossillon, where the French
were lying, was disturbed, and even in Navarre,
which the familiars could not reach, all Friends of
Light were eager to protest against the founding of
this new tribunal in a neighbouring state.

5. Fray Tomas named as deputies in Zaragoza,
Gaspar Inglar, a Dominican friar, and Pedro Arbues,
a Canon of La Seo; but the King, who had his
worldly purpose, caused these agents to appear as
deputies, not of Torquemada, the Castillian friar,
but of his son, the bastard primate, and the pet of

every pilgrim, artizan, and vagrant on the Ebro. Inglar and Arbues were to take instructions from Gomedes, and the office was to be in the Archbishop's house.

6. The Cortes, meeting in the Casa Blanca, sent a deputation to the camp at Jaen. They put their trust in Sanchez and Clemente, who were in the camp, and in Abravanel, who was oftener in the royal tent. Abravanel was not a man to think of violent courses; but he had authority with the King; and, if his voice were raised at all, he would be certain to support the Friends of Light. Clemente had a grievance to avenge. The Sanchez family had also reason to distrust the new inquisitor and his familiars. Every thing in time, and place, and person, led the Friends of Light to think they could control their worldly and ambitious Prince.

A spiritual court, they held, had certain functions to discharge; it might advise, exhort, and censure an unfaithful citizen; but such a spiritual court could lay no finger on that citizen's goods. Fray Tomas claimed a right to seize and to retain some portion of a heretic's goods. This claim was contrary to law. The Cortes begged the King to listen to their voice—the voice of free and loyal men, and strip his new inquisitors of these lawless powers. The deputies laid no stress on any other point. They raised no cry against the Church. If once Arbues and his colleague were deprived of their authority to seize a person's goods, they thought these new inquisitors would give them no more trouble than the old. Arbues could be trusted to

retire the moment he was asked to seek out error
at his own expense.

7. A second deputation started for the Roman
court.   A new Pope, Innocent the Eighth, had just
succeeded Sixtus; and the deputies were sent to tell
his Holiness how papal grants were being abused
in the subjected Caliphates, and to protest against
this planting of a new tribunal in their free and
faithful towns.

———

CHAPTER IV.

Sacrilege and Murder.

1485.

1. ARBUES, who in pride and daring was a second Torquemada, when he found the Cortes bent on sending deputies to the Pope and King, resolved to strike a blow by which he fancied he could force these nobles to desist. Repairing, with his colleague, Inglar, to the rooms of Juan de Gomedes, in the primate's palace, he despatched his agents through the town, with orders to arrest a number of reputed Friends of Light. Arbues found them wanting in some article of faith. Fray Tomas had supplied him with a score of tests by which he was to know a secret Jew. He might be seen to drink Caser wine, and heard to ask a blessing on his cup. He might be found eating fish and olives in honour of the dead. A man who wore fine clothes on Saturday—a man who cast the horoscope of his child,—was likely to have been a Jew. One who looked carefully at the blade of a knife before he killed a kid, was probably a Jew; one who recited a Psalm without the *Gloria Patri*, was certainly a Jew. Arbues found the citizens at fault, and judged them worthy to be burnt. A fire was lighted in the public square; the men were marched into a

neighbouring church; and while the deputies were
on their ways to Rome and Jaen, Arbues caused
two batches of his victims to be burnt alive.

2. The blow had now been struck, the war begun. Not only men who were the foes of Arbues
because Arbues was a foe to learning, but those
stiffer patriots who were always boasting that their
country was a land of law and freedom, were excited to the point of frenzy by this daring deed.
"If such things can be done," they cried, "we are
no better than Castillians, who have suffered Isabel
to rob and burn them for the past three years."
From Aragon to Cataluña and Navarre, the passion
of resistance spread. In every province, and in almost
every village, threats were hurled at the tribunal and
its agents. Never had the Friends of Light appeared
so strong. The fundamental pact was on their side;
the custom of the land was on their side. They had
a strong majority in the Cortes, and this strong
majority was backed by the most active citizens in
the capital and in provincial towns. But all these
great advantages were thrown away in passion. Gotor
and Cerdan read such notes from Sanchez, that they
thought the King was with them; that the short way
was the safest way; that they might kill Arbues with
no other risk than of fighting with a monk who
might be aided by a mob. They showed these
notes to Juan de Abadia, Blasco de Alagon, and
other friends. At every word from Sanchez, men
took fire. A Lord Treasurer, waiting on the King,
could hardly, they imagined, be mistaken in the
royal mood. To kill the man whom they regarded

as a murderer, seemed at once the quickest and
the surest way; a way that gave them eye for eye
and tooth for tooth; and answered by an Act of
Justice to his Act of Faith. The friars had tried to
scare the Friends of Light; the Friends of Light
would see if they could scare the friars. If Arbues
should be slain, what man would step into his shoes
and brave his fate? Blasco de Alagon and Juan de
Abadia took the leading parts in what was meant
to be their counter-stroke. Alagon was to raise the
necessary funds; Abadia was to find the necessary
men.

3. In no long time the money and the men were
found. Alagon got ten thousand silver marks. Abadia
found a man of gentle birth, Juan de Sperandeo,
who was willing to avenge the dead. Sperandeo
had a French domestic, Vidal de Uranso, who engaged to help him. Alagon was appointed banker
to the fund; Abadia was entrusted with arrangements
for the actual deed of blood.

Arbues, when he heard that men were hired to
track and kill him, put a coat of mail beneath his
gown, a cap of steel below his hood, a bar of oak
behind his chamber-door. He seldom went abroad,
and never in the light of day. Abadia hung about
him, with the two avengers at his back. Arbues
feared to pass from the seclusion of his cell to the
cathedral of La Seo; even at the altar he was hardly
safe. At night he stole into the temple, said his
office, and retired as swiftly as he came. But he
could only do so safely in the dead of night.

4. One dark September night, between eleven

and twelve, Arbues left his cloister, picking up a
lantern and a bludgeon as he stepped into the street.
Going up the Calle del Sepulcro, and across the
Plazuela de San Bruno—not a minute's walk in all
—he entered the cathedral by its eastern porch.
Dim lights were hanging in a vast and empty space;
a Moorish mosque, with Gothic choir and shrine.
A lamp was hanging here and there, and priests
were singing matins in the dark.   Arbues set his
lantern on the ground, and leaned his club against
a shaft; the first great column as he entered from
the porch. At once, he knelt, pulled out his beads,
and hurried through his office.   In the gloom a
figure was observed—a figure muffled in a cloak.
This figure came and knelt beside him. Steps were
heard behind the pillar, and a voice was raised in
tones unusual in a church. The figure drew a sword,
and slit Arbues through the elbow. "Strike him on
the neck!" Abadia shouted from behind the pillar,
when Uranso, who was close upon the canon, struck
him on the neck. A cry of murder rang through
the cathedral! Monks and priests came forward;
lights were brought by shrieking women; and the
murderers, on seeing they had done their work,
drew off in haste. In less than thirty hours the
wounded man was dead; but ere he died, the city
mob was roused to fury by the monks. Some men
in hood and gown ran up and down the streets,
exclaiming that the New Christians were murdering
the old. "The canon is the first to fall," they
cried, "but others have been marked for death; no
man is safe until the murderers have been hunted

down." From every narrow lane and dirty quay—
the alleys of Sepulcro, Pilar, and Valero, the paseo
of the Ebro, and the arco of the Dean—poured
out a troop of spare and tawny men with matted
hair, red belts, and hempen brogues. This savage
crowd soon filled the public square, and clamoured
at the primate's door for blood; nor would they
cease their cries until the boy-Archbishop came into
the streets and promised in his father's name that
justice should be done.

Alarmed by the Archbishop's words, even more
than by the fury of his partizans, the Friends of
Light made haste to fly, and by their flight gave up
their cause as lost.

5. When news of this great crime arrived in
camp, Fernando rode to Cordova, where his consort kept her court. His officers tried to guess his
mood; but he was not a man who wore his purpose
in his eyes. At Cordova, their hearts began to
faint. The Queen seemed fierce, and no one knew
what course the King would take. The nearest to
his person disappeared. His Secretary fled; his
Treasurer, his Paymaster fled; his Protonotary and
Vice-Chancellor fled. His highest offices were without their chiefs, and many of the courtiers thought
he must recall these servants and support them in
their contest. On the other side, the King was
urged by two of his most active passions—by his
greed of gold, and by his lust of power—to turn
against them. He required no hint that if these
men were hung, their goods and rents, their lands
and castles, would be forfeit to his crown. Alagon

and Urrea, men with rent-rolls only less long than
their pedigrees, were at his mercy. Cerdan had
heaps of money. Sanchez was believed to own a
mine of wealth, and several counts and knights
were in his jails. Five hundred citizens were under
guard, and there were many more who might be
seized if he should give the sign. Yet hoards of
money were but part of what Fernando had to
gain. By ruining the foremost Friends of Light,
the liberal party in his Cortes might be broken and
dispersed.

6. Fernando's war, though managed in the name
of heaven, was a dynastic war. A cardinal, three
archbishops, and a host of prelates, stood in mail
about his tent. Whole groups of friars, black,
white, and grey, were in his wake; and hosts of
martyrs, saints, and angels, were imagined in his
front. His standard was a silver Cross. As many
a text and sermon told, his objects were to win
back souls from error, and extend the limits of the
Christian world. Yet those who knew him saw that
his pretence of fighting for the Cross was nothing
but a cloak. Fernando lusted after soil and sway.
He hoped to win the Caliphate by force; and after
driving out the Moors, he meant to turn his sword
against his native states. It was no secret in his
council that he found the law a curb on his ambitious flights. In Aragon, a free and liberal country,
with a fundamental pact, his powers were limited
on many sides; in Cataluña, her republican sister,
they were limited on every side. In Barcelona, then
the richest port in Spain, the King had scarcely any

power at all. Castille and Leon, free and ancient states, with rights and charters older than the reigning house, were no more docile to the Queen than Aragon and Cataluña to the King. Fernando wished to free his hand from these restraints. In Cordova and Seville, where the people had no ancient laws, the crown could levy taxes, raise recruits, imprison, heretics, and banish citizens by word of mouth and scratch of pen. A conquered district was a crown estate. Both King and Queen preferred to live among these vassals in the South, where parliaments never met to vex their souls. The war was serving them in many ways. It gave them the command of armies which might overawe Toledo and Zaragoza while they menaced Baza, Malaga, and Loja. It enlarged from year to year those conquered lands, in which they owned no law but their despotic will. It brought them, and secured to them, a compact with the church, the military class, and the religious orders. More than all, it gave them many a chance of acting on the Cortes of their independent states. This war was not as popular in the town as in the camp. A man who wished to live and trade, to keep the freedom handed down to him in full, to cultivate the arts of peace, could feel no joy in victories which brought fresh strength to King and Queen, which kept the court and council in the south of Spain, and threatened to transfer his capital to a conquered town.

7. This war was turning to a war of race, and many of the higher classes were connected with the

persecuted race. In every town there was a group
of doctors, artists, advocates, and bankers, who had
sprung from Oriental roots. In every noble house
there was an Arab teacher, and in many a noble
house there was a Jewish wife. Men married
Jewesses more frequently than women married Jews;
yet almost every city saw some splendid matches
made by Jews. Davila, when he married into the
proud family of Mendoza, shocked no national sentiment. In Isabel's closet and Fernando's tent, the
ablest and most trusty officers were of Hebrew race.
Few families in the higher ranks were free from what
the new inquisitors were calling "taint of blood;"
and when these fathers and their rabble raised the
cry of "Out with the infidel!", this war-whoop from
the cloister and the street was met by many a flashing eye in court and camp. The crime of Zaragoza,
which had stained a sacred edifice with human gore,
was but a scene in this hot warfare of the cloister
and the world.

CHAPTER V.

King Fernando.

1485.

1. At thirty-three, Fernando was a small, brisk man, alive in every sense, alert in every nerve. A chubby cheek, thick lip, brown eyes and raven hair, were lighted by a cold metallic smile, like that which shimmers on a well-worn front of bronze. His skin was tawny gold. Though he was squat in frame, his thews and joints were steeled by frugal diet and by exercise in sport and war. A sleek and comely face led many into deeming him a man of careless mood, more likely to be hunting lovely eyes than poring day and night through plans for conquering rival kings and overturning native laws. Yet he was one of those rare men who will not let their right hand guess the purpose of their left. In using men to serve his turn he had no rival. While he rode against the Moors, he made the Caliph of Granada trust him as a friend. When he attacked the Fundamental Pact of Aragon, he put his monks and priests in front, and threw the odium of his victory over law and justice on the Holy See.

2. By birth and training he was meant to be a Friend of Light. His father was a patron of the great

revival.   In his father's house the leading influence
was that of Abraham Bibago, an accomplished
Hebrew.   In his father's days the printing-press was
brought to Spain, and both the first and second
books were printed in his native states.   The house
he lived in, called the Aljaferia, was a Moorish
palace; the church he knelt in, called La Seo, was
a Moorish mosque.   In every street his eye was
gladdened by the sight of Moorish arch and star.
On every side—in wall and tower, in quay and
gate, in shrine and court—he saw the traces of a
nobler art than that of the ascendant race.   Fernando
was too open-eyed and active to become a bigot;
but the love of power and lust of money might induce him to betray his natural cause.   All causes
were the same to him.   The man was light of love,
but never light of heart.   His virtue was a clear
and intellectual insight; his defect a want of sympathy and humour, and the moral insight which
depends on sympathy and humour.   In Fernando's
eyes all men were rogues; some rich and royal
rogues, some poor and lowly rogues; but in their
several spheres they all were rogues.   No living
creature had his confidence.   He kept a hundred
secrets from the Queen.   He named confessors by
the dozen, but he told these monks no more than
he allowed himself to tell his wife.   A councillor
had to guess his meaning from his looks.   Yet Nature
had not given him the expression which deceives
without an effort to deceive.   His mouth was big;
his left eye turned askant; his voice, which issued
through a broken tooth, was an unpleasant hiss and

snap. It was not hard to see that under the metallic dimple beat a heart of brass.

3. Once only in his youth, Fernando had been stirred into romance. He fell in love with Isabel and her fortunes; nay, he put on rough disguise; he travelled in the night; he sought adventures in her name. But these wild oats of poetry were quickly sown; and he had long ago found out, while he was under twenty, that a man may thrive in love without the burthen of a heart. The Queen suspected him; for he had always cheated and abused her in a woman's rights. To gain her hand, he had not scrupled to concoct a papal breve, to wed her with a lie upon his lips, and cast her into what he knew was mortal sin. Untrue to her in heart, although he prized her as a queen, he took no pains to hide from her his amours with the ladies of her court. In convents up and down the country, there were children whom he owned. His son by Countess Eboli was made Archbishop of Zaragoza at the age of six. A favourite child, Juana, borne to him by a noble Portuguese, and in his bridal year, he hoped to give a yet more lofty seat. Another son, a Catalan, was at Lerida, where he afterwards slept in peace beneath a splendid tomb. Two girls, each called Maria, were the fruit of other amours. These Marias were in convents, over which they were in time to live and reign as Lady Abbesses in virtue of their birth.

Though Isabel strove to treat the King with grave respect, she could not always bear his falsehood. In her fits of rage, she fled, and shut herself

behind some convent wall; but he was younger than
herself, and had a wheedling way no woman could
resist. He was her soldier, statesman, and crusader;
in his absence everything went wrong.   In all their
quarrels, victory lay with him.

4. A younger son, Fernando was not born to
reign; but he had fought his way, assisted by a
beautiful and wicked mother, Queen Juana-Enriquez,
second wife of Juan the Second, king of Aragon, to
what was properly his brother's place and throne.

5. Carlos, that elder brother, had the happy
fortune to unite the heirship of two neighbouring
crowns; his father, Juan, being king of Aragon; his
mother, Blanca, princess of Navarre.   A union of
these kingdoms would have put an end to quarrels
which had fired the Pyrenees for centuries, and
would have closed against the French all passages
and inlets into Spain.   A student worthy of Bibago,
and a soldier worthy of the Cid, Don Carlos was
the charm of every college and the pride of every
camp.   A "perfect prince," he seemed ordained by
nature to unite the scattered crowns and coronets
of Spain.   But all these qualities had made him hateful to the young and wicked woman whom his father
had espoused and made the mistress of his house.
That house, the Aljaferia, standing in the Ebro
vineyards, close to the Portillo gate, was shut against
his feet.   He had to find a home elsewhere.   The
Queen was young, the King her husband old.   A
witch in malice, she had turned her husband's heart
against his handsome son.   The prince had been
arrested, thrown into a dungeon, treated as a rebel,

branded as a man unfit to reign. She had compelled him by her policy to retire from Spain; she had induced him by her falsehood to return without his father's leave; she had betrayed him by her perfidy into taking arms. On finding he was strong enough to crush her, she had offered to become his ally. She had started on a journey with him, hoping to undo him with his friends the Catalans; and some hours after she had left him, with a cordial greeting, he had sickened of a strange complaint and died. A storm of public rage had burst upon the Queen, whom every voice accused of murder. Cataluña had revolted from the crown, revived the old republic, and pronounced the King a traitor to his oath. These Catalan republicans had not been crushed without assistance from the French, who had despatched some troops to Barcelona, and received in pledge two Catalan duchies, Rossillon and Cerdaña, with the fort of Salsas and the port of Perpignan. It was Fernando's mother who had brought these foreigners into Spain; it was for crushing liberty in Cataluña that the French had got these duchies in the Pyrenees.

6. Navarre the Queen had not been able to secure. As Carlos left two sisters, Blanca and Elinor, to succeed him in their mother's right, Fernando had no claim, remote or near. All hope of a pacific and immediate union of the kingdoms had been buried in Don Carlos' grave. But if the Queen had lost Navarre, and pawned Rossillon and Cerdaña, she had won by her dexterity a richer prize than either, in the kingdom of Castille.

7. A King of Aragon was always ready to disturb his neighbours in Castille. His people lived
on rocky heights, from which they poured at will
into the plains, and swept the pastures of their flocks
and herds. What Scotland was to England, Aragon
was to Castille. When Isabel had risen against her
brother, Enrique the Fourth, and sent to Aragon for
help, the beautiful and wicked queen had named
the price of her support—the rebel princess must
espouse her son and share with him her future
throne. Three obstacles had seemed to bar this
union. Isabel was engaged elsewhere; the Prince
and Princess were of kin; and King Enrique was
not likely to consent. Her lover, Pedro de Pacheco,
was a man to claim his bride. The Roman curia
was unwilling to annoy a reigning prince by granting Isabel a dispensation on the score of blood. No
one supposed the King would give his sister, then
in arms against him, to the foremost enemy of his
crown. Yet all these obstacles had been swept
away. Pacheco had been poisoned on the road; a
papal dispensation had been forged; the King had
been distracted and defied; and on this ruler's death,
Fernando, as his sister's husband, had secured possession of his crown.

CHAPTER VI.

Queen Isabel.

1485.

1. IN person, Isabel was like her father's mother, Catharine of Lancaster; tall in stature, full in bust, and fair in tint, with auburn ringlets, cold grey eyes, and cheeks on which two full-blown roses burned. In figure, as in mind, she held a vast reserve of strength. She knew the female arts; could broider, trifle with her lute, and speak her native tongue with grace; but she was not a queen of song, still less a queen of learning, as her scribes gave out. She kept a dozen priests and monks to praise her; writers like Alonzo de Palencia, who could tell the story of her life in unctuous periods, and like Pietro Martire, who could sound her virtues in the ears of cardinals and kings.

2. These priests were bound to Isabel by stronger ties than love of food and hope of place. She was their child, their banner, and their pledge. The books she read were lives of saints; the court she kept was one of monks and nuns; the method of her life was service to the Church. She entered a religious order; she arrayed herself in cord and sack; she took upon herself the customary vows. Beneath her purple robe—and she was fond of

wearing silk attire—she wore a long chemise of
serge. She strove, and not in vain, to make herself
a type of monkish and monarchical Spain; that
Spain which had not heard of ancient Greece, and
hardly heard of ancient Rome; that Spain which
knew no pagan poetry, no Spartan heroes, no republican cities; and, in happy ignorance of what
our race had done in nobler ages, was content to
follow in the wake of holy monks and kiss the rod
of native kings.

3. A sister of the Order of St. Francis, Isabel
had a fancy for the lower classes, and could dazzle
and mislead them, like her English kinsman Richard
of Bordeaux. A rogue in rags was pleasant in her
sight. Like other princes who aspire to rule beyond
the law, she liked to turn the rich against the poor,
and to excite the poor against the rich. A wish to
set one class against the other led her to revive the
Santa Hermandad; a league of towns and villages
which in ancient times had risen against the nobles
and the crown. She hated what was new, and still
more what was liberal. She suspected learning as
a snare for loyalty no less than as a snare for faith.
A man who lived in Plato's Athens and in Scipio's
Rome, might grow impatient of Toledo; even as a
man who spent his days in reading Homer and
Cicero might turn in weariness from the book of
saints. The printing-press and classical revival, she
was taught, were leading men to doubt the power
of holy Church. She put the presses under strict
control of mayor and monk, and kept the promise
she had given to Torquemada, her confessor, that if

God should raise her to the throne, she would devote herself to rooting out of Spanish soil all creeds and rituals hostile to the Catholic Church. That pledge had made her queen; and when she was a queen, her masters, the Dominicans, had held her to a full redemption of that pledge.

4. A royal saint had been selected by her party as the model of her reign. This saint was San Fernando, one of her foregoers on the throne; a man of her own house and blood; a prince who had united Leon and Castille; who had commenced the shrines of Burgos and Toledo; who had carried fagots on his back to burn a heretic; who had conceived the project of a holy war; and who had won for Holy Church the mosques of Seville, Cordova, and Jaen. To crown the labours of this royal saint had now become the passion of her soul. She yearned to be a saint; like that Elizabeth of Hungary who had lived in San Fernando's days, and caught her fervour from the Spanish prince. One lady of her husband's line, an Isabel of Aragon, had been canonized. This saint was born at Zaragoza, in that very palace of the Aljaferia which the living Isabel occupied as Queen. Her room was treated as a shrine, and every one at Zaragoza spoke of her with love and awe. What Isabel of Aragon was, her namesake of Castille desired to be. The living Isabel built a convent in Segovia, which she dedicated to this sainted dame. Three objects always stood in Isabel's sight:—to spread the empire of her creed; to live in favour with the orders; and to get her name inserted in the roll of saints. To gain these

objects she had laid out all her life; had married,
sinned, and fought; had risen against her brother
and dethroned her niece. To live in favour with the
orders, she had built the great Franciscan convent
of San Juan at Toledo; curbed the printing-presses;
fixed her chief inquisitor at Seville; founded the
Dominican convent of Santo Tomas near Avila; and
bestowed her offices of state on friars, monks, and
priests.

5. If she had gained her ends—a crown on earth,
and something like the promise of a crown in heaven
—she had been forced to pay the price of her success.   The upper classes of her people feared her
as a tool, and when their feelings broke into expression she was hailed by words of scorn and
hate.

6. Fernando, as became a pupil of Bibago, kept
some taint of liberal culture in his household, where
a man of talent, such as Gabriel Sanchez, might be
used in State affairs without regard to subtleties of
faith.   Fernando never troubled his astronomer Zacuto on account of his belief. Chabillo of Mouzon,
and Paulus of Heredia, could pursue their studies
under him in peace, though they had never knelt
before a cross. But Isabel would have no servant
in her house, no teacher in her schools, on whom
her grand-inquisitor refused to set his seal. Two
Popes, Eugenius and Calixtus, had forbidden parents
to allow their children to be taught by Jews; how,
therefore, could a Christian prince permit his chairs
of history and science to be filled by men of that
forbidden tribe? Fernando used his priests when

he could turn their cloth against a foe; but Isabel, who had the weakness of her sex and country, sought, in what she termed her pious duties, a protection from the stings of conscience and the phantoms of remorse.

7. These stings of conscience and these phantoms of remorse were not the vapourings of an idle fancy, bent on delicate questionings of the heart; but ministers of outraged nature, such as every man and woman may expect who wades through treachery and bloodshed to a throne. The ghost that came most frequently to the couch of Isabel, that scared the sleep of innocence from her eyes, and fed the daily fever in her blood, was that of a fair girl, her niece, and queen; a girl whom she had wronged, dethroned, and buried in a foreign convent cell. No rite performed by an inquisitor could lay for Isabel this royal ghost. Nor was Fernando, as her partner on the throne, less troubled by the royal maid. In every word he wrote, in every pledge he gave, Fernando had his eye and thought on her. She was his evil genius, and the only human being who could force his game. How he might act at Zaragoza towards the Friends of Light depended on the course he had to take in reference to the exiled queen.

CHAPTER VII.

A Royal Exile.

1485.

1. This exiled queen was lodging in the convent
of Santa Clara of Coimbra, in the bare and lonely
district north of Lisbon, under watch and guard of
John the Perfect, King of Portugal, who held towards her a jailor's office, and received from Isabel
a jailor's pay.

2. Juana, only child of Enrique the Liberal, was
born the lawful heiress of his kingdom; but her
father had not pleased the great religious orders
which were striving for the mastery of Spain; and
she had lost her crown in the mischances of a civil
war.   All through Enrique's reign — a reign of
foreign trouble and domestic strife—the brethren of
St. Francis and St. Dominic had been striving with
that Greek revival which Antonio de Lebrija and
his learned friends were preaching in Castille. The
King, a poet and a friend of poets, had been a
patron of these liberal studies, a protector of these
earnest men.

3. Enrique was a Friend of Light, and therefore
had been called an enemy of the Church. He sought
his councillors and companions in the liberal schools.
Pacheco, his most potent minister, was descended

from a Lisbon Jew. Castillo was his councillor as well as poet-laureate. Arias de Avila, an accomplished Jew, was master of his exchequer. Don Gaon was his farmer-general. A Moor was captain of his guard. A Jew was bishop of his favourite seat, Segovia. Jacob Nunez, a distinguished Israelite, was his physician. Many of his architects were Moors. His palace at Segovia and his sepulchre of the Cid at Miraflores proved his taste in art. All guests who visited his court were struck by what appeared its gay and liberal aspect. Lisbon may have been more enterprising; Granada may have been more splendid; yet the arts of peace, and notably the minstrel's craft and mason's trade, had found no truer patron than Enrique of Castille. In taste, in study, in amenity of life, his court had been a Moorish rather than a Gothic court.

4. The Spanish brethren of St. Dominic had called his court a libertine court. Religious orders lean to the ascetic and despotic sides of life; for they are founded on the principles of abstinence and submission; and the members of such guilds are apt to fancy that the rules by which they live are good for all mankind. In leaning to the harder sides of life, the brethren of St. Dominic went beyond the Carmelite and Benedictine monks. They hated freedom even more than they suspected light. Their mission being to strengthen and defend the Pope, as one who held the keys, they wished to have a prince, who, in his sphere, was like a pope—a man above the reach of law. By word and deed, they taught the duty of submitting to all popes and kings, as

men submit their souls to God.   But in the Greek
revival they could find no sanction for the doctrine
that obedience is a virtue, poverty a grace.   The
glory of that learning which was stirring all the
youth of Alcala and Salamanca was a glory of
Olympian gods, free commonwealths, and independent scribes.   A pope had told them that a man
who studies Homer in his youth will worship Jupiter,
in his riper years.   Against this great apostasy, the
brethren of St. Dominic had been trained to fight;
and those of Santa Cruz were brooding on a plan
for silencing such teachers as preferred the Georgics
to the Book of Saints.   But they required a partner
on the throne, and agents in the royal judges and
provincial mayors.   They had not cared to combat,
as their founder meant, by written books, by spoken
words, and by the precepts of a holy life.   A classical teacher had the gift of speech.   To write and
preach against him was to court reply.   The brethren
yearned to crush their enemies by force; and enemies
like the Friends of Light were only to be beaten
down by men who held the civic sword.   A ghostly
weapon would not smite them; but the subtlest
brain and nimblest tongue might quail before a
secret judge, a searching rack, and a chastising fire.

5. A royal architect and poet was no partner
for a crusade on these learned men, and he who
could not be a partner must be dealt with as a foe.
At first the brethren had been prudent in their
work.   A king has many eyes and hands; but
preachers like the brethren of St. Dominic have
means of acting on the public mind unseen.   They

have the cloister and confessional at their service. As an architect, Enrique loved the Moorish arch and star, and strove to imitate the Moorish dome and tower. This taste for foreign things might be presented to the faithful as a danger for the Cross. Would not indulgence towards the Arab's art beget indulgence towards the Arab's creed? Were not the Moorish arch and star the sign and light of Moslem faith? Enrique's faith had never been robust. His father, who had also been a poet and a builder, was suspected of conversion to the Moslem rite; and who could tell the brethren of St. Dominic that his daughter, trained amidst a court of Jews and Moors, would live to be a faithful and obedient queen? Enrique had abused his royal power. Not only had he filled his court with foreign artists, but had given the care of Christian souls to men whose fathers had crucified Our Lord. Juan Arias, Bishop of Segovia, was a Jew, and Pedro de Aranda, Bishop of Calahorra, was a Jew. The fathers had been no less puzzled than enraged by such appointments in the Church. Resolved to fight for sway, and if they won, to tear the ancient codes and pacts as Pedro of the Dagger had destroyed the Instrument of Union, they had cast about them for a tool; a ruler who should owe his crown to them, and who would hold it in subjection to their will.

6. In order to impeach Juana's right, the fathers had been forced to blast her mother's fame. That lady was their queen; but in a friar's presence queens are only dust. A sister of Affonzo, King of Portugal, and of the Empress Leonor, that queen

had brought into Castille a mind as happy as her
face was fair.   In seeking to disturb her daughter's
claims, they had been forced to whisper that her
cheery temper was the cloak of a corrupted heart.
She was a Portuguese, and any tale might be received
against a Portuguese.   No proof of her disloyalty
has ever been produced, nor were the prince and
princess who had reaped the harvest of her wrongs
deceived.   But scandal may be raised without a
shred of proof.   A doubt once planted in the ear
is sure to grow; and in a kingdom torn by civil war,
it is not hard to sow the seeds of doubt. They had
suggested Beltran de la Cueva, one of the King's
companions, as a lover of their Queen.

Although of indolent artistic nature, apt to
shrink from cares of state, Enrique had been stung
by these reports, and roused to take some measures
for his own defence. With triple force, as husband,
king, and father, he had met these scandals of the
cloister; first, by showing confidence in his partner;
next, by taking oaths of fealty to his child; and last,
by giving them his best affection, service, and respect.   He had procured a wife for Beltran in a
kinswoman of the Cardinal of Spain.   Before the
papal nuncio and legate, he had caused the Queen
to make an oath on her salvation that the stories
told of her were false, and that Juana was a true
and lawful daughter of the King.

7. When king and pope, council and parliament,
had proclaimed Juana's right and sworn to guard
that right, a crowd of princes had proposed to
marry her and her estates; Prince John of Portugal,

Alonzo of Castille, Fadrique of Naples, Charles of France. Charles, Duc de Guienne, had been the favourite suitor, and the land had hailed Juana and Guienne as future Queen and King; all Spain, except the mother of Fernando, and those brethren of St. Dominic and St. Francis, who were fighting for supremacy in Spain. That woman could not hope to get the princess for her son, and the religious orders wanted a less powerful pupil on the throne. A sovereign with a perfect title would be strong enough to reign without their help.

8. Fray Tomas having made his bargain with Enrique's sister, the Dominicans had held her to her pledge. The stony region, lying round the two strong cities of Valladolid and Avila, had always been devoted to the Church. Alonzo Carillo, primate of Castille, a restless, vain, and domineering priest, had recently demanded that the Moors and Jews should be expelled; and on the King refusing his request, he had retired from court in anger, and the brethren knew that for the moment they could count on his support against the Queen and her unhappy child. But they had not been able to go forward at a stride. Enrique had a brother, Don Alonzo, who was next in order of succession to his crown. Alonzo was a child, and therefore a convenient tool. At Avila, a rock-built town, with walls and towers as solid as the earth on which they stand, Carillo and a party whom his influence carried into opposition had deposed the reigning prince and set the boy-pretender on his throne. A band of discontented men had gathered on that rocky

height, and from those rebel towers had hurled defiance at their sovereign lord. A war had then begun; Alonzo as pretender in the front, and Torquemada with his purpose in the rear. Enrique, knowing that the boy was not to blame, had held his troops in check. Avila is the centre of a district noted as producing the most stupid peasantry in Spain. By help of ignorant and superstitious boors, Carillo had kept the kingdom in a state of chronic feud. Avila could not be attacked. The great cathedral was a fortress; and the walls defied the largest guns. At twelve the boy had played his part and disappeared; and then the fathers and their party, going to the convent of Arevalo where the Princess Isabel lived, had offered her the crown. Already they had got her promise. If they made her queen, she was to be with them in heart and soul. They had in her a platform and a principle. Enrique was the Liberal; his sister Isabel was to be the Catholic.

CHAPTER VIII.

Señora Excellenta.

1485.

1. UNBOUND by either oath or edict, vote or pledge, the fathers had been free to come and go, to jest and sneer, to feign and fawn, as suited them from year to year. They had the pulpit, eucharist, and confessional, under their control. They had the choice of time and method of attack. They had a fort in every convent, and a spy in every house. A thousand scribes had helped to spread their lies. The women and the rabble had been always on their side. Resolved to win, and pitiless towards the victims of their plot, they had denounced the child as Little Beltran; they had stung their Queen to frenzy; they had fixed an epithet more odious than the Liberal on their King. Against these secret arts, the Queen had not been able to defend herself; and she had bowed her head before the blast—a lily broken in a storm.

2. Each movement in this drama had been watched and aided by Fernando's mother, who had thrown her soul into the strife; and after years of civil discord, she had partly teased, and partly terrified, Enrique into signing articles of peace.

These articles had been the cause of future wars;
for while Enrique fancied he was placing Isabel, his
sister, next in order of succession to his daughter,
Isabel's party and the Queen of Aragon contended
that the articles he had been induced to sign had
placed her next in order to himself. Although he
was too just and generous to deprive his sister of
her proper rights, Enrique would not leave the offspring of Fernando to ascend his throne. When
the Infanta Isabel was born, Enrique had denounced
the marriage of his sister as unlawful, and her child
as base in blood. All Europe had been told that
Isabel's marriage was illicit in the eyes of God and
man; and as the Pope had not yet sent a lawful
breve to Spain, her eldest child was "born in sin."

3. Fernando, careless of these paper edicts and
political oaths, had waited for Enrique's death, and
then appealed to arms; aware that words are vain,
that might is right, that victory is law. At first his
partner's cause had seemed a desperate cause.
Right, law, and power were on Juana's side. The
girl was hailed as Queen. She had the Cortes and
the capital in her favour. When her father died,
the crown was on her head, and every act of government conducted in her name. Around her stood
the Cardinal of Spain, the Grand-master of Santiago,
the Grand-master of Calatrava, the Duke of Arevalo,
the Marquises of Cadiz and Santillana, the Counts
of Benevento, Haro, and Tendilla, with a crowd of
other counts and cavaliers. Carillo was the only
man of name who had declared for Isabel. Yet
Fernando had not been dismayed; believing in the

power of priests and women to upset the strongest thrones.

4. Enrique had erected at Segovia, on the platform of a Moorish alcazar, a palace which he meant to be his house, his fortress, and his bank. This house, which he had given in charge to Andreas de Cabrera, one of his most trusty knights, contained ten thousand silver marks, the ready money of his kingdom. If Fernando could secure this fund, the insurrection might begin; if not, the cause was hopeless. So it lay with Andreas de Cabrera to arrest or to provoke a civil war. Cabrera's wife had caused her husband to betray his trust, to yield the alcazar, and place his silver marks in Isabel's hands. Too soon defection had begun to spread. Beltran de la Cueva was among the first to violate his oath. Mendoza, too, was won; but Isabel, in order to secure his favour, had been forced to sacrifice Carillo, her most powerful prop. One kingdom was too small for two such spirits; but the rebel queen, in giving up Carillo for Mendoza, was securing for her flag the craftiest head and wealthiest family in Spain. Five years this civil war had raged. The learned and commercial classes had sustained their lawful queen; the great religious orders, with the rabble they could drive afield, together with the feudal counts and feudal bishops, had supported her aspiring aunt. Carillo, vexed to find his service spurned by Isabel, had made some efforts to undo the mischief he had wrought. He had returned to his allegiance to the lawful queen, had written, preached, and fought for her; but he

had not been able to unite the great religious
orders to a liberal court. "The Church in danger,"
that exciting cry, which has so often roused an
ignorant mob to madness, had been raised. The
Queen, a child of twelve, had been presented to
her people as an enemy of God; her aunt, the rebel
princess, as a child of God and an obedient servant
of His Church. All persons who were faithful to
their oaths, had been denounced as bad Christians,
bad Catholics, evil-doers, heretics, and thieves. All
those who fought for Isabel, even knights like
Beltran de la Cueva, had been called the friends
of Christ. From every part of Europe men of
desperate fortune flocked to Spain. Italians, Moors,
and Switzers flung their swords into a strife where
every act of rapine was rewarded as a service to
the Cross.

5. Juana had no soldier who could cope with
Isabel's husband. When this able general pressed
her hard, Pacheo, as her father's minister, had im-
plored her uncle, Dom Affonzo, King of Portugal,
to aid her by his arms. In earlier days Affonzo
had been thought a soldier. By his wars in Barbary
he had gained his name of African; and both as
king and kinsman he had seemed to be the natural
champion of Juana's right. It was proposed in
Lisbon that Affonzo should espouse his niece Juana,
and her cause together; so that he might march and
combat for an interest of his own. A dispensation
would be needed; but a dispensation could be got
from Rome. Affonzo had despatched his agent, Ruy
de Sousa, to demand from Isabel the recognition of

Juana's rights as only daughter of Enrique the Liberal. Isabel had denied her niece's right; on which the King of Portugal had crossed the frontier with his troops. As city after city hailed his troops, Affonzo had received this cry of welcome as an invitation to assume the crown. At picturesque Plascentia, in the Moorish palace, he had met the Queen, his niece, whom he had then espoused, so far as he could marry such a child. Had he been swift of foot and strong of hand, he might have crushed the rebels at a stroke; but he had stayed his march in order to amuse his knights with feasts and shows. Fernando, taking full advantage of these errors, had renewed his strength. The King of Portugal had waited till it was too late to strike, and when it was too late to strike, had struck. One battle had dispersed his army and compelled him to retire, with an engagement to renounce his claims and those of his pretended bride.

6. Affonzo had not kept this treaty long. The French, who hoped to keep the Catalan duchies, and the Austrians, who detested Isabel as a usurpress, had induced the King of Portugal to try again. Once more his troops had been defeated and dispersed; once more the poor old soldier had been forced to sue for peace. Juana was a prisoner in her uncle's house; and yet her aunt was not content. What surety had she that Juana would not slip away to France or Germany? The Emperor was her uncle, and the fighting Archduke Maximilian was her cousin. Isabel had proposed a league between the royal families of Spain and Portugal, of

which her niece should be the victim.   John, then
Prince of Portugal, was dreaming of a union of the
crowns of Spain, and Isabel suggested through her
agents that his schemes might come about in concert with her, but could never ripen through alli-
ances against her.   John was dreaming of Juana.
He had once before proposed to her.   Since then
his father had espoused her; but their union was a
form of words, and nothing had been done to give
that form a spark of life.   Juana was his cousin;
but a dispensation from the Pope would clear away
impediments of blood.   Yet Isabel's suggestion, as
he saw, was true.   The Princess Isabel, though born
in sin, was obviously a better match.   A papal breve
had wiped away her shame.   Her parents were in
full enjoyment of the crown; her claim to follow
them was not denied.   The Exile had at best a
birthright in Toledo, while the Princess Isabel might
live to wear the crowns of Sicily, Sardinia, Aragon,
Leon, and Castille.   John had accepted Isabel's hint,
and signed a treaty for the marriage of his son
Affonzo to the "child of sin."

7. Juana, living as a queen in Lisbon, with a
court of pages, minstrels, maids of honour, and confessors in her house, had seen her servants sent
away, her title taken from her, and her liberty
abridged.   Yet something had been done to satisfy
her pride.   Her aunt had set before her maiden
eyes the choice between an earthly and a heavenly
crown.   Would she elect to marry Juan, Prince of
the Asturias, or go into a convent as a spouse of
Christ? Mendoza was not easy in his mind; for he

had been Juana's guardian, and was well aware that
all the stories told about her birth were false. He
felt the evil they had done, and feared the danger
they had braved. Guienne was dead; but Louis
took the Exile's part. The Empress Leonor was
outraged by the treatment of her sister and that
sister's child. For years Mendoza had been seeking
for the means of reconciling aunt and niece. This
task had been too hard for even his elastic conscience and inventive brain. Juana would not take
the veil, and Isabel would not yield her royal state.
What could he do? One throne would not ac-
commodate two rival queens. At length, he saw
his way. As soon as Isabel bore a son, Mendoza
put the case before her. Juan must espouse Juana,
and unite the elder with the younger branch. The
Queen adopted his suggestion; though by offering
to accept Juana for her son, and thus restore her
to her kingdom, Isabel made confession that the
rumours she and her adherents had been spreading
for so many years against the mother had been
false. Confession came too late to save that injured
queen. The outraged woman's last few weeks of
life had been so sweet and saintly, that the fathers
had been moved to pity her. They set aside the
injuries they had heaped on her; and when her dust
was laid at rest, they pointed to her end as that of
one, who, sorely tried on earth, had passed into her
rest a perfect pattern of the Christian life. But
though the words were tardy, it was something to
the Exile that her aunt had been compelled to own
by public acts her knowledge that the dead queen

was innocent, and that the living queen, her daughter, was not born in shame.

8. Yet Queen Juana was not able to accept the match proposed to her by Isabel, her aunt. The Prince was eight months old; the Queen was in her eighteenth year. When Juan would be twenty-one, Juana would be thirty-nine. If she agreed to wait for twenty years, how could she feel assured that Juan would redeem his mother's pledge? As she would not accept this child, they carried her from Lisbon to Coimbra, where they lodged her with a trusty abbess, under orders that the sisters of her convent were to worry her until she took the veil.

In time, they got her to profess; for she was soft of mood and full of saintly grace; but they had not induced her to pronounce the final vows. No art, no menace, had succeeded with the lonely child; though prince and prior had essayed to work upon her mind. She had not ceased to claim her own; she had not dropt her style of Queen. The Church was asked to curse her, and such cardinals as Borgia had not stayed their lips and pens. All princes, dukes, and knights, who owned Juana, even in their secret hearts, were cast out bodily from the fold. Yet Isabel, in her palace and her chamber, could not rest for fear. If anything was wrong with her, as sickness in the house, disaster in the field, disorder in the towns, cross purposes in foreign courts, she felt that every eye was turning from the alcazar of Cordova towards that cloister of Santa Clara in Coimbra, where the holy maid was ready with her stainless banner and her popular name. The Emperor wished her to resume her throne; the court of France desired her to resume her throne; the people of Granada and Navarre expected her to resume her throne. Nor was she less desired at home. Juana had become a parallel to the Perfect Prince. As people prayed before the tomb of Carlos, they revered the Exile as a sort of living saint. All laymen of her kingdom, from the councillor at Isabel's table to the shepherd on his mountain, called upon the Exile by her popular and endearing names of Excellenta, Lady Excellenta, and Señora Excellenta of Castille.

CHAPTER IX.

At Alcala.

1485.

1. THE summer had been hot, and Isabel was suffering in her physical and moral health. With autumn came a flood of rain. The Guadalquiver rose above her banks, and swept through maize-field, melon-yard, and croft. Mosques, tombs, and houses, were surrounded by a flood; the lower city was a lake; and people had to paddle up and down in boats. Below the city wall, the river broke her dykes, and poured in one wild sheet across the plain. Trees, mills, and herds of kine, were swept away. From Cordova to Seville, in the basin of the stream, her country was a wreck. In Seville, too, a lake was formed in every square, and torrents roared against the walls and gates. A watcher on the Golden Tower could see the drovers floating through their fields on rafts. Triana, on the farther bank, where Torquemada held his court, was drowned. These floods brought pestilence; for out of lake and swamp steamed up a hot mephitic vapour which infected man and beast. Great battles had been fought around these cities, and a host of corpses had been left to whiten on the ground. A cry of pest was raised. At Cordova, around the

alcazar and mosque, now purged into a palace and cathedral, many of the poor and homeless drooped and died. The cry of pest was followed by a cry of flight; and those who had the means of flight prepared to fly. Fernando, no less startled by his news from Cordova, than by his news from Zaragoza, hastened from his camp, and snatching up his queen, his children, and his household, bore them towards the high and healthy ridge of Central Spain.

2. It was already autumn in the year of Bosworth-field and Ronda, when the royal company set out from Cordova. In front rode Don Fernando, King of Aragon and Sicily; Doña Isabel, his consort, Queen of Leon and Castille; Don Juan, Prince of the Asturias, their only son; the pale Infanta Isabel; the fair Juana and the child Maria, with their several abigails and knights. Behind the Queen, and prouder than the Queen, rode Pedro de Mendoza, Cardinal of Spain. Mendoza, from his pride of place, was called a king, the Cardinal-king of Spain. Not far behind the Cardinal came his kinsman, Diego de Mendoza, Archbishop of Seville; after whom, with no great pause and distance, came a crowd of prelates, friars, and chaplains; prelates like Alonzo de Fonseca, Archbishop of Santiago; friars like Tomas de Torquemada, Grand Inquisitor of Castille and Aragon; chaplains like Fernando de Talavera, prior of Santa Maria del Prado and confessor to the Queen. A tail of pages, cooks, and slaves, with many friars, black, white, and grey, were followed by the royal guard; a band of knights

in Moorish armour, riding Moorish horses, and commanded by that gallant Count de Cabra who had marked the recent summers by a great success and a severe reverse.

3. Where could Fernando find a place of rest —a place of strength as well as rest—in which his Queen and children could remain while he was wrestling with the Friends of Light? He dared not take them to the Aljaferia. A mob was howling in the streets of Zaragoza for the blood of Jew and Moor. The citizens of Tudela were protesting in the name of law and liberty against this cry for blood. In Teruel there was a rising of the people, headed by the magistrates and priests. In Barcelona every one was quick with rage, and every day produced some conflict with the royal troops. Valencia was unquiet, and his neighbours in Navarre were ready to support the Friends of Light. In spite of genius and success, Fernando was not loved in his hereditary states, where people knew how he had risen to power, and every lip was praying to the Perfect Prince. The jails were full of knights and citizens, the abbeys and cathedrals of a surging and excited crowd. Fernando's officers were flying to their lonely castles, to the liberal towns, and into foreign lands. He dared not venture to the Aljaferia, even though his wife might wish her infant to be born in the auspicious room where Santa Isabel had first beheld the light of day.

4. Where could he rest? Toledo and Avila were too far away from Aragon. He must be near his frontier, yet beyond the reach of an avenging

knife. The Cardinal who rode beside him had a
house at Alcala; at Alcala, the holy city, lying in a
green and fertile vega near the royal forests of
Madrid; and, save Toledo, the most populous town
in New Castille. This house Mendoza offered to
the King and Queen.

5. When seen afar off by the muleteers who
trudge in dust and heat through Central Spain, this
city has a look of age and strength becoming her
renown. Yet her renown is old, is widely spread,
and is of many kinds. She is the city of San Juste
and San Pastor, and enjoys the special patronage
of these infant saints. For centuries she was a
citadel of Moslem pride, a centre of Arabian wealth
and art. In later ages she was wrested from the
infidel; became the scene of Don Bernardo's vision,
and the prize of King Alonzo's arms. When captured by the Christians, she was consecrated to
religion as a temporal holding of the Church. For
ages she remained a home of cardinals and primates,
who enlarged Bernardo's cell till it was vast enough
to lodge a royal household. Consistorial and in-
quisitorial courts were held within her walls. She
was the school and the retreat of Ximenes. A
printing-press which rivalled that of Venice spread
her fame abroad. Her college of San Ildefonso
was a nursery of sacred learning, and the workshop
out of which came forth the Complutensian Bible.
For a century her doctors and professors held a
rank in letters hardly less conspicuous than the
doctors and professors of Salamanca held in law.
Not often have so many glories met in one small

city; yet the pride of Alcala is in a cradle and a
grave. In Alcala Cervantes was born, and there
Ximenes died.

6. A corner of the town was covered by the
primate's palace, with a garden lying in the shadow
of a Moorish wall and tower. Approached by
spacious courts and splendid stairs, the halls and
chambers of this palace were the pride of Spain.
The Allelujah hall, the Inquisition hall, and the
Banqueting hall, were royal rooms. Mendoza placed
these chambers at the service of his sovereigns,
while those sovereigns were engaged in dealing at
a distance with the Friends of Light.

CHAPTER X.

Catharine.

1485.

1. IN siding with his monks, the King made many foes whom he could ill afford to front. The nearest officers of his court were under ban. Navarre was friendly to the fugitives. The people of that country, clinging to the memory of their Perfect Prince, disliked Fernando for his mother's sake. Navarre received the Jews who fled from Aragon, and, as the exodus increased, provided them a separate quarter in Pamplona and allowed them to erect a synagogue. Ambassadors were coming from the Pope. The Emperor was hostile; and the Austrian court regarded Isabel's niece as lawful queen. The French were pouring troops into his duchies, and conducting their affairs in Perpignan as though Rossillon were a part of France. A change of rulers at Pamplona, where Catharine, wife of Jean d'Albret, had recently succeeded to her brother's throne, gave Charles, a leading influence in Navarre. Fernando saw the gateways of his kingdom in the west, as well as in the east, thrown open to an active and unscrupulous foe.

2. Nor was the outlook closed for him by Germany, Rome, and France. What sort of king, he

had to ask, was reigning in the English court? A pirate named Columbus, kinsman and companion of the navigator, had received a patent as vice-admiral of the French fleet in Portuguese waters, mainly with a view to harass the Venetian trade. Columbus hated the Venetians like a Genoese, and when their galleys hove in sight, with spices, cotton, wine and gold on board, he fell upon them, fought them for a summer day, and forced them one by one to strike their flags. On board these ships he found rich store of Spanish goods and produce; bales of spice and bags of cotton, butts of wine and heaps of silver coin; all which he seized and held as spoil of war. But having doubts if such a haul was lawful prize, he sailed for England, where he hoped to find a market for his spoil.

3. By treaty right, Fernando could demand from France the restitution of these bags and bales, and he was sending his request to Paris when he learned that the Italian corsair had retired into an English port. Columbus knew a little more of England than Fernando knew. Aware that Richard had been slain at Bosworth-field, he knew that Richard's death had put an end to treaties made between the courts. Until those treaties were renewed, no rule of law prevented him from selling in an English port his captured bales of silk and butts of wine. Fernando was so far behind in knowledge, that he could not learn what king was seated on the English throne. While he had been afield against the Moors, dark tales had reached

him from that distant court, in which his children,
as the heirs of John of Gaunt, had an eventual
claim. A king was dead; his sons were murdered
in the Tower; the murderer had seized his crown.
Plots, risings, and assassinations, marked that murderer's reign. An exiled prince had tried to land
and failed; a second effort of that prince had met
with more success. But who had won the fight
Fernando had not heard; and when he wrote from
Alcala, complaining of the corsair, he was forced to
write in blank; his letter being addressed to no one
in particular, but only to "the serene and powerful
prince" who happened, when his note reached London, to be King.

4. Fernando sent his orders into Aragon. A
hall and chamber in his palace of the Aljaferia
were prepared for the Dominicans, who henceforth
were to sit beneath the royal roof, and issue
sentences of fine and death. His hand fell heavily
on the Friends of Light. These counts and citizens,
the flower of his estates, were hunted, tried, and
hung; nay, every one who gave them shelter, even
for a night, was seized by royal officers, handed
over to familiars of the Holy Office, hid from sight
in dungeons, tortured till he answered, and condemned to ruinous fines, to penance in the church,
and haply to the flames. Uranzo turned king's
evidence on the promise of a pardon, and was
hung; Fernando saying, as he strung him up, that
by a pardon he had meant to spare the fellow's
hands, but not his head. Abadia slew himself in
jail. From every town in Aragon, the fathers took

at least one victim; so that every town in Aragon should know what punishment had been awarded to the Friends of Light. Among these victims was a royal prince, Don Jaime of Navarre, Fernando's nephew, who was charged with having sheltered one of the unhappy fugitives in his house. Don Jaime was a son of Elinor, late Queen of Navarre, and uncle of Catharine, the reigning queen. Fernando loved his elder sister and her offspring, as he had loved his elder brother Carlos. Jaime was seized by the familiars, flung into a vault, compelled to yield his secret, and condemned to suffer personal shame. This prince, whose crimes were royal blood and noble sentiment, was carried from his jail to the cathedral of La Seo, where, in presence of Fernando's bastard son, the boy-Archbishop, and a crowd of monks and citizens, he was stript and beaten round the choir with rods. This act of shame, inflicted on a royal prince, was called a penance of the Church.

5. From Alcala, a fortress and a sanctuary, the King and Queen directed all these acts of vengeance. Upwards of two hundred citizens were put to death. The Cortes and the council-board were purged of Friends of Light. Arbues was adopted by the Queen. Though he was dead she named him her confessor, and the King decreed him a magnificent tomb. Amidst this reign of fire and blood, the Queen fell sick. She fainted in her chair, was borne into her room, and on the sixteenth day of December, 1485, was delivered of a female child,

6. This female child was born beneath a troubled star. She came into the world too soon; her sex was a surprise and a regret; and she was born, not only far from her imperial home, but in a fortalice of the Church. It was an open question with the judges whether she was not the Cardinal's subject; but the child was born as she would have to live and die—away from home, the sport of time and chance, the prey of rival priests and kings.

BOOK THE SECOND.

CATHARINE'S CHILDHOOD.

CHAPTER I.

The Cardinal of Spain.

1485-6.

1. MENDOZA, Cardinal of Spain, received the infant from her nurses and adopted her by book and bell into the Christian fold. Her name was Catalina, the Castillian form of Catharine. When the rite was done in church, Mendoza gave a banquet in his splendid hall in honour of the child. She was his infant, born in his own city, and he wished to mark her baptism by a feast which minstrels would rehearse in song, and chroniclers would celebrate in prose.

2. Pedro de Mendoza, known in story as the Great Cardinal of Spain, was born of noble race, and in the mind of every monk and priest he was the noblest of his race. His father was the famous Marquis of Santillana; his elder brother was the famous Duke of Infantado; his cousin was the famous Count of Tendilla; yet the Cardinal of

Spain had risen beyond all reach of rivalry outside the reigning house.

3. A man with brimming eyes and shaven chin, you saw in him at once a pleasant mien, unruffled temper, and prolific force. In youth, a rhymester and a student, he is said to have translated Ovid into Spanish verse. In riper years, a friar, a councillor, and a soldier, he had brethren in the cell and colleagues at the board who put that pagan poet to the ban. Though he was neither ignorant friar nor stupid councillor, he chose to fight beneath the flag that led him by the easiest road to fame and power. A member of the Order of St. Francis, he was vowed to poverty, to chastity, and to obedience; yet, in every stage of his career, he was devoured by greed of gold, by love of women, by ungovernable pride. He kept a table and a harem. In Mendoza's day, a prelate who retained one lady only in his house was deemed a model priest; but he had taken to himself as many favourites as the King. Two ladies of the highest rank bore children to him, whom he owned without a blush of shame, and whom he gave in marriage, with befitting fortunes, to his equals in hereditary rank. These pleasures of the table and the harem were the themes of many a stave and sermon, which the young Franciscans, starving on their peas and rye, gulped down with water, loved to launch against their powerful and indulgent chief. Mendoza listened to these censures with a humorous smile. One day, an earnest brother, who was preaching in his presence, made a bold allusion to his fondness for

the sex, his craving after money, and his appetite
for meat and drink, as incompatible with his vows,
and even with a Christian life. Some bishops who
were in the church rose up in rage, and would
have torn the insolent varlet from his pulpit; but
Mendoza stilled them by a movement of his eye;
and going in to dinner, which was cooked as for
an emperor, he took a dish of highly-seasoned
game, together with a purse of dollars, and despatched them to that brother's cell. His meat and
money were not thrown away, for in his next dis-
course the preacher undertook to show that Gospel
liberty means a special license which is given to
men of high estate.

4. Mendoza's feast in honour of the young Infanta was prepared in the great banquet-room. The
King and Queen, Don Juan, and the lords and
ladies of two royal households, were received in
state, and fed with dainty food and warmed with
costly wine. Fonseca, the Archbishop of Santiago,
graced the feast. Mendoza's banquet had a rare
success.

5. Yet there was hot debate between the royal
mayor and clerical judge. At Alcala, Mendoza
claimed to be supreme. The place belonged to
God and not to man. It was a city of the Cross,
recovered by a miracle, and held in virtue of that
miracle by the Church. A storm began to rage
round Catalina's crib in Alcala, like that which was
to rage about her closet at Kimbolton in her dying
hour. The royal mayor asserted that his powers
were absolute. He was the royal mayor—in Alcala

the same as in Toledo and Zaragoza. "No," the clerical judge replied, "Toledo and Zaragoza own another rule than Alcala; those capitals are temporal cities; Alcala is a possession of the Church." Each party called upon his chief. Mendoza said his officer was right. Fernando, speaking for his consort, said her officer was right. All processes of law were stopt; nor could the baby's birth be certified in the usual form. The Queen, when told of the affair, would not give way, because the matters in dispute were held to touch the unity and splendour of her crown; the Cardinal, on his side, could not yield, because the matters in dispute were held to touch the freedom and authority of his Church.

6. For Alcala was not a sacred and ideal city only, but a fastness lying in a fertile valley on the road from Aragon into the heart of Spain. It closed the shortest line from Zaragoza to Toledo. In Carillo's days the town had proved a sure defence; for though the Queen detested her archbishop, she had never sought to pluck him from this safe retreat. Mendoza could not say how soon such days might come for him. Carillo had been once as near to Isabel as he was now; yet, in his later years, Carillo had been glad to toy with magic and pursue the elixir of life behind a gate which neither King nor Queen could pass on penalty of stirring up the ire of holy Church.

7. A feud seemed ready to break out between the crown and church; in which event the Excellenta might have been recalled, the priest of Zaragoza might have died in vain, the Inquisition might

have been arrested at an early stage, and Catalina might have lived the abbess of a convent in some Spanish town. A sense of common peril checked their tongues. To turn upon each other while Granada still held out, while Aragon was burning into fever, while the French were stirring in the Pyrenees, was ruin to the aims alike of church and crown. Sage doctors met in council and proposed a truce. Fonseca showed the way. His plan was to refer the case to certain learned men, with power to study the original grant, and make reports to Cardinal and Queen. No one disputed Don Alonzo's grant. No one denied that this original grant had been confirmed by various kings and popes. The Queen herself had recently confirmed the grant. One question still remained—to what extent the sovereign right had passed, in virtue of these grants and confirmations, to the primate of Castille? Was Alcala, like Rome, an absolute property of the Church? Five learned men were chosen by the Cardinal; five other learned men were chosen by the Queen. Fonseca was to act as president and moderator. These men were wise enough to take much time. Before Fonseca made his full report, the Queen and Cardinal were in their graves, the Caliphate of Granada was destroyed, the German court was reconciled, the Inquisition was at work in every part of Spain, the liberties of Aragon were outraged in the name of Christ, and baby Catalina was a widow in a foreign land.

CHAPTER II.

A Holy War.

1486.

1. The feast of blood being over and the Friends of Light dispersed, the Inquisitors having moved into the Aljaferia, and the offices of state being filled by orthodox counts and knights, Fernando and his consort quitted Alcala, in company with the Cardinal of Spain. They rode to Cordova, their conquered city, and the pestilence being abated, Isabel took up her residence in the alcazar. The children stayed with her, together with a crowd of tutors, chaplains, and confessors, while her husband and his generals bore the bars of Aragon and lions of Castille into the south.

2. A small, but beautiful and fertile part of Spain still owned the sway of Moorish prince and Moslem seer. That Andalus, of which Granada was the capital and Malaga the port, was painted by an Arab bard, Salami, as a land of gentle hills and fertile plains, sweet air and wholesome food; a land of useful animals, abundant fruits, and constant seasons, neither hot like Barbary, nor chilly like Castille; a land of flowing streams, bright groves, and pleasant homes; and peopled by a race of men endowed with ready wit, clear intellect, high courage, manly pride;

6*

a people in whose hearts there beat a passion for the highest and most gracious things.   In picturing Andalus to men who had not seen that earthly paradise, an Arab poet drew on all the riches of his fancy and his memory.   "This land of Andalus," wrote Abu Obeyd-illah, "is like Syria for the sweet-ness of her water and the pureness of her air; like Yemen for the mildness of her climate, which is one perpetual spring; like India for her wealth of drugs and spices; and like China for her mines and precious stones."   Of this poetic land, Granada was the pearl.   "Granada" cried her rhapsodists, with oriental flush of metaphor, "has no equal on the earth; not Cairo, not Bagdad, nay, not Damascus can compare with her; she is a bride, of which these cities are the dower."   Granada was the throne of Andalus, protected by a ring of strongholds worthy to defend so rich a prize.

3. Much fighting lay between Fernando and his prize, and he depended for the conquest of Granada rather on the Caliph's weakness, on the discords in his household, on the factions in his capital, and on the feuds between his towns, than on his own superior strength; even though the armies he could put in line outnumbered his opponents ten to one. The Moors were strong in art, in science, and in engineering skill.   Their troops were better armed and better drilled than Spanish troops.   Their swords were finer and their guns of longer range.   The Moors were swifter riders, better shots, and more adventur-ous scouts.   But they were few in front of many, and they had no leader equal to their foe.   Though

brave as lions, they were pushed from town to town,
from ridge to ridge, which, once abandoned to the
Goth, could never be recovered; yet the war was
less a conflict of the Goths and Moors, than a particular duel between the King and Caliph. An unscrupulous general, master of the art of war, as clear
in aim as he was dark in means, was matched against
a learned, restive, and poetic dreamer, who desired
to live in peace, to please his mother, to amuse the
rabble of Granada, and to spend his days in the
apartments of a favourite slave.

4. Abd-allah, this easy Caliph, was the eldest
son of Hassan, a refined and restless prince, who
had been no less hapless in his wars than in his
loves. This prince had lost Alhama,—

Ah de mi Alhama!

and the loss of that strong post had helped the faction of his wife, Zoraya, to dethrone him. Jealous
of a captive Greek, on whom the Caliph doated with
poetic frenzy, she had whispered through the city
that her husband meant to raise the offspring of
this Christian slave. A civil war had broken out.
"The Mosque in danger" is as fierce a war-cry as
"The Church in danger." From the kennel and the
college surged the champions of the mosque. The
son rose up against his father; and the aged Caliph
who had vexed his partner was expelled. Their
country parted into hostile camps; one caliph reigning at Granada and a second caliph reigning at
Malaga. In evil hour the hero, Az-zaghal, a younger
brother of the Caliph Hassan, yielded to the clamour

of his troops, and he, too, was invested with the
sovereign rank. A province less in size than York-
shire had to bear the burthen of three reigning
princes, each of whom required a court, a harem,
and a royal guard.

5. Of these three caliphs, Az-zaghal alone inspired much fear in Spain. Abd-allah won no battles
save against his father. At Lucena, he had fallen a
prisoner; but Fernando, who discovered that his
absence from Granada might induce all parties in
the country to unite beneath the flag of Az-zaghal,
allowed him to return. Fernando got Abd-allah to
accept a body-guard of Christian knights; well knowing that the presence of these knights would rouse
the fiercest anger of the Moors. Fernando sowed
his tares in fertile soil. One town grew jealous of
another; jealous as Zoraya of the Christian slave.
Granada flouted Loja; Gaudix hated Baza; and Illora
envied Malaga. Instructed by his captor how to
rule, Abd-allah offered peace with Spain to every
city that would own his sway, and war with Spain
to every city that should close her gates against him.
These appeals to Spain were backed by a display of
Christian troops. Surprise, disorder, and division,
showed themselves on every side. The aged Caliph
was restored and was again expelled. His death
brought no composure to the land; for Az-zaghal,
though followed as a soldier, could not reunite the
factions as a prince. Granada was at issue with
itself; one bank of the Darro being for Abd-allah,
the other bank for Az-zaghal. The rabble were on
one side, the nobles and professional classes on the

other side.   That rabble spoke of Az-zaghal, their
only soldier, as a tyrant who was fighting to deprive
a nephew of his throne.   Fernando watched this
Moorish leader with a wistful glance; for whether
his campaigns were brisk or sullen, nothing was
decided even for a moment while this brilliant horse-
man was afield.

6. Good news saluted King and Queen on their
arrival in the south.   Fierce strife, they heard, had
broken out between the two great factions of Granada,
the Antiqueruela and the Albaycin. The Antiqueruela
were the knights; the Albaycin were the roughs. These
factions lived in different quarters of the city, and
supported different Caliphs.   All the upper ranks,
the captains, advocates and mollahs, were for Az-
zaghal; the lower classes, porters, smiths, and muleteers, were for Abd-allah.   Az-zaghal was marching
on Granada to support his party and repel the foe;
Abd-allah was flying on the road towards Seville,
calling out for succour to his Spanish friends.   A
band of Christian horsemen bore Abd-allah back;
and then a war of fire and sword consumed the
capital.   Az-zaghal was posted with his knights in
the Alhambra; Abd-allah in the suburb of the Albaycin, secured by Christian troops.   While they
were tearing at each other's throats, Fernando made
a dash at Loja—strong and lovely Loja! rising on
her verdant hill, and closing by her gates the beautiful and fertile vega of Granada. Troops from many
countries flocked into Fernando's camp, and found
a joyous welcome from the King. Earl Rivers, uncle
of the Queen of England, rode into his camp,

attended by a troop of English horse, and asked no
other favour than to ride in front. Abd-allah stole
away from the Albaycin, and appeared among the
Christian tents. Lord Rivers and his English troops,
dismounting from their horses, raised their battle-
axes in the air, and rushed upon the Moorish line.
Struck senseless from the wall, his teeth knocked
out, his visage mauled and spoiled, the English Earl
was carried to his tent. But men as stout as Rivers
followed, and the siege went briskly on. Granada,
torn with discords, would not send a man to help
her neighbour in the hour of peril. Loja fell; and
then the out-work of Granada was in Spanish hands.

7. Illora, Modin, and some other places fell with
Loja. When the vega had been opened to his raids,
Fernando sent his Caliph to the capital, with offers
of a league of friendship if the people of Granada
would desert the flag of Az-zaghal and drive that
warrior from his throne. Abd-allah entered the Albaycin in disguise, and in the dead of night convened
a meeting of his partisans. He told them Spain
would lend them arms and powder to expel their
tyrant. If they wished for more, the King, his friend,
would send them help in men and guns. Would
they not rise? Would they not storm the tyrant in
his purple hall? His cry was answered by a shout
of joy; the treacherous aid of Spain was welcomed;
and a raid on the Alhambra was proposed.

8. On hearing that their plans were speeding
well, the King and Queen rode up on pilgrimage
from Cordova to Santiago, one of those great
Spanish shrines which hardly yielded in importance

to the chapel of Our Lady on her jasper shaft. St. James, the brother of our Lord, had taken shape in Spain as Santiago, a saintly Hercules, a mundane Michael; and the people saw in him at once a saint, a patron, and a god of war. He was commander of all Spanish troops; the highest military order in the country bore his name; and every soldier of the Cross, on rushing into battle, was reminded by his captain and his priest that Santiago and a host of angels would be fighting at his side. So great a victory as that of Loja called for an unusual rite, and so the King and Queen, attended by their son, their daughters, and their household, rode into the north and threw themselves at Santiago's shrine.

CHAPTER III.

Malaga.

1487.

1. NEXT year Fernando turned his face towards Malaga; that shining city on the sea—the port of figs and olives, grapes and almonds, mulberries and limes — of which the royal poets loved to sing. Blue waters washed the feet of purple hills, on which there seemed no speck of soil that was not garden, vineyard, olive-ground, and fig-walk. Every city of the East, from Smyrna to Bagdad, received the figs of Malaga with rapture. "God has given to Andalus," the poets wrote, "a blessing which He has withheld from Barbary and Fez." No less delicious were the grapes, both dried and pressed. "O Lord," a caliph on his death-bed cried, "among the pleasant things of paradise, let there be Malaga wine and Seville oil." White mosques and houses glistened on the slopes. A mountain stream, which leapt into the city, fanned the narrow streets, and cooled the glowing air. High walls of ancient date ran round the place, and one great mosque, of special sanctity, with a noble court adorned by orange-trees, attracted every eye. The people were a quick, mercurial, and artistic race; professors, craftsmen, minstrels; men whose thoughts were

given to art and trade, and who were mainly anxious to pursue their lives in peace.

2. First sending help in men and money to Abd-allah, who was hovering in and out of the Albaycin, in the hope that he would give employment to the rival prince, Fernando marched on Velez Malaga, a famous outwork of the still more famous port. Alhama gave the Spaniards access to Velez Malaga; a fortress which could only be assisted by an army coming from the east by steep and arid mountain roads. Yet Az-zaghal no sooner heard that foes were sitting down in front of Velez Malaga than he mustered troops for her relief; and hoping that the Moorish factions would forget their feuds in presence of so great a danger, rode from the Alhambra with his troop of horse. He sought his foe, and pressed him hotly; but his squadrons were too light to raise the siege; and in his absence from the capital, the rabble of the suburbs stormed his palace and proclaimed his nephew Caliph. He withdrew to Gaudix, whence he watched the enemies whom he could no longer meet. Attacked by sea and land, the fort of Velez Malaga surrendered to the King, who instantly pushed on his troops to Malaga, and called upon that port and town to yield.

3. In this extremity the Moors bethought them of their brethren at the farther end of the great Midland Sea. A poet of their creed was seated on the greatest throne on earth. This poet, Bajazet, whose arms had smitten kings and khans, was master of two continents and seas. If any man on

earth could help them he was Bajazet. An agent
of the Moor was sent to the Serail, where Bajazet
received him kindly. In romantic strain this agent
prayed the Sultan to assist the Princes of the Beni-
ahmer, Sons of Crimson, in Granada, who were
pressed and harried by Fernando, King of Aragon,
an enemy of their holy faith. His pleas were
elegies, composed in Arab measure, and adapted
to the prince whom he addressed. For Bajazet
was not an ordinary Turk; a young barbarian, hot
with pride and strength, who fought from wanton-
ness of blood; but a pacific prince, who loved to
strike his tent and fold his flag, and grieved when
he was forced to draw his sword and mount his
horse. They told of what the Moors were suffering
by the war. They spoke of what the Moors had
done for Spain; the cities they had built, the
mosques they had adorned, the gardens they had
planted, and the poems they had written, in a reign
of many hundred years. Yet they were pressed,
they said, by infidels on every side; they feared
the faith itself might perish in the wreck; their only
hope was in the justice and compassion of their
Moslem brethren. If the Sultan would not aid
them, they were lost.

4. A poet and a zealot, Bajazet was touched by
these appeals. But Spain was far away; Kazan
was crying out for help against the Russ; and he
was much averse to entering on a distant war. If
he could do them good without declaring war he
was inclined to serve them. Calling for his page—
a page called Kemal, "perfect," from his personal

beauty—he commanded ships to be prepared for sea. Page Kemal was to head this fleet; he was to visit Spain; he was to lend what help he could to the outnumbered Moors. As Kemal Reïs, this page soon made himself a name of fear; but plundering caravels at sea and wasting woods and villages on shore, could not arrest the progress of Fernando's arms.

5. Though weak in numbers and divided in opinions, the southern Moors, in these last months of independent rule, exhibited the virtue of those nobler days when their supremacy in arts had been supported by supremacy in arms. A trading and artistic city held a mighty enemy at bay for six long months, disputing every rood of ground as he approached their walls, and beating him in many a fair and open fight. Once succour seemed at hand. From Gaudix Az-zaghal sent out a troop of horse to throw relief into the town, as proof to the defenders that they were not left to fight alone. But Abd-allah, who was afield with a superior force, waylaid this party of relief, and having either captured or destroyed it, sent the news of his success into Fernando's camp, with presents of Arabian horses, with congratulations on his victories, and meek entreaties for his friendship. After a resistance which has given the Malagans a place in history, they had to yield the sword, and trust the mercy of a man and woman who had now become their king and queen.

6. No age of time, no zone of earth, has witnessed a more brutal use of power than followed

this surrender of the port and town of Malaga.
When King and Queen rode in, together with their
troops, they seized the alcazar and public baths,
they threw a company of friars into the mosques,
they occupied the gates and towers, they tore the
Crescent from all vanes and minarets, and, after
chanting mass and burning incense in the mosque,
now named Our Lady's Church, they sentenced
every man, woman, and child, without regard to
age and station, to be sold as slaves.   In vain the
elders interfered in favour of the young.   In vain
the males protested on behalf of female innocence.
The Queen was pitiless.   Some Moors reminded
her how differently their caliphs had behaved at
Cordova, and in other cities where their arms had
been resisted by a gallant people fighting for their
homes.   To spare a broken enemy was not in
Isabel's nature.   Men of rank and learning were
exported to the Barbary coasts and sold for slaves.
Young girls were given to soldiers and to priests.
A few of the most noble and accomplished were
reserved as presents, such as queens might give
and pontiffs might receive.   Mendoza sent one
band of noble Moors to Rome.

7. So far was Isabel from sparing these poor
innocents, she pressed to have her share and choice
of spoil.   The prettiest captives were reserved for
her, and she bestowed these captives into slavery
far and wide.   She sent one batch of them to
Lisbon and a second batch of them to Naples. She
dispensed them freely to the ladies of her court.
Her tent, her stables, and her alcazar, were crowded

with these sad and dusky forms.   Ten thousand
innocent men and women, many of them more accomplished than her husband and herself, were
given by her to slavery in a single day.

———

CHAPTER IV.

Santa Hermandad.

1487.

1. When the campaign of Malaga was over, and the troops were lodged in quarters to await the spring, Fernando, with his wife, his children, and his household, rode into the north, and took up his abode at Zaragoza, where his Cortes were about to meet.

2. His Holy Office was unpopular with the upper classes, who were but too well aware that even in its milder form, the office of St. Dominic was forbidden by their fundamental laws. His capital was in mourning for the Friends of Light. In every noble house there was an empty chair. In almost every noble house there was a widow with beseeching eyes, a son with burning cheek, a brother with revengeful heart. Of those who were not called to mourn the dead, too many were compelled to mourn the absent. Princes, counts, and councillors were in flight. A father was in France, a son in Zürich, and a brother in Milan. Some desperate men had taken shelter in Granada. Like the dead, they were removed from time and space, and only felt by instinct in the void and pain created by their loss. A chill, a silence, as of rage and sorrow, sat on Zaragoza, and if fear restrained

the lust of vengeance, nothing but an armed band
supported by a brutal mob could keep the citizens
down. All Aragon was seething with the same
white passion as the capital, and the dependencies
of Aragon were seething like the parent state. To
a demand for information as to any fugitives who
might have entered Tudela from Zaragoza, the
magistrates of that liberal city answered they had
none to give. Lerida, with the bishop at its head,
was actually in arms. Valentia was excited, and
the Catalans, still new to Torquemada's black familiars, were kindling to the heat of civil war. Majorca,
Sicily, Sardinia, were as warm against his Inquisition as the cities in his older states.

3. Fernando met these movements of his people
with the cold and forward eye of one who had
prepared his work. Abravanel was at his side, a
pleader for compassion to the innocent, if not the
guilty; but a greater than Abravanel was also at his
side. The Queen could show no clemency to men
whose friends had slain her priest. Fernando, fighting for the monks, was fighting for himself. The
mob was on his side. Though jealous of the crown,
this rabble was obedient to their Church. By putting
an inquisitor in front, and tearing up the charter
of his kingdom in the name of holy Church, he
could secure his ends, and yet incur no blame.
Nor were these future benefits the whole of what
he had to gain. The fines were heavy, and the
seizures frequent; but beyond this flow of money to
his chests, he had a pressing need for men. His
holy war was a consuming fire. Pay, license, love

of arms, and chance of plunder, would not fill his
ranks. To drive more soldiers to his camp, he wanted
sharper spurs and stronger prods. These sharper
spurs and stronger prods he found in the inquisitor's
rack and brand. A man who put on armour for
the Cross could hardly be accused of heresy; and
hundreds who would otherwise have been content to
tend their vineyards rode afield in order to escape
the logs and pitch. An Act of Faith was fruitful in
another way. It kindled holy rage. It set the
looker on athirst for blood, and most of all for paynim
blood. From every Act of Faith a group of men-
at-arms came into camp. On every ground of policy,
Fernando saw a motive for supporting his Inquisitors against the Friends of Light. He therefore
sent fresh troops to Teruel and Barcelona, where
the clergy and the craftsmen had been making common cause with the superior ranks against the
deputies of Torquemada, and repressed these risings
in the name of law and liberty with unsparing hand
and hoof.

4. The Friends of Light being mostly counts
and knights, who lived in towers and castles up
and down the land, in lonely districts, difficult to
reach and still more difficult to storm, Fernando
formed a league of friars and villagers against them.
In Castille his consort had revived an ancient
democratic union called the Santa Hermandad; a
league of villagers and town-folk, like the bands and
brotherhoods in the Rhetian Alps; which, under
popular chiefs, had served in times of rapine to
protect the weak against marauding nobles and

rapacious kings. In her revival of this democratic league, the Queen had grasped the reins, and put the Bishop of Cartagena, one of her most trusty partisans, in the chair of president. She turned the Santa Hermandad against the upper ranks; so that a league which had been framed to check the royal power, was changed into the firmest bulwark of her throne. Though hating leagues, Fernando saw in such a brotherhood the means of checking knight and count, who lived on crested heights away from towns and royal fortresses. A league of peasants, governed by the brethren of St. Francis and St. Dominic, offered him, without expense, a troop of friends in front and rear of every castle in his realm. That league, as in Castille, could be directed from the royal chanceries. In brief, the Santa Hermandad was necessary to the Inquisition, and Fernando asked his broken and dispirited parliament to revive that ancient and forgotten league.

5. The Casa Blanca was in no condition to resist the Aljaferia. Fernando was a victor, flushed with fame and rich with spoil. He only needed to pronounce his will. His palace was a fort; his army lay about his gates; and no one doubted that his soldiers would obey their chief. In arming him against the Moor, his people had been arming him against themselves. A sword will cut with edge and point, and with the backward like the forward sweep. A regiment can wheel to either left or right, and face to either front or rear. One year of war transmutes an army into a machine of brass

7*

and steel—hard, bright, unreasoning, irresistible—
and his battalions had been many years at war.
The Moors were not subdued; yet he who should
have been the magistrate of a republic with the
name of King, was fast becoming through his army a
despotic prince. Such councillors as might have held
him back were either dead or ruined, either exiled
or imprisoned; and the liberal benches in the Casa
Blanca were too weak in number and in spirit to
insist on standing by their fundamental law. Fernando had no need to press them much. Averse
by instinct to such unions as the Santa Hermandad, he only meant to use that league of monks
and rustics for a little while. When they had
served his purpose, they would have to go. He
asked his Cortes to revive the union for a term of
years, and, after some debate, that term of years
was limited to five. His brother, Don Alonzo,
Duke of Villahermosa, had been already named
by Isabel her Captain General of the Santa Hermandad.

CHAPTER V.

Matrimonial Schemes.

1487.

1. DON JUAN, Prince of the Asturias, now nine years old, was heir to more than twenty crowns and coronets; to the kingdoms of Castille, Leon, Aragon, Sicily, Toledo, Valencia, Galicia, Majorca, Seville, Sardinia, Cordova, Corsica, Murcia, Jaen, Algarve, Algesiras, and Gibraltar; to the duchies of Athens, Neopatri, Rossillon, and Cerdaña; to the marquisates of Oristan and Goceano; to the earldoms of Barcelona; and the lordships of Biscaya and Molina. This inheritor of crowns was in the market as a marrying man. In order to improve his value as a match in foreign courts, his father wished to have him recognised as heir in Aragon and her dependent states. It was a form, and nothing but a form. No question as to title could exist in Aragon, whatever doubts might linger in the minds of men about his mother's title in Castille. In foreign countries he was known as Prince of Aragon, rather than as Prince of the Asturias. As Prince of Aragon he had been offered in marriage to Lady Catharine of York. He was the only heir, and so his right in blood and law, as Prince of Aragon, was solemnly proclaimed.

2. Don Juan was heir to every part of Spain, except the caliphate of Granada, and the kingdom of Navarre. Granada, as an enemy's country, might be won by force of arms. Navarre, a friendly country, governed by his cousin, might be gained by marriage. To a king who meant to play a leading part in general politics, Navarre was more important than Granada. She commanded every pass into his kingdom on the western side; the pass of Ronces-valles, the path of Maya, and the road through Irun; so that he who was the master of Navarre could pour his legions into either France or Spain. Navarre, a mountain fortress, was the key to either realm. To France she was the counter-part of what Rossillon was to Spain—an outwork, pushed beyond the mountain crests, from which an army could deploy. A Spanish prince, not master of Pamplona, was like a Frenchman who had lost his hold of Perpignan. He had to check a foe entrenched within his lines.

3. Catharine of Navarre was young and lovely, but her youth and loveliness were little in her kinsman's eyes. She was a liberal, and she held the mountain roads. By law and right she was his heiress, should his children fail him; it was good for both that they should keep on terms; and he desired her to regard him as her nearest friend. He meant to get her states by either love or law, by either force or fraud. Navarre, he said, was part of Spain, and he must push forward his frontier to the Pyrenees. While Phœbus was alive he had proposed to give him Juana, his second

daughter, for a wife. But Madeleine of France had put his suit aside. A sister of Louis the Eleventh, Madeleine had brought into the Pyrenees a soul devoted to her native land. All questions took with her one form, "Is this the thing to do for France?" Navarre was little in her eyes; Castille and Aragon were less. The house of Valois—Louis—France; these were to her the first and last. She had refused Fernando's suit because her brother wished to see Navarre and Aragon at feud. An embassy from Madeleine and Phœbus had been sent to Lisbon with an offer for the royal Nun; but in the midst of his alluring projects, Phœbus, like so many who had crossed Fernando's path, had died a sudden and mysterious death. When Catharine rose, Fernando's course seemed easier. If the Queen would marry Juan, all that he required was won:—Navarre would be united to the rest of Spain. If she had asked her country, Catharine would have married for the love of Spain. She asked her mother, and her mother, Madeleine, rejected peace and union for the sake of France. In place of Juan and his twenty crowns, she took Jean d'Albret, son of Alain d'Albret, one of the petty seigneurs in the Pyrenees. Jean d'Albret, now King-Consort of Navarre, was liegeman to the King of France.

4. If he were left alone, Fernando felt that he could reach Granada; but he had to ask how many of his neighbours would be glad to see him there? Would France, would Portugal, would Austria? France was anxious for her safety on the Catalan coast. Unless she were a partner in his conquests,

Portugal would note them with regret and fear. Austria, which had every reason to dislike Fernando, would be weakened in her chief Italian states. As King of Sicily and the Sardinian Isles, Fernando was a dangerous neighbour to Italian princes and republics; and the King of Naples, as a member of his house, might die at any hour and leave him heir. No Kaiser could have wished to see Fernando grow in strength, and Kaiser Friedrich's family hated him with burning bitterness of heart. A league of neighbours was a thing which any week might bring about. To keep the duchies, France would venture much. Being mistress in Navarre, she could attack him by the western passes while she took him in the rear by way of Perpignan. If either France or Germany could move the court of Lisbon to renounce the treaty and proclaim the Exile, his offensive war against the Moors would have to cease, the Caliphs might have time to stay their feuds, and all his forces might be found too weak to hold in check the arms of Austria, Portugal, and France.

5. His bargain with the Portuguese, by which the Exile was to be secured, was ten years old; the child was grown into a woman; yet the years had failed to soothe his anger at the way in which his allies carried out the peace. Fernando had proposed to use the Portuguese, and found the Portuguese were using and abusing him. If more than half the shame was theirs, they took good care that more than half the profit should be also theirs. No sooner had Fernando signed the articles,

than he felt himself a slave; a slave to what his
country, in her pride and passion, called a paltry
court and despicable race. No man in Lisbon paused
to think of Spanish pique. The Portuguese could
now be haughty and exacting in their turn. They
held the key, and could unlock the gates. In every
squabble over frontiers, water rights, and trade, the
weaker party had compelled the stronger one to
yield. By each affair Fernando had to wound the
pride of Spain. In dealing with the outer world, in
Paris, Augsburg, Ghent, and Rome, he had been
bound to ask what Lisbon would approve. The
Portuguese had never been content. As soon as
John the Perfect had been crowned, he talked of
tearing up the articles, renouncing Isabel for his
son, espousing the royal Exile, and restoring her by
force of arms. These insults galled Fernando sorely.
No man likes to have his child refused, his treaties
cast into his teeth. Fernando was too great for
such an insult to be borne.

6. He turned his eyes towards France, and
thought of making her a friend. Could he destroy
the Austro-French alliance? France and Austria
were his enemies, and a connexion of their princes
would perpetuate a line of foes. Could France be
tempted to forswear the Austrian match? His eldest
girl was pledged to Portugal; but pledges were to
him a form of words. As Portugal could only in-
jure him through the French, he would not need to
fear her malice after he had made his game with
France. A treaty with the House of Valois would
secure his dynasty from all attacks. If Charles the

Eighth, who had succeeded to his father, Louis the Eleventh, could be induced to marry Isabel, and call his troops from Perpignan, all Spain might soon be at his feet; but he was careful not to lose his hold on John till he was sure of Charles. A clever agent, Ruy de Pina, was despatched to Lisbon, where he was to hear objections to the articles, and offer Isabel's younger sister, Doña Juana, to the Prince of Portugal. Juana was a lovely girl, the pride and darling of her race. Yet Pina was to offer a great sum of money, if the Portuguese would only take the younger and more lovely for the elder and more homely girl.

CHAPTER VI.

Cross-proposals.

1487.

1. CHARLES THE EIGHTH, of France, had been engaged for many years to marry Marguerite, a daughter of Max, Archduke of Austria and King of the Romans. Louis, his sagacious father, had arranged this match, by which the French and German courts were to be bound by family ties, and France was to divide the sway and empire of the world with Germany. Charles was bound to Marguerite by many ties; his father's pledge, his own assent, the custody of his betrothed, a treaty with the Flemish towns, an understanding with the King, her father, and a clear advantage to his crown. For Marguerite had the dowry of a princess in her lap; two provinces, and many lordships, on the frontiers of his kingdom. Yet Fernando thought the youth, a son of Louis the Eleventh, would look to nothing but his gain, and therefore might be brought to cast off Marguerite in favour of his daughter Isabel and her contingent claims in Italy and Spain.

2. Fray Bernard Boyl, Prior of Monserrat, a famous shrine in Cataluña, was intrusted with the task of showing Charles, and Charles' sister, Madame Anne, how much they had to gain by breaking

faith with Max. Fernando's daughter Isabel would have a royal dowry, and in case her brother were to die she would be Queen of Spain, and Queen of no small part of Italy. Of course, the French must give up Rossillon; but after peace was signed that duchy would have less importance in the eyes of France. As Charles was governed by his sister, Fray Bernard addressed her secretly; but Madame Anne, who knew her father's secret purpose, was in favour of the Austrian match, not only as a thing decided by her father, in his wisdom, but as being the best for Charles as well as France. The girl he was to wed was fair and young. Her father was a King and would in time be Kaiser. She was then at school in Paris; and if only eight years old, she was already French in wit and style, and showed some dawning of the talents that in after seasons were to crown her queen of epigram and song. But more than all to Madame Anne, this young Archduchess was to bring the provinces of Artois and Franche Comté to her husband; districts which would carry France some marches nearer to the German Rhine and Flemish Scheldt. No claims of a contingent sort outweighed with Madame Anne such clear and instant gains. If Juan lived, his sister would have nothing but her dowry and her dubious birth; and yet a main condition of the league with Spain must be surrender of the fort of Salsas and the town of Perpignan. Fray Bernard used his eloquence in vain.

3. Fernando having failed with Madame Anne, his consort seized her pen. If there were any word

to say and any deed to do of special darkness, Isabel's pen was sure to be employed. She told Fray Bernard he must wait on Madame Anne; present her with a purse of money; ask her if she wished to seize the regency; and offer her, in case she had a mind to rule alone, the whole support of Spain. But nothing came of this attempt on Madame Anne. Fray Bernard found that princess quick to take his purse and slow to enter on a plot against the King, her brother. As a pious lady, ripe in years and rich in faith, she knew that Doña Isabel had been "born in sin," and that her birth had been denounced in legal acts. She knew that Charles, her uncle, had proposed to wed the Exile, and that Louis, her congenial father, had sustained that Exile from a feeling that to help her was the safest thing for France. She would not change her course. Alliance with the empire, and retention of the frontier, were her corner-stones of policy. When Fray Bernard came back to the Aljaferia with news of his repulse, the King took up his former game in Lisbon, settled every point with John the Perfect, and rejoiced to find the Exile changed into a prisoner of the Portuguese crown.   .

4. But John, though useful as a jailor of the exiled Queen, was not an ally who could help Fernando in a contest with the French. A prince whose blows would draw the French from Perpignan towards Paris was required, and only two such princes could be found alive. Max, King of the Romans, lying on the north of France, could scare her by his lancers from Namur and Metz, while

Henry, King of England, lying on the west, could harry her by his fleets at any harbour from Boulogne to Brest. If he could make these kings his allies, and procure a triple league of England, Flanders and Castille against the French, he might regain his duchies in the Pyrenees and yet complete his war against the Moor. But such a league would be a difficult work. The passions of all parties were against it. Max detested him, and he detested Max. Fray Bernard had been recently employed in trying to inflict on Max a personal insult and a public wrong. Nor was the feeling better in the north. Max hated Henry: Henry hated Max. All evil things were said, all evil deeds were done, by Max against the Tudor prince, whom he regarded as no better than the Queen of Spain. Each had seized a cousin's crown. Connected with the House of York by marriage, Max could see that Henry's rise cut off his children's claim to what their birth had seemed to give them; an immediate place in order of succession to the English throne.

5. This fair-haired Austrian, known in song as Last of the Ritters, and in sarcasm as a man "more Knight than Emperor," though as brave as a poetic war-god, was a comic politician, teased by turbulent burghers and an empty pocket. Husband to the Duchess Marie de Bourgogne, the only child of Charles the Bold and Lady Margaret of England, he was left, at twenty-three, a widower, and the guardian of his children, Philip called the Fair, and Marguerite the Sprightly; but the task of guiding two such heirs had been beyond his strength.

Though Max could take a lady by his condor nose and golden locks, he was unfit to rule the burghers of her Flemish towns. He joined one party in these towns against another, and had entered into every brawl of Cod-fish mobs with Fish-hook mobs. The Flemings claimed a right to train their duke, his son, and pledged the sister of that duke, his daughter, to the King of France. This contract gave the French an interest in his states which they were but too swift to press. If Cod-fish gained a battle, Fish-hook called upon the French for help; and Maréchal de Querdes, their captain in the border counties, marched on St. Omer, and pushed their fortunes at Bethune, while Max was wrangling with the citizens of Bruges and Ghent. In spite of their engagement, Max and Charles were usually at strife; but Max, instead of helping others, was in need of help himself.

6. No ally seemed of use except the prince who fought at Bosworth Field. But how could Henry be induced to draw the sword? This ruler was the nearest friend of Charles; the prince who helped him in his voyage and hailed him as a king when he had won his crown. He had no motive for a war with France. Before he sailed from Honfleur he had pledged his honour to renounce all claims on Normandie and Maine. Since his accession, Charles had kept on the most friendly terms with him, while Spain had held aloof and Germany had treated him with scorn. Could any bait induce him to revoke his pledge and draw his sword? Yes; playing in the chambers of the Aljaferia there

was such a bait. Fernando glanced at Catalina. Some obscure and nameless agent had been whispering in his ear that Henry would be proud to have that young infanta for his son. Fernando seized the hint. Might not a step be taken towards a match, and under cover of that match a treaty of defence be urged and signed?

7. Fernando would not venture far. As yet the Tudor reign was hardly two years old, and anything might come to pass in England. Such a scheme was sure to please the Queen, his wife, who bore a personal grudge against the House of York. While she was lodging in the convent of Arevalo, Edward, King of England, had proposed to her, and after asking her in marriage, had rejected her in favour of a subject and a widow, the poetic Lady Grey. Their dynasty was also touched. A sister of the man who had insulted Isabel in her youth, the Lady Margaret of England, had bestowed her daughter, Marie de Bourgogne, in marriage on the son of Empress Leonor. Philip, grandson of these women, would be Emperor, and it was easy to believe that boy would be an enemy of Spain. Isabel would consent to any step that would annoy the House of York. The English crown was always in the dust. Events would guide Fernando; but a promise which he need not keep unless he liked, might bring an English army into France.

CHAPTER VII.

The Secret Agent.

1487.

1. FERNANDO cast about him for an agent who could go to London, see the King and Queen, inquire about the Prince their son, observe the humours of the people, and prepare in silence the conditions of a league against the French. He was to speak about a treaty of alliance first, and only in the case of need to back that hint by reference to a match between the royal houses. Any agent he might send to London must proceed with prudence; France being on her guard, and Henry on the friendliest terms with Charles. The object of his mission must be kept a secret, and if Madame Anne should find it out, the agent must be one who could be censured and disowned. It was no easy thing to keep such matters secret in a place like London, where the public policy was free to public comment, and a topic of the day in Council was a topic of the morrow at St. Paul's. The Spanish agent to be used must, therefore, be a man obscure, adroit, and close; a priest, a lawyer, and a man of business; who might claim the help of monk and prelate, who might bandy terms with doctors and attorneys, who might hope to hold his own, on points of detail,

with experienced men. He ought to be a man so
little known that he could travel unperceived, and
labour unsuspected, by the outer world. He must
be one who would submit to serve for scanty pay,
to take his orders like a trooper and a monk, to
ask no question as to means employed, and in the
case of either failure or detection, to become a willing scape-goat for his Prince.

2. In riding through those border towns which
had no rights, Fernando met the man he wanted in
a lean and learned cripple, Rodrigo de Puebla,
mayor of Ecija, on the river Xenil, some few leagues
from Seville. Puebla was a canon, out of orders,
and a doctor not unlearned in the civil law. The
man was gaunt and swarth, a scare-crow in appearance, and a pedagogue in style; but he was full of
quips and wiles, a careless Christian, and a zealous
servant of the Crown. What else he was—what
else he might become when tempted by the sight
of gain—Fernando, having neither sympathy nor
humour, and observing men with cold, mechanical
eyes—could hardly guess. How far the cripple
suited him, he saw; how far he also suited Puebla
he could only learn in time. The man was very
poor and frail; so poor that he would serve on
easy terms, so frail that he could raise no scruple
as to means. His craving was to grow with time
and chance, but even when his master called him
out, he knew some tricks by which a mission into
England could be made to pay. Corn, tin, and
cloth were dear in Seville and Toledo; raisins,
leather, oil, and wine were dear in London. Trade

was cramped by laws and customs, which a royal license only could remove. A man with friends at court might get a license now and then, and there were merchants from Coruña and Bilboa in London who would buy his favours at the market price.

3. On many grounds Fernando thought his offer would be well received. The change of dynasty had broken up all former treaties with the English crown. In neither country had the merchants of the other any legal rights. The risks of trade were much increased at sea, and almost every port was closed on their respective flags. No week passed by without some deed of violence being done, for which the innocent victim sought redress in vain.

4. A treaty that should open out the English ports and markets was desired on every hand in Spain. That country wanted corn and tin, which England had to spare. She also lacked the finer kinds of wool; her fibre being too short in staple and too coarse in grain to weave. She had her dates, figs, raisins, leather, goat-fell, soap and wine to sell. Large works and factories had been built by her in Bruges and Ghent, and some of her ad-.venturers had already crossed the Straits. Such merchants as Diego de Castro and Pedro de Miranda found a mine of wealth in London. Living with the men of Cheape and Fleet Street, they became aware that English palates, though they liked the Spanish wine called bastard, had a wholesome craving for the vintage of Guienne. These men had houses at Bilbao, and ran their barks, the Santa Maria and Santiago, from the Garonne to the Sluys

and Thames. De Castro knew Machado, one of the foreign heralds, Nanfan, one of the King's body-guard, and Savage, one of the King's advisers in affairs of law. Through friends at court he got a license for himself and others to import from France no less than five ship-loads of claret. At a later date, about the time when Puebla was about to start, he had procured a license for himself and partners to dispose of cargoes brought from Spain; no doubt of raisins, leather, Seville oil, and goat-hair; all of which were in demand at London Bridge. De Castro was a man of family, who lived in princely style at Burgos; and the younger sons of many gentle houses in Castille were tempted by success to seek their fortune in the northern isle.

5. The fame of Catharine of Lancaster was fresh in every mind. Her name and presence were the themes of popular songs; her name and presence having been to Spain a flag of union and a pledge of peace. Her going into Spain had been con-nected in the mind of every one with sheep and ships; good mutton, better wool, fresh customers for raisins, leather, goat-hair, dates and Seville oil. In olden time the families of England and Castille had been allied in marriage. Edward the First had married Elinor of Castille. Two sons of Edward the Third had married daughters of Pedro of Cas-tille. Edmund of Langley had married Isabel, and John of Gaunt had married Constanza. Thus the blood of Lancaster was in the veins alike of Enrique the Liberal, Isabel the Catholic, and

Juana the Excellenta; every party, therefore, in the land might find their hope and interest in a royal match.

6. No nation but the English offered them unbought support against the Moors. Peer, knight, and man at arms repaired to Spain, as soldiers of the Cross, and fought for the recovery of Granada with the valour which their sires had shown at Azincour. Lord Rivers and his troop of horse, all men of gentle blood and richly dight, were seen in front of every charge, until the Queen, amazed at so much will to serve her cause, had sent the English peer twelve horses and an almost royal tent. Some pilgrims from this country were observed at Santiago and Monserrat, and the land they sailed from was itself an Island of the Saints. Canterbury was as great a shrine as Santiago, and St. David's more than matched Monserrat. Every county in the island had a holy well and tutelary saint. A Spaniard, therefore, looked on England as a field in which he might improve his fortune and refresh his soul. A daughter of Castille, descending from the House of Lancaster, the young Infanta was an English rose. She came from John of Gaunt by no concealed and crooked line; the links connecting her with John being reigning kings and queens. A bride for Arthur who had known no taint of blood was much to be desired by Henry; and the King was sure to see this merit in the girl proposed. It was his wisdom to supply his own defects of title by a marriage with Elizabeth of York; and in allying Arthur with a Spanish princess, he would be

giving his issue the security of a second claim derived from John of Gaunt.

7. "Induce the King of England to engage in war with France; induce him, if you can, by promises of aid and friendship on our part; if promises of aid and friendship fail you, offer an Infanta for his son; at any cost, induce him to engage in war." Such, briefly stated, were the cripple's orders from his master's lip and pen. Puebla was never to forget that what Fernando wanted from an English treaty were his duchies in the Pyrenees. He had himself no means of wresting them from France, nor could he offer much assistance to an ally who was fighting for him while the Moorish war was on his hands. He wanted England to incur the largest cost and run the highest risk. In drawing up the articles, Portugal must be excepted from the clause which treated friends as friends and foes as foes. On no account could Spain admit a quarrel with the court of Lisbon. Even for the sake of winning back Rossillon and Cerdaña, she could take no step that might offend the Portuguese and liberate the royal Nun.

Alone, in secret, and without his papers, Puebla started for Coruña; carrying, in a sealed message from his King and Queen, the germ of treaties and events that were to change the maps of Europe and divide the streams of Western thought.

————————

BOOK THE THIRD.

ENGLAND.

CHAPTER I.

After the Roses.

1487-8.

1. How stood the land which Puebla was to drag into a foeign war?

Between the empire left by Henry the Fifth in Paris and the fragments of that empire found by Henry the Seventh on Bosworth Field, there was the difference of a first-rate and a fifth-rate power. The ancient pomp of words was left; but men and means to back this pomp of words were gone. As King of England, France, and Ireland, with his seat in Paris, Henry he Fifth had been as strong as either Kaiser Sigsmund or Sultan Amurath. As King of England, France, and Ireland, with his seat at Windsor, Henry the Seventh was not much stronger than a Doge of Venice or a King of Scots. In thirty years of civil strife, extending from the onset in the streets of St. Albans to the clash of swords on Redland marsh, the country had been

wasting all her stores of strength.   No one had
time to think of Normandie and Maine, except as
duchies lost for ever.   Save the March of Calais,
not a rood of soil remained to her in France.   In
fact, the tides of war were rolling back.   A French
and Breton fleet was cruising off her coasts, and
hardly any of her ports were safe from Margate to
Penzance.

2. Through these unhappy years the country
had been burning in a never-dying fire.   The French
were either left alone in France, or called by York
and Lancaster to throw fresh fuel on the flames.
From year to year these broils had been renewed,
and every spring-time with a deeper hate and fiercer
ire.   St. Albans, Towton, Wakefield, Barnet, were
but samples of a hundred fields on which the
noblest blood had soaked into the earth.   Battles
were fought of which the names are lost.   Whole
shires were ravaged by contending troops; for victory had passed from red to white from white to
red, and every chieftain had been able to enjoy his
day of sweet revenge.   If York killed Somerset,
Margaret had in turn killed York.   If Edward
drove out Henry, Henry had also driven out
Edward.   Each had been by turns a suppliant,
prisoner, exile, despot.   In that reign of violence,
two kings were murdered in the Tower, ten princes
of the royal house were slain, and half the peers
of England swept away.   When Leo von Rozmital
came to London, in the reign of Edward the Fourth,
he saw the Queen, Elizabeth Woodville, seated in
the midst of eight duchesses and more than thirty

countesses and other great ladies. Nearly all these families had been broken by the civil war. Large towns had fallen to decay, and lands, which in the reign of Edward the Third were sold for twenty-five years' purchase, would hardly sell for ten in that of Edward the Fourth. With every change of prince the price had fallen. If a man had money, like an abbot, he could buy up manors and manorial rights, and get in every case a shilling for his groat. A man with wood to sell could hardly find a buyer. Every one had wood to sell. This wood was used for making beams and shafts, but while the torch of war was burning through the shires, what man had heart to build him house and barn? Land almost went a-begging. One who asked for largess from the King was better pleased to get two hundred pounds in money than a hundred pounds a-year in land. All men could tell how much a hundred pounds in gold would buy; no man could tell how little an estate in land might fetch. The coin was sure; the field might suffer from the tramp of man. Great tracks were often left untilled; for no one felt assured that he who ploughed the soil would live to bind the sheaves. Loose gangs, with pike and fire-lock, wandered up and down, in search of captains; willing to engage their arms in any cause; infesting every yard and inn, and when their wants were pressing every glebe and hall. A thousand crimes, unnamed and nameless, were committed by these roving bands.

3. Amidst this general wreck, the martial spirit of the isle had all but died. In the unruly gangs

who vexed the public roads, here robbing hedges,
there abusing women, it was hard to see the sons of
yeomen who had drawn their bows at Azincour.
The warlike virtues are the last to go; but as the
nobler spirits of the country fell, their ranks were
filled by rogues and scare-crows from the styes and
stews.   At Wakefield and Northampton there was
something of the fury which had swept the fields of
France.   At Bosworth there was hardly any fight
at all.   Some companies would not lift a pike; some
archers shot their arrows into empty air; some captains turned against their flag.   Two thousand
strangers marched into the midland shires unchecked;
and with a band of uncouth allies gathered from
the mines of Pembroke, seized the crown in what
was hardly other than a country brawl.

4. When Henry called his peers, one duke, nine
earls, two viscounts, and fifteen barons, answered
to his writs.   Not one of the great dukes of Edward's
reign was present.   Buckingham had been put to
death at Salisbury.   Bedford had been degraded
from his rank because of poverty.   Suffolk had been
butchered on his way to Calais; and his son, now
duke, being married to a sister of King Richard,
was a fugitive.   Exeter had been attainted and his
honours lost.   Norfolk had been out at Redland
marsh.   The only duke who met the King was one
whom he had made; his uncle, Jasper Tudor, whom
he had created Duke of Bedford.   Of the earls who
answered Henry's summons—Arundel, Oxford, Kent,
Nottingham, Wiltshire, Rivers, Derby, Huntingdon,
and Devon—two had been created by himself;

Thomas Stanley, Earl of Derby, and Edward Court-
ney, Earl of Devon.   One, the Earl of Oxford, he
had purged in blood.   A Viscount, William Beau-
mont, and a Baron, Henry Clifford, he had also
purged in blood.   The Earls of Warwick, Surrey,
and Northumberland, had not been summoned to
attend the King.   Warwick, a Plantagenet, was
under guard.   Surrey was a traitor; and Northumberland, who had refused to fight on either side,
was in the north.   Zouch, Lovel, Ferrars, had
to answer for their necks.   Of all the Nevills,
only one, Lord Abergavenny, came into the House
of Lords.   In brief, the temporal peers were so
reduced in wealth and numbers that the spiritual
peers were found to have the mastery of vote and
voice.

5. Letters and science had suffered even more
than the temporal peerage by these years of warfare.   Art and song were dead.   The convents
which were wont to pour out poems, chronicles,
illuminated hours, and golden missals in a copious
stream, had now become the homes of wounded
men, the centres of political life.   No work of note
in letters had been written in those barren years.
Such versifiers as Adam of Cobsam and Richard of
Hampole, only served to show that art was stag-
gering under loads too great to bear.   The race
of poets who had followed Chaucer was no more;
the race which was to herald Shakespeare had not
come.   Lydgate was dead, and Surrey was unborn.
If English maid or matron pined for song, she had
to read the chansons of the Prince of Orleans.   If a
king desired to grace his court with laureates, he

must call them to his side from Italy and France.
All Henry's poets were of foreign birth.   André
was from Toulouse, Giglis from Lucca, Carmeliano
from Brescia.   Where could Henry seek for native
song? Skelton, the coming bard, had still his earliest
rhymes to write.

6. Even popular quip and stave—those old and
pleasant strains, in which our language is so rich—
had all but ceased to drop from unknown pens. A
scrap of dolorous verse on "civil war," a chant on
the "recovery of the throne," and a political tract
in rhyme on our "commercial policy," are nearly all
that English thought and humour gave the world in
thirty years.   Nor was the country richer in respect
of prose. Walsingham was gone. Capgrave, Elmham, Otterborne, were gone. The muse of history,
driven from her cloister at St. Albans, had to seek
asylum in a city ward.   Robert Fabyan, of the
Drapers' company, an alderman of Farringdon-
without, was chief of those who chronicled events
in prose. He kept a ledger of events, in which he
noted, as of equal mark, the fighting of a battle, and
the selling of a cask of fish.

7. Not a single work on mathematics, not a
single work on astronomy, saw the light in England
in this troubled time.   John Rous· of Warwick
feebly represented antiquarian study. Lyttleton and
Fortesque, the early lights of English law, were
dead, and no one had presumed to hold the torch
of law.   Two peers, indeed, had graced this period
by their genius: Tiptoft, Earl of Worcester, and
Woodville, Earl of Rivers; but the axe that was
beheading England cut them down.

CHAPTER II.

Church and Cloister.

1487-8.

1. But while the country was a prey to fire and sword, the Church stood high above the wrack and waste. A state within the state, she claimed to live in virtue of an older gift and higher rule than those of ordinary men. A king was but an agent of her will; a code was but an accent of her grace. She claimed a power to bind and loose at pleasure; nay, a power to make a wrong thing right, a right thing wrong, by simple scratch of pen and press of seal. Nor were the faithful people slow to take her word. When Edward, Duke of York, had risen against the reigning prince, all men accounted him a traitor till they heard that an Italian priest whom they had never seen, whose tongue they could not speak, had granted him a dispensation from the penalties of his violated oath. As England fell, Rome rose. From year to year the pontiffs had assumed a loftier tone; and Sixtus used a language which Eugenius had not dared to hold. The Roman court had come to look on England as a patrimony of the Church.

2. This change of tone was but an index to the change of fact. The miseries which had weakened

other classes had increased the strength of priest
and monk. A people harassed and opprest will
seek the nearest help, and in our civil broils this
help was found at convent doors, and taken from
the hands of holy men. A fugitive from battle ran
into the nearest sanctuary. A hedger wanting bread
would seek it at the abbey gate. A dying soldier,
fainting for a drink of water, caught the cup and
blessing from a monk, and thanked with dying eyes
the man who had not fled from scenes of woe. A
family bereaved by sudden death could look for
comfort only to their priest. If any one went out
to face the fury of contending troops, he was some
aged abbot, who, like Father John, the abbot of
St. Albans, stept into the street, with cross in hand,
to stop the slaughter and protect the town. What
wonder that a people, urged by fear, and worn by
fasting, should have turned towards mother Church
with confidence that she could feed and save them
when all other help was gone? In that long night
of trial she had always been in sight—a rock above
the wave, a star beyond the cloud, a port within
the storm.

3. Her fanes were guarded by a host of saints.
A castle might be sacked and burnt, and the ad-
jacent chapel left untouched. Amidst the wildest
fury of the war, it had been rare for either convent,
cell, or shrine, to be profaned. The shrines were
rich in gold and precious stones, and every wastrel
in the land believed them richer than they were in
fact; yet they were safe from men whose hands
were black with fire and red with blood. A shrine

was shielded by the saints whose relics it contained, and in a spot like Canterbury, these saints were of the mightiest in the heavens above and in the earth below. Rozmital saw at Canterbury a fragment of the robe of Christ; three splinters from the crown of thorns; 'a lock of Mary's hair; a shoulder-blade of Simeon; a tooth of John the Baptist; blood of John the Evangelist and Thomas the Apostle; bones of James and Philip; part of the cross of Peter and Andrew; tooth and finger of the proto-martyr Stephen; hair of Mary Magdalene; a lip of one of the innocents slain by Herod the Great; and heaps of minor relics, such as a head of Thomas à Becket, a leg of St. George, the bowels of St. Lawrence, a finger of St. Urban, a tooth of St. Benedict, bones of St. Clement, bones of St. Vincent, bones of Catherine the Virgin, a leg of Mildred the Virgin, and a leg of Recordia the Virgin. That the saints were present near their shrines was proved by miracles. Rozmital saw a fountain in the cloister brimming with a fluid which was sometimes water, sometimes milk, and sometimes blood. Five times the water had been changed to blood, and just before Rozmital's visit to the cell, it had been changed to milk. A layman while engaged in holy things was under care of these all-potent saints. When every road in Kent and Norfolk was beset by roving bands, a pilgrim wending to the chapel of St. Thomas of Canterbury, to the altar of Our Lady of Walsingham, might trudge along in peace. A rogue who stript the hedges would have doffed his cap to one who was returning from Our Lady's shrine.

4. While every other corporation in the land was losing ground, the clerical body had been gaining ground. As duke and baron fell on tented field and prison block, the abbot waxed in riches, and the prelate rose in power. A prelate was a man of peace, who seldom took a side so long as there were actual sides to choose. His precept was obedience to the power ordained of God, and in his spiritual eyes success was God. All princes suited him. Hence, every year of civil strife had seen more bishops at the council-board, more abbots in the ante-room, and more confessors in the privy-chamber. Every year had found more legates going to and fro, and higher pomp and glory in the service at St. Paul's. More cardinals had come to London; more ambassadors had been sent to Rome. More foreign monks had been employed in offices of trust; more papal "nephews" had been stalled and mitred in the English Church. An abbot, through the right of sanctuary, might easily become the host of kings and queens. All parties had to seek the Church and make that Church their friend and judge. A king might offer terms; but a pretender had to take her at a price. The Church had sometimes favoured York; but York was liberal, Lancaster conservative; and she had oftener set her face against the elder branch. Her policy in Spain had been her policy in England; for a ruler who was weak in law would have to pay her any price she chose to ask for help.

While he was yet in exile, Henry had proposed to hold his crown in fealty to the Pope; and Rome, which had not often found an English prince so meek, had armed him with her hosts and sent him forth to conquer in her name.

5. When he had won the crown, he caused his Papal title to be read in public at St. Paul's, not by a simple herald and his men in cap and tabard, but by the Lord Primate of England, with the Bishops of London, Winchester, Ely, Worcester, and Exeter, standing at his side, arrayed in full pontificals. These prelates cursed with bell, and book, and candle every one, who should presume to doubt if he who had become the King in fact was King in law and right. Thus clothed with ban and curse, he held the crown; held it, as he conceived, of Rome and God.

6. A few days after Lincoln fell at Stoke, he wrote to Innocent, his patron, some account of an event in which he traced the hand of heaven. Some partisans of the House of York, who had been moving in the city, fled for sanctuary to St. Peter's, Westminster, in which they stayed till news—false news—arrived in town, that Henry had been worsted in the field. Distracted by the papal ban and curse, these fugitives were in a painful plight. But one of them stood up and spoke. "A certain John Swit," wrote Henry, "who was rather rash than brave, cried out, when all the rest were dumb, 'What force is there in such ecclesiastical and pontifical censures? You see that these decrees are idle, since you have before your eyes the very men who hurl them at you put to rout and shame!' No sooner had he spoken than he reeled and fell; his face becoming

black as midnight, and his corpse so foul that no
one dared go near it. So, most holy Father, fell
this matter, which we should not write unless we
knew it for a truth. We give our ample thanks to
God, who in His own ineffable mercy, has given in
this our realm, this great miracle for the Christian
faith. We also give your Holiness our grateful
thanks."

CHAPTER III.

Henry Tudor.

1487-8.

1. HENRY, King of England, and Fernando, King of Spain, were men well mated for a game of high political craft. Both kings were in their early prime: Fernando thirty-five, and Henry thirty years of age; with time in front of them, through which they could afford to plot, and wait the harvest of their toils. Each prince was short in stature, closely knit in frame. Each wore a frank expression in his eyes, and threw a coaxing tone into his voice; yet neither let his left hand guess the object that his right was raised to strike. Each came into the levels from a poor and hilly country, and was counted as a stranger in the land he ruled. Each found a title in his sword, yet made a show of justice in the birthright of his wife. Each fought his way to rank and fame; but Henry, having no such helper as the beautiful and wicked queen, had won his way through greater hardships and in later years. In neither prince had Spain and England crowned their types. Fernando was not much a Spaniard; Henry was not much an Englishman. In gazing at their portraits as they hang at Windsor side by side, a stranger to their faces might mistake them

9*

for each other. Henry, who was spare and sallow,
had a rather Spanish face; Fernando, who was sleek
and rosy, had a rather English face. Ayala, the
acutest judge of men whom Spain sent out to London,
told his master there was nothing "purely English"
in the English king.

2. Yet in the higher grades of character no
princes could be more unlike. Beside Fernando,
Henry seemed a child of nature, nay, a child of
grace. By birth a Celt and prone to superstition
from his youth, the English King believed in signs
and acted on the promptings of an unseen spirit.
A rose-bush growing in the Temple Gardens put
out buds, which blossomed into red and white.
Men ran into the grounds to see the wonder; and
a people who were sick of civil warfare blessed that
bush, and said it was a type of peace. A red rose
and a white rose on a single stem must surely mean
a union of the Earl of Richmond and Elizabeth of
York. In striving for his crown the King obeyed
a cry of nature, and expected to receive the help
of heaven. No Spaniard put more trust in Santiago
than the Earl of Richmond vested in St. George.
"God will aid me," he had cried to his companions
as they sailed from Harfleur in the scantiest craft
that ever ventured for a crown. Of other help
there seemed no chance. But Henry had not paused
to count his forces, like Fernando when Affonzo,
King of Portugal, had crossed the frontier of his
states. "Let God, the giver of victory, judge!" He
looked upon himself as one appointed to fulfil the
purposes of heaven. "In the name of God and of

St. George, advance!" and in the name of God and
of St. George he won his crown.

3. The bards and monks who had been near
him from his birth had fired him with two mystic
and unselfish yearnings; yearnings which became
a part of him, and helped to govern him through
life; a passion for the legends of his native land,
as sung by Cymric bards; a passion for the cross
of Christ, as monks and friars conceived the cross
of Christ.

By birth a Celt, and trained among a Celtic
people, Henry had a feeling for those border bards
who sang—

> Our land's first legends, love and knightly deeds,
> And wondrous Merlin and his wandering king.

At Pembroke Castle and at Begar Abbey he
had toyed with these Arthurian myths, which in
their Cymric form present the picture of a happy
and romantic court, and not that drama of a doting
lord and guilty wife which the Provençal troubadours
had wrought from them in France. To Henry's
fancy, Arthur was a light, a beacon, and a guiding
star. If not an actual saint, he was a pattern prince
and perfect knight. The King regarded Arthur as
the glory of a line of princes older than the Saxon
times. Even more than what St. Louis was to
Charles, and San Fernando was to Isabel, King
Arthur seemed to Henry. In his mythic ancestor
he saw a Christian knight and national hero, who
had spent his life in fighting with a foreign and
idolatrous foe. To him, this warrior was the noblest

hero of the British soil. In spite of history, he told
Italian agents that the Order of the Garter was
King Arthur's work and badge. A knowledge of
this mystic side of Henry's genius is the key to
many of the secrets of his life.

4. His passion for the cross was no less ardent
than his passion for the legendary court. In truth,
these passions fused and centred in one radiant
point. King Arthur fought with paynims for the
cross of Christ, and Henry set this glory of the
cross before him as his own peculiar star. He was
the last great prince in whom the spirit of a Templar
raged. A crusade was his daily dream; a crusade
to regain the Holy Sepulchre, and liberate the host
of Christian slaves. To gain these ends, he strove
to stir up popes and kings; he wrote to the religious
orders; and he offered to conduct the liberating
force. He wished to measure swords with Bajazet
as Richard of the Lion Heart had measured swords
with Saladin. He would have risked his life, and
even lost his crown, in order to regain that sacred
tomb and liberate those Christian slaves.

Nor was his zeal the fury of a day. It burned
in him through many years, and only died at length
in the cold prudence of an honest Pope.

The Knights of Rhodes elected him Protector
of their Order; and the King of Portugal proposed
that if a crusade were attempted, Henry should be
marshal of the Christian troops. And even when
his dream of winning back the Sepulchre was past,
he clung to what had been the better part of his
design, the hope of freeing Christian slaves. Unable

to release them by his sword, he could and would
relieve them by his purse. He set apart some portion of his income as a sacred fund; which fund
was yearly spent in ransoming unhappy captives
from the various Moslem ports.

5. Yet Henry was as fond of money as Fernando. Poor and pinched in youth, he set a store
on gold beyond its natural worth. He too could
feed a hunger of the eye with coin. He liked to
count his pieces, weigh his plate, and note the value
of his cups and rings. He learned to prize the
cup beyond the wine; and yet he seldom put the
weight of dross before the chaser's art. Fernando
looked no higher than his personal gain; a gain
that he could see and touch; while Henry, though
he looked to have his groat in either meal or malt,
could take some part of his return in things unseen.
Each sank a fortune in a shrine; but Henry was an
artist, and his wealth was lavished with an eye for
beauty rather than for pomp and show. He loved
to build a house, to plant a field, to decorate a
church. Retiring from his council-boards, he strayed
to chat with monk and priest, and watch the progress of their favourite works. His monks and
priests were mostly artists. Father John, of Westminster, afterwards known as Abbot Islip, copied
hours and missals for the Queen, with borders
twined through painted puns and happy marriages
of leaves and flowers. Sir Reginald Bray was drawing plans for the King's new chapel in the abbey.
Father Christopher Urswick, afterwards dean of
Windsor, was an architect. Father William Smyth,

archdeacon of Surrey, was the founder of Brazen-
nose college. Poets, who were also monks and
priests, enjoyed his friendship and received his pay.
André held the office of his laureate and historio-
grapher. Carmeliano, who had now become a
denizen, was his Latin secretary. Giglis was his
bishop of Worcester and his minister in Rome.

6. Unlike Fernando, who was fond of war for
war's own pastime, Henry was a man of peace.
Unless to fight for Zion, he would never of his own
free choice have drawn his sword. Though young
in power, he laboured to acquire the title of a
Friend of Peace; and when his people urged him
to the field, he strove to put them off with what he
called a show of war; a squeak of fife and roll of
drum, in place of ghastly wounds, of ruined trade,
and desolated homes. The Roman poet wrote to
Innocent, "The King is so pacific and so prudent
that we have the promise of a general peace."
Another day that poet wrote, "This prince prefers
a fair peace to a just war." Sancho de Londoño
summed up Henry's temper in the words, "He is a
man of peace." No cause less pressing than a
danger to his crown and life could make him face
the miseries of actual war. His heart was sick of
strife. "When Christ was born," he said, "peace
was sung on earth, and when He died, peace on
earth was what He left." To him the name of a
pacificator seemed a nobler heritage than that of
either prince or pope.

CHAPTER IV.

The English Court.

1487-8.

1. THE English court was pure; the royal home a model of domestic peace. Three ladies who had each been chastened by her sorrows, ruled in Henry's house; the Queen, Elizabeth the Good; the Queen's mother, Queen Elizabeth Woodville, widow of Edward the Fourth; the King's mother, Margaret of Richmond, widow of the Tudor Earl from whom the King derived his Celtic blood. The Queen, a bride of twenty-one, and of surpassing beauty, was of shy and homely temper, fonder of her husband and her child than of that pomp of state, to which, as eldest daughter of a king, she had been born. The virtues of denial and obedience flourished on her hearth. Elizabeth was the soul of charity. She portioned good and penniless girls. She paid the fees of novices too poor to take the veil. She liberated debtors from the London jails, and gave a decent burial to penitent rogues and thieves. She liked to keep old servants in her house, and had a separate purse for the support of orphan boys and girls. As well became a daughter of the House of York, her tastes were liberal and refined. She

kept her poets and reciters; her singing men and
singing boys; her minstrels who could play on lute
and pipe.   The greeting of her bridal morning was
a poem from the pen of Giovanni de Giglis, her
Italian laureate, whom the King rewarded for his
service by a prebendary stall in York. One present
she received from Henry was a book of noble verse;
the chansons of that Prince of Orleans who had
sung in exile and imprisonment his passion for an
absent wife.

2. Her mother, Queen Elizabeth Woodville, was
the tender and poetic woman for whose lovely face
King Edward had incurred the wrath of Isabel.
This Queen had borne her share of tragic sorrows.
Gray, the husband of her youth, had perished in
the field. Her boys by him had been deprived of
their estates.   Her union with the King, although
he loved her well, had brought misfortune to them
both. She had been separated from the King; she
had been forced to enter sanctuary; she had suffered
siege and stress. Her father had been put to death;
her mother had been charged with sorcery; her
brother had been also put to death. She lost her
royal partner at the early age of forty-two; and in
that year of woe, had taken sanctuary with her sons,
had seen the princes torn from her embrace, and
learnt that they were murdered in the Tower.
Forced to quit her lodgings in Westminster Abbey,
she had suffered every agony of restraint until the
victory of Bosworth set her free.   Since Bosworth,
she had been at court, except when she retired to
Bermondsey Abbey for repose, acknowledged as

Queen-Dowager, and pensioned as became her rank.

3. Lady Margaret, the King's mother, was the most commanding figure in his court. Tall, stern, and proud, she moved about the palace, where she held a lodging near her son, like some pale prophetess of ancient days. To her all ears were bent, and most of all her son's; for he had proved her love, her courage, and her wisdom when his fortunes had been dark and low. Her chaplain, Father Christopher, was his almoner and agent. In his early days, she had directed all his movements, but since Bosworth had enthroned him, she had kept herself to the domestic side of life; arranging for his union with Elizabeth of York, and fixing on a residence for the future Prince of Wales. She was a scholar and a friend of scholars. Fisher owed to her his first promotion in the Church. Caxton was indebted to her kindness. Pynson printed several works which she translated from the French. These works were books of piety; for Lady Margaret was rapt and fired with holy zeal. She wore a shirt of hair, like Isabel. She fasted long and often, and her body seemed to waste in prayer and vigils. Learning and piety were objects of her care, and Lady Margaret's name is warmly cherished on the Isis and the Cam.

4. The Queen had four sisters, who were also in her court; Lady Cecily of York, Lady Anne of York, Lady Catharine of York, and Lady Bridget of York. These girls were younger than herself. Lady Cecily had just been married to the King's

uncle of the half-blood, John, Lord Welles. Lady
Anne had been engaged to Philip, son of Max; but
this engagement had been broken off by Edward's
death. Lady Catharine had been pledged to Don
Juan of Aragon, and afterwards to James, a younger
son of the King of Scots. Lady Bridget, who was
only eight years old, preferred to lead a holy life,
and took the veil at Dartford when she came of
age.

5. When Henry found his Queen was near the
time when she might hope to bear a son, he had
removed her from the Tower, in which the kings
of England had been mostly born, to Winchester,
the legendary seat of Arthur; that the future ruler
might be born in Camelot, and breathe the very
air from down and sea which Arthur breathed. The
Queen took up her room and kept her state, according to the rules drawn up by Lady Margaret, who
was more of a religious mystic even than her son.
The infant had been christened Arthur, and a pair
of ancient Britons stood beside the font. The King
felt proud that Arthur of Winchester was born to
be a Prince of Wales. A seven months' child (like
Catalina), he was small and comely, needing every
care from Stephen Bereworth, his physician, who
was pensioned to attend on him. The King arranged
his cradle so that when his eyes should open to
receive the images of outward things, the objects to
salute him first should be the mystic dragon and
the sacred leek. The King had fixed his heart on
a revival of the ancient names and ancient ways.
A second Arthur should renew the first, and live a

perfect hero in a court of perfect knights and dames. This hero must be consecrated from his cradle, and in after years he should be sent to live among his ancient kith. A castle on the Teme should be arranged for him; a house less wild and stern than Pembroke; yet a place of border name and fame. In royal and romantic state, the second Arthur was to emulate the first.

6. As yet the English people hardly knew this hero's name. Pendragon was to them an ogre, and his leek the symbol of a thief. King Arthur was a Celt, whose arms had been arrayed against their Saxon sires. At best, he was a foe whom they had crushed. The Paris press had long been scattering tales about him and his deeds; in London, not a single legend had been printed till the year of Bosworth Field. Malory had been gathering out of French romances an account of Arthur and his knights; that work which Roger Ascham was in after days to scout. It is not known who this Malory was; but from his love of these old tales it has been commonly inferred that he was Welsh. No man of English birth was likely to have cared about a knight who fought against his fathers, till the advent of a British sovereign taught him to regard with sympathy the legends of a friendly and poetic race. No less than fifteen years elapsed before Malory's version could be put to press; but while the Tudor prince was hiring troops in Normandie, some knights and gentlemen had gone to Caxton and requested him to set Malory's book in type. The sheets were on his blocks when Richmond was at Harfleur; when

the victor came to London they were in the public hands. In Henry's advent, ancient prophecies appeared to be fulfilled, and some of Henry's bards affirmed that he—the wandering knight and prince —was Arthur in the living flesh.

CHAPTER V.

The Spiritual Power.

1487-8.

1. A MYSTIC and usurper, Henry felt the need of ghostly help in his affairs, and wished his country to become what she had been in olden times, an Island of the Saints. He envied France St. Louis, and desired to have a saint of his own name and blood. England had given a host of martyrs to the Church, but no one of the name of Henry; so he begged the Pope to canonise his uncle, Henry the Sixth. St. Henry would have been a great supporter of the House of Lancaster. He also asked the Pope to grant a privilege to a tomb which Lady Margaret, his mother, was preparing for herself. Outside the walls of Rome, there was a chapel of the Virgin called the Stair of Heaven. This chapel had been favoured by a line of Popes; a prayer recited at the altar took away a load of sin; and Henry asked the Pope to grant him patents for his mother's tomb as rich in virtue as the bulls which had been granted to the Stair of Heaven.

2. In doing homage for his crown, he told the Pope that all the kings, his predecessors on the throne, had rendered reverence and obedience to the reigning pontiff. Henry was deceived. No king

had done so, even in appearance, since the days of
Henry the Third; no king had done so in reality
since the days of John. A hundred times the Popes
had striven to make the English yield; but neither
Peers nor Commons would consent to such an act.
"I will not do it," said the second Henry to a papal
legate. "Neither do we, nor will we, nor can we,
nor ought we, to permit our lord the King to do
so," said the Parliament of Edward the First. When
Urban the Fifth was seeking to revive these papal
claims, the peers replied, "That act of John was
done without consent of the estates, and contrary
to his oath." The commons added, "If the Pope
appeals to force, we will gainstand him to the ut-
most of our power." Edward had already struck
the note. "If both the Emperor and the King of
France should take the Pope's part, I am ready to
give battle to them in defence of the liberties of my
crown." All England stood behind the prince who
spoke these words. But after Bosworth, England
was no longer what she had been after Créci, and
the King who ruled her was not Harry the Fifth.

3. Henry had only reigned two years, and in
his second year he had been forced to fight for
crown and life. The sword had given, and what
the sword had given the sword might take away. If
he had failed at Stoke, he must have been a fugitive
or a corpse. The Spanish sovereigns had a royal
nun to fear; but Henry had a dozen rivals like that
royal nun. The Perfect Prince being dead, Fernando's title to the crown of Aragon was free from
doubt, and if the exiled Queen could ever be in-

duced to take the veil at Santa Clara, Isabel's title
in Castille would stand beyond the reach of doubt.
But no removal of a prince and princess here or
there from Henry's path would make the English
ruler's title good in law.

4. He traced his lineage back to John of Gaunt;
but every step in his descent gave way beneath his
weight. A doubt had long ago been raised about
the birth of John of Gaunt; his mother, Philippa,
having told her priest that she had changed a girl
for him at birth. John's elder brother, Lionel, had
issue still alive; the princes of the House of York.
So long as any of these princes lived, the King
could have no legal right to reign. Nor were these
obstacles the whole. John Beaufort, son of John
of Gaunt, was basely born, and though a papal brief
had made him pure of blood, a papal brief could
not create for him a right denied by English law.
When Henry the Fourth confirmed that papal brief,
he carefully denied this house of Beaufort's claim
upon the crown. In Richard's days this bastardy
and this exclusion of the line of Beaufort had been
openly proclaimed. If even these great obstacles
had been removed, the King would still have had
no lawful claim. His mother would have been the
Queen, and he no other than a Prince of Wales.
On every side his title failed. The house of Lancaster was a younger branch; and he was not the
head of even that younger branch.

So conscious was the King of these defects of
title, that he made no reference to his birth and
lineage in the act of settlement. "The crown shall

be, rest, remain, and abide," in Henry and his heirs
at law,—so runs this famous act. No pedigree is
cited; he is king in right of war; and will be king
while he can hold his seat. The law was silent; for
his sword had set aside the law. His only title,
other than the sword, was that derived from Rome.

5. Having laid his crown before the Pope, the
King had placed his highest offices in clerical hands.
His foremost ministers were Primate Morton and
Bishop Fox. John Morton was Archbishop of Canterbury, Lord Chancellor, and first minister of the
crown. Richard Fox was Bishop of Exeter, privy
councillor, Lord Privy Seal, and second minister of
the crown. Their power was only shared by monks
and priests who hung about the royal closet, and
were sometimes asked to give advice; such men as
Father Christopher, the royal almoner, Prior John
of Clerkenwell and Rhodes, William Smyth, Archdeacon of Surrey, and Thomas Savage, priest and
doctor of the canon law. The primate, Morton,
was the greatest pluralist alive. This man had been
appointed vicar of Bloxworth, sub-dean of Lincoln,
prebendary of Salisbury, principal of Peckwater Inn,
prebendary of Lincoln, privy councillor, Chancellor
of the Duchy of Cornwall, Master of the Rolls, rector
of St. Dunstan's in the East, prebendary of St. Paul's,
archdeacon of Huntingdon, prebendary of Wells,
prebendary of York, archdeacon of Berkshire, archdeacon of Leicester, bishop of Ely, Lord Chancellor
of England, and archbishop of Canterbury. Some
of these rich offices had been yielded out of shame
—not many of them—and the grasping prelate was

not yet content. He hungered for a cardinal's hat, and Henry was beseeching Rome to gratify his servant's pride. The primate was a stout supporter of the Holy See.

6. One other step the Church had gained. For close upon four hundred years, the Church had claimed a place outside the statute-book. A court for clerks, in which the bishop was to sit as judge, had been created by the Conqueror as the price of clerical support against the people and their laws. This court had been resisted and renewed from reign to reign:—the people asking to be judged according to their native laws; the clergy wishing to condemn them by a foreign code. A man like Arundel might sweep both prince and judge along with him by force of will. But priests like Arundel had set the country in a blaze. To see a man licked up in fire for saying that he could not understand how bread was actual flesh and wine was actual blood, drove many wild with rage. A secular judge could hardly help some pity towards a prisoner of the Church; and when that prisoner came before him, by attorney, he would grant his *habeas corpus*, have the man brought up, peruse the warrants and the pleas, and if he found him wrongly seized, discharge him on the spot. A judge could only go upon the statute-book. This claim of bishops and their ordinaries to be the sole interpreters of law for clerks, had never been admitted by the crown. A case is given by Coke. The crown referred this question to the bench; the bench reported that the law could only be interpreted by

the ordinary courts. A civil court could scan the
sentence of a spiritual court; a common judge reverse the sentence of a clerical judge. Such acts
had always pleased the English people, whether
gentry in the shires, or craftsmen in the towns; for
people liked to know that rich and poor, that clerk
and layman, had the benefit and protection of his
English law.

7. But if the clergy could not gain their point,
they never ceased to urge their plea. At every
change of dynasty they tried to make their terms.
When Bolingbroke murdered Richard and usurped
his throne, they had procured the act for burning
heretics. When York defeated Henry the Sixth,
they had obtained a charter giving them immunity
from the charge of civil courts. When Richmond
struck down Richard, they had asked to have that
charter strengthened by an Act of Parliament. Being
masters in the closet, in the council, in the upper
house, and being backed by Henry as their partner,
they had passed their bill; a bill which had conferred on bishops and their ordinaries that power
beyond the law which they had always claimed and
sometimes won; a power to seize suspected clerks,
to lock them under ward, and hold them in restraint. All right to scan their acts was done away.
A clerk arrested by his bishop was without appeal.
All pleas of wrongful verdict were annulled; redress
for false imprisonment was denied. For every man
who could be called a clerk—the bishops and their
ordinaries being the judges as to who was properly
a clerk—the guarantees of English law were swept

away. The King and kingdom were committed to the Church; committed to her teaching, her pretensions, and her fortunes. Each enjoyed the gain and bore the burthen of this close connexion with the Papal court; for if the King was mighty in the strength of Rome, his realm was feeble with the feebleness of cardinal and pope.

CHAPTER VI.

Puebla in London.

1487-8.

1. WHILE he was waiting in Coruña for a ship
to carry him across the sea, two English barks arrived in port.   As Spain had signed no treaty with
the English crown, these barks were held to be fair
prize, and Pedro de Segura, captain of a Spanish
ship of war, compelled these barks to strike their
flag.   The canon saw this act of piracy with his
own eyes; and though some forty ships were lying
in the harbour, not a hand was raised to check
Segura's deed.   All articles of peace, the Spaniards
of Coruña said, were held to die with those who
signed them.   If the English wanted peace and
trade, another treaty must be drawn and signed;
and Puebla crossed the sea to study how that treaty
could be turned to good account.

2. For weeks he had to labour in the dark.
When he arrived in London, every one was busy
with the young Queen's coronation, which the King
had ordered after the events at Stoke.   He had to
see his traders, to collect his facts, and learn to
tread on English ground.   By choice, he lived in
slums and taverns; herding with the poor, and even
with the vile; and selling all the favour he could

win. His habit of consorting with the low and
profligate never left him, even when he might have
lived in mansions in the Strand and kept a barge
and boatmen on the Thames. A mason took him
in, and lodged him in his house at twopence a day
for bed and board. This mason kept a small and
dirty inn; a house of call for shameless women and
apprentice lads; and Puebla, canonist and cripple,
took his seat at table with these dollies and their
mates. But though he lodged in cheap and nasty
dens, of which the rough and ready skippers of
Bilbao were heartily ashamed, his cloth enabled
him to seek those monks and priests who formed
an innermost circle round the King.

3. Of those who held no secular office, yet were
always heard and oftentimes employed on public
business, Father Christopher stood the first. This
father had been near the sovereign from his boyish
days; he was his mother's chaplain and confessor;
and his own most constant friend. When Henry
lodged at Begar Abbey, Father Christopher was always flitting from the mother to her son. They
had no secrets from him. To his faithful hands was
given that message from Elizabeth of York which
led to union of the red rose and the white. He
followed Henry to the palace, where a lodging had
been found for him. The highest offices lay within
his reach, but he would only take such posts as left
him near the King; the place of almoner, the
rectory of Hackney, and a prebendary stall in London. As the royal almoner, and as Lady Margaret's confessor, he had greater power to make

and mar than any other priest.   Beside this Father
stood John Weston, Knight and Prior of St. John in
Clerkenwell.   This knight was called the Prior of
St. John of England, and in virtue of his rank was
premier baron of the English Parliament.   He was
a link between the west and east.   No man could
tell so soon as he what Bajazet was doing in the
Grecian waters and the Holy City.   He inspired
the King with a crusading spirit, and supplied a
channel of communication with the Grand Master
in Rhodes.   Of higher reach than these advisers of
the King was Thomas Savage, doctor of the canon
law; a man of learning and ability, and silent as
the grave itself.   On every point of law, the King
consulted Savage, and in matters needing special
secresy the silent doctor was employed.

4. At first the Spaniard spoke of peace and
trade between the states, and only hinted at a plan
for giving aid and comfort to each other in the day
of need.   As Henry's ministers were alive to the
advantages of peace and trade, they listened to his
tales in hope that good might come of them. Since
Bosworth neither peace nor trade had been secure
with Spain.   A league of peace would stop such
acts as those of Pedro de Segura, and might bring
a profitable fleet into the western ports.   The
Spaniards wanted corn and cloth; the English wanted
wine and oil; and most of all they wanted Bordeaux
wine.   An act had just been passed forbidding any
other than an English ship to bring this wine 'to
England, save on special license granted by the
King himself.   To favour an exchange of what his

people had in plenty for the things they needed—
corn for wine, cloth for oil, and tin for soap—the
King was granting letters somewhat freely to the
Bilboa merchants then in Cheape. Nor was the
King averse to framing articles of peace. The
country needed peace, even more than she was
willing to confess. He, therefore, on the Spanish
case being put before him, named the Prior of St.
John, Father Christopher, and Thomas Savage, his
commissioners, to settle matters in dispute between
the crowns of Spain and England, and confer with
Puebla on articles of mutual aid and comfort to be
given on either side in case of war.

5. On hearing how his agent sped, and careless how and where that agent lived, Fernando sent
a letter properly conçeived, appointing Puebla his
ambassador at the English court, with full authority
to treat of peace and to conclude a match. When
sending out these powers, he also sent a spy, one
Juan de Sepulveda, knight and trooper, to observe
the cripple and report to him how things went on.
The canon and the trooper were to push the treaty,
rather than the match. Their object was to draw
the English into war with France. While Max was
pounding in the north, Fernando wished the English to be thundering at the gates of Brest. If
that design could be achieved without committing
him to give the English prince his daughter Catalina.
he preferred to leave his daughter free.

CHAPTER VII.

First Proposals.

1488.

1. Though Henry was annoyed to see a nameless cripple sent to him instead of bishop, count, or councillor of state, he still received the Spanish agent with his winsome smile. "They do not know me yet in Spain," he said to those about him, with the spirit of a man who means that they shall know him. Keeping Puebla at his side, as though he were a friend like Father Christopher and Prior John, the King observed him in and out. Ill bred, ill fed, ill dressed, the King soon learned to read the man he had to deal with, and he took good care to feed his hunger and indulge his love of praise. He asked the agent to his palace; when he came to court, the King invited him to stay and dine. A dinner at the royal table suited Puebla's taste far better than a penny mess with drabs and prentice boys. He came so often that the pages laughed, and Henry, quaint of humour, sometimes joined these pages in their sport. "Look you, my masters," cried the King, as Puebla hobbled up an avenue, "here is the Spanish ambassador—what does he want?" At once the merry voices rang, "To eat; he wants to eat!" The King took care that he should have

his fill. He lodged his servants in a convent, and
the bursar was instructed not to charge him for
their food. When dining at the court, he sometimes asked, on leaving, for a loaf of bread and jug
of wine for supper; and having got these dainties
from a servant, carried them away beneath his cloak.
One day, when Lady Margaret heard him begging
this and that, she asked him if the King and Queen
of Spain could not afford their minister meat and
drink?

2. But Henry held his course of favour to the
cripple; glad to find that for a royal smile, a loaf
of bread, and now and then a pardon or a license,
he could buy Fernando's agent; nay, convert him,
as the Spanish traders said, into a minister of his
own affairs. To put some coin into that agent's
purse he granted him a license for a merchant, Juan
de Scover, to import two hundred tuns of claret
free of charge. To tickle his conceit, and raise his
credit in the pool, he called him in the license his
"beloved Doctor de Puebla." Whatever they might
think of him as priest and man, the Spanish traders
from Bilbao and Seville soon had solid proof that
this ungainly priest could serve them at the English
court.

3. For Henry saw his gain in such a match,
and even such a peace, as Spain proposed to him.
He had become aware that even in the face of
Isabel's dislike to Edward, articles of peace and
trade had been arranged in 1481, which were to be
in force ten years. Those years had not expired;
and Henry held that while those articles were in

force, the seizure of a ship with English goods on board was piracy. A case had just arisen. A Spanish ship, the San Stephano, sailed from Bristol for a port of Spain. When she arrived, one Martin de Miranda, who had letters of marque in his possession, got her seized by the provincial governor, and held to ransom for two thousand crowns of gold. A cry arose in Bristol, where the goods were owned; and Henry wrote an angry letter to the King and Queen of Spain.   But there were doubts about his case, since many of the Spaniards held that with the change of dynasty those articles of peace had lapsed.

4. Nor were these trading interests all. In many ways it might be well for Henry to be sure that Spain was at his back. As two usurping kings, supporting and supported by the Church, Fernando and himself had common enemies in the liberal ranks. As yet, this name of Liberal was not used in English speech. The odious word was Lay. "Lay-men" and "Bible-men" were Bishop Pecock's terms of menace and reproach; by which he stigmatized those Wycliffites and Lollards who desired to read the Scriptures and uphold the English law.   A century later Shakespeare caught the word in a transition stage. Lord Say, in speaking of the state of England in the days of Cade, describes the men of Kent as "liberal, valiant, active, wealthy." Say had been a Liberal, for he founded schools and set up presses. Many of the King's opponents were suspected of a liberal mood, and if the Inquisition had been introduced from Seville into Canterbury

many of these enemies might have perished in the flames instead of on the block.   John Swit was not alone in laughing at the thunders as they rolled from Rome.   Though many of the people were extremely pious, many were disposed to smile at such impostures as the winking saints and pools of milk and blood.   Some people put no trust in saints; some passed an image with an unbent knee; some mocked the wandering friars; some trolled their staves and cracked their jests against the parish priest.   Some people spurned the temporal verdicts of the Holy See.   In most affairs of conscience they were with those Bible-men whom Bishop Pecock had denounced as lost for saying—that Scripture is the only rule of life; that every man should read and judge; that those who live a goodly life may hope to understand the word; that image-worship is idolatry; that pilgrimages have no merit; that the Church should own no property in land; that calling on the saints for help is useless; that the monkish brotherhoods are vicious; and that laws decreed by papal and prelatical authority are null and void. These scorners of the bishop and the pontiff made the strength and glory of the House of York, and hence the court of Rome was swift to put them under ban and curse.

5. A singular event beyond the straits induced the King to draw near Spain.   King Max had so incensed the popular party that a mob had hustled him in the streets of Bruges, arrested him in a shop, and borne him to a lonely tower, where the Last of the Ritters was kept a prisoner, while his councillors

were spiked and headed in the market-place below.
All Europe shook with rage and merriment at his
mishaps. Kunz von der Rosen, the imperial Fool,
had tried to swim across the moat to him. A flock
of swans and geese had set on Kunz and driven
him back in rage and pain. The burghers were as
savage with the King as geese and swans had. been
with the imperial fool. Before they let him go,
they raised a scaffold in the market-place; they
made him mount that scaffold with a paper in his
hand; they made him read that paper; and they
made him swear on his salvation to observe the
terms laid down. He was to yield the government
of his son to them; he was to keep the peace towards France; he was to recognize the liberal rule
in Bruges and Ghent; he was to separate the duchy
from the empire, and to send his German troops
across the Rhine. Ashamed and angry, Max had
gone into the Tyrol, while the Emperor, his father,
broke into the duchy with a great array. All kings
and dukes were called upon for aid, and some who
owed the man no love were angry at the insult
offered to a prince of his exalted rank. Even Henry
melted towards a fugitive who still refused to recognize him as a reigning king. The Kaiser, though
he broke his son's most sacred pledges, could not
batter down the walls of Ghent, and when he turned
away in rage, no king in Europe felt his person safe
from outrage. If an insult could be offered to a
King of Rome, what might not happen to a sovereign
less august?

6. To tickle and delight the canon, Henry named

as his commissioners a famous prelate and a still
more famous peer; Richard Fox, privy councillor,
King's secretary, and Bishop of Exeter; Giles, Lord
Daubeney, privy councillor, and lieutenant of the
fort and town of Calais. The provincial mayor,
whom Henry never treated otherwise than as a great
ecclesiastic, was beside himself with joy. The King
invited him and his companion down to Sheen, presented them to his consort, carried them to his
nursery, and let them gaze in wonder at his infant son.

7. They saw Prince Arthur in his cot asleep; they
saw him naked in his bath; they saw him in his
royal robes and state. In every form they liked the
round and rosy child. "We find in him," they wrote
to Catharine's parents, "so many excellent qualities
as no one would believe." But they were still more
taken by the Queen and her attending maids: the
young and lovely queen, now twenty-two years old,
being served "by two-and-thirty ladies, each of whom
is of angelic beauty." Henry wished the Spaniards
to inform the King and Queen, their lord and lady,
that if the match went forward, he should like the
Princess Catalina to be sent to England early, as
Archduchess Marguerite of Austria had been sent
to France. It would be well for Catalina to acquire
some use of French, the language of his court and
household, in her youth, as well as get accustomed
to the island mist and rain. It would be wise, he
added afterwards, if the Princess were allowed to
drink some wine. The Spanish agent was already
Henry's man.

CHAPTER VIII.

Articles of Marriage.

1488.

1. ALTHOUGH an advocate for the Spanish marriage, Fox would willingly have dropt all question
of a league. A match would give him peace with
Spain and with the friends of Spain. A match
would check such corsairs as Segura and Miranda,
and would open Cadiz and Coruña to the outer
trade. Beyond these points he had no boon to ask
from Spain. All thought of war was absent from
his mind. His countrymen were restless, and would
shout for war on anybody's call; but Fox was well
aware how much his country needed rest. In twenty
years they might be strong again; but even those
who burned to win new Crecies in the plains of
France, could see that they must first endure some
years of peaceful growth. "There is no need to
talk about the treaty; let us go at once upon the
match," he said, as soon as the commissioners met.
The Spanish priest was taken by surprise. His
orders were to push the treaty and postpone the
match; and Fox proposed to push the marriage and
postpone the league. As his ecclesiastical superior,
Fox had some advantage in the contest over Puebla.
After praising heartily the King and Queen of Spain,

he came abruptly on his point: "What sum will the Infanta have?"

2. "It would be seemly," answered Puebla, "if you were to name the fortune you expect." Fox named a sum so large that Puebla started to his feet. "We must refer this matter to our masters," he observed in wonder. "No," said Fox, "that course will never do; the King and Queen of Spain will not consent." "You ask for things beyond the scope of reason," answered Puebla, losing temper; "if one only bears in mind what happens every day to English kings, it is surprising that our royal masters should consent to give their daughter to the Prince of Wales." These words were hardly out of Puebla's mouth before he felt that he had gone too far. The stately prelate and the dashing soldier were not men whom he could flout in that Castillian style.

3. Fox brought the Spaniards to their senses by a hint that Enrique the Liberal had offered to give his daughter (now the royal "Nun"), to an English prince—who was not even Prince of Wales—together with a dowry of two hundred thousand ducats. Fox was satisfied with throwing out this hint. He wished the Spanish agents to perceive how well he knew the state of things; how much the Exile weighed in any bargain to be made with Spain. Fox had no thought of starting her as a pretender, but he kept the fact of her existence in his mind. If Puebla had replied by asking where that English prince now was, he might have heard some hint, far off, and yet too near, about the Perfect Prince. He felt it would be wiser to withdraw his speech. He had

to recollect that though the English King might be
defeated in a year or so, he could immediately
despatch an army into France.

4. "It was a jest," said Puebla, harking back.
In his report to Spain, he boasted of his skill in
fence. He let the English know, he said, the state
of things, but in a form so courteous that they could
not take alarm. His hint was fruitful in results;
"the English lowered their terms one-third." The
sum required by Fox was still too high. "Since
there is time enough to think of details," Puebla
urged, "let us refer this point to umpires; two or
four, as you shall judge." "No, no," the English
councillor said; "that course will never do. We
are the umpires. If we cannot settle the amount,
no other persons can." They felt that he was right.
"Then name your price at once," said Puebla.
Fox set down his price; two hundred thousand
crowns. The Spaniards offered him a hundred
thousand crowns. "Why should your masters not
be liberal?" asked the Bishop; "they will not have
to pay the money; they will raise it from their subjects; why this haggling over what will cost them
nothing?" From a drawer he took some marriage
treaties; Scottish treaties, French treaties, Flemish
treaties; and in every one he showed them that
a larger dowry had been paid. The country was a
dear one, he insisted, and an English penny was as
much as thirty-two Spanish maravedies. People
spent vast sums in keeping house. An English
duke was rich. When Catharine came to London
she would have a third part of the revenues of

Chester, Wales, and Cornwall for her separate use; not less in all than eighty thousand crowns of gold a-year. The county, principality, and duchy had some thirty thousand vassals; hundreds of villages and castles, many forts and harbours, and a few considerable towns. All these would be her own.

5. Fox held his point; two hundred thousand crowns; if less were offered him, he had no more to say. At length, the Spaniards yielded. "Here," said Fox and Daubeney, "is a memorandum of agreement—sign it."

Richard, Bishop of Exeter, and Daubeney of Daubeney, in their quality of Commissioners of Henry the Seventh, declare to Rodrigo de Puebla and Juan de Sepulveda, ambassadors of Fernando and Isabel, that the dowry of the Princess Catharine is expected to be two hundred thousand gold crowns, each crown worth fifty English pence.

"Add one word more," said Puebla, "that we only sign in order to consult our masters." Puebla's words were added to the clause, and then the Spaniards signed.

CHAPTER IX.

Articles of Peace.

1488.

1. NEXT came the articles of peace.   The case was ticklish, hardly less so in respect of Portugal than in respect of France.

The King of Portugal could scarcely be omitted from a treaty which engaged the Kings of Spain and England to regard each other's friends as friends, each other's foes as foes, since Spain, on no account whatever could expose herself to risk of quarrelling with John the Perfect, while the Excellenta was alive and in his power.   Yet Puebla saw that John would be exasperated by the treaty, let it take what name and shape it might.   A treaty with the English monarch would diminish John's authority in the councils of Castille.   It was a blow at France, and John's importance in Castille was measured by his means of stirring up the French.   The English, too, had something to reserve.   Their friendship for the Portuguese was one of ancient date.   They could not lightly cast away old friends, nor would they treat the Portuguese as friends and foes to suit Fernando's politics.   In everything that touched the Exile, Fox and Daubeney wished to keep their hands unbound.   If Spain should go to war with Portugal, they meant to hold a neutral course. Beyond this point they would not move. "It is sufficient," Puebla wrote to his employers, "better even than if more had been obtained. The friendship of both countries may be so secured. It will be wise to say no more about it. If the King of Portugal were to hear of what is going on, he would be wild with rage." But neither Fox nor Daubeney would give this clause about the Portuguese in writing, as a portion of the articles of peace.

2. More delicate still was the affair of France; for Henry was at peace with Charles, and had no motive, like Fernando, to engage in war.

No state in Europe showed so wonderful a power of growth as France. The land of wine, of oil, of silk, of corn, no folly in her rulers, no misfortune of her armies, could depress her long. Not more than fifty years had passed since English dukes had reigned in Paris; yet within these fifty years the French had entered Rouen and Bordeaux as masters; had acquired possession of Provence; had re-annexed the province of Bourgogne; and got a footing in the frontier duchies of the Pyrenees. What they had gained they kept; and only foes who smote them as the English smote at Azincour, had ever forced them to disgorge their prey. One province of the France of Charles the Great resisted their attacks; the sea-washed Duchy of Bretagne. But though the Breton folk were Celtic, and had never learnt the language of their neighbours, France had partizans among their nobles, such as Rohan and Laval, who thought it finer to be counts and dukes in Paris than in

Rennes.   That prize was tempting to a king of
France; as tempting as Granada to a king of Spain,
as Scotland to a king of England; for a province
that would round off France by sea, and give her
all the ports from Bayonne to Boulogne, might
make her mistress of the narrow seas, enable her
to strike the Spanish trade, and give her what she
had been striving to obtain—a virtual primacy in
the West.   No prince in Europe liked this growing
power in Paris, but Fernando liked it least of all.
On every side the French were knocking at his
gates; disputing the possession of his duchies, stirring up his kinsfolk in Navarre, intriguing with the
royal Nun, exciting the nobility of Naples to dispute
his rights.   Of all these burning questions, that of
Rossillon and Cerdaña touched him nearest to the
quick.   For five-and-twenty years, since they were
pledged to France for crushing the republicans of
Cataluña, these two districts had been subjects of
dispute between the crowns; each party to the
bargain striving to deceive and cheat the other;
France to keep the duchies in defiance of her
pledge, and Spain to get them back without the
payment of her debt.   The tract had been restored,
invaded, and reduced by turns.   No Frenchman,
looking at the ridge of mountain as his natural
frontier and defence, could bear the thought of
yielding up a fort like Salsas and a town like Perpignan into his adversary's power.   Salsas was the
key of Languedoc.   Perpignan was a Calais in the
south; an open gate by which an active foe could
push his legions into France.   The people, Catalan

by race and speech, were ardently attached to Cataluña. Charles was only master in his actual
camp; but while he held a sword, and while the
royal Nun maintained her right, he was not likely
to relax his grip on these important border lands.

3. To Henry, too, this growth was matter for
regret and fear, though French support had helped
him to obtain his crown. What France had done
for him she might be tempted to repeat for others
after him. Yet he was slow to cause her just offence,
and loth to think of goading her to war. "My
orders are," said Puebla, "to insert an article in the
treaty binding either party to wage war on France
when France makes war upon the other." What
he wanted was a mutual guarantee. "Why name
the King of France at all?" asked Fox; "when marriages and treaties are concluded, other things come
after. England will be glad to act with Spain,
especially as English friendship for Spain is of old
standing." "If the friendship is so great," said
Puebla, "it is easy to do what is now asked." If
Puebla gave a true report of this important con-
ference, Fox replied, "It is not well to put such
things in writing; first, because a treaty signed and
sealed remains, and nothing should be signed and
sealed but what is just; next, because the insertion
of such an article is unusual; and, third, because
the balance of advantages will lie with Spain." Fox
and Daubeney had consulted jurists who replied,
that the insertion of a clause engaging Henry to
make war on Charles was contrary to conscience,
honesty, and God. "I showed them," Puebla wrote,

"from books, that both by canon law and civil law, it was according to conscience, honesty, and God, that England should make war on France." The Spaniard said the French had robbed their neighbours north and south; had stolen Guienne and Normandie from the King of England, just as they had stolen Rossillon and Cerdaña from the King of Spain. "It is notorious," answered Fox and Daubeney, "that the King of England is indebted to the King of France for many services, and it would not be honest to insert an article against him." So the article about the King of France was laid aside.

4. The articles were drafted into form and signed. Prince Arthur was to marry Princess Catharine when he came of age; the dowry was to be two hundred thousand crowns; one half the money was to be paid on landing, a second on the bridal day. All Spaniards then in England were to be security for this sum. Fernando was to send the princess over, in a decent manner, at his own expense. Her parents were to give her dress and jewels suitable to her rank. She was to own all property that came to her in virtue of her birth. All articles of peace and commerce were to be the same as they had been for thirty years. Each party was to help the other when attacked; the party asking the assistance to defray the cost. The rebels of one prince were not to be received by the other. If either of the high contracting parties made a treaty with another prince, his ally was to be included in the league. The commissioners were to meet again at Easter in the following year.

5. Fernando read these articles in no easy mood. He scanned the letters brought from Puebla, and he read the articles drawn up and signed. They seemed to him like papers on two different matters. "How is this?" he called to Sepulveda, who had carried the despatches over. Sepulveda could not tell him. "How is this?" Fernando wrote to Puebla; "the English ask two hundred thousand crowns, because Enrique had proposed to give that fortune. Puebla must reply that Enrique had one daughter only to endow." At most, he would consent to pay one hundred thousand ducats in the money of Castille. He would not hear of ducats being taken at fifty pence; if that were in the treaty they would cheat him in the weight. Nor would he pay this money down, as stipulated in the draft. He would consent to pay one half his daughter's portion when her marriage was consummated, not a day before that time; a second half in two years after that event was certified by officers of his own. He would not give security; his word must satisfy the King. Nor would he give his daughter ornaments and plate, unless he were allowed to count them as a portion of her hundred thousand crowns. He thought it wise to say no more about the cost of sending Catharine to an English port. As to her rights in Spain, no other property could be secured to her than what she held by birth—her claim in order of succession to the throne.

6. But more than in these details of the match the English seemed to have outwitted Puebla in the articles of peace. These articles gave Fernando

scarcely any of the things on which his heart was
fixed. He wished to have a treaty covering all his
friends, uncovering all his foes. He hoped to isolate
John the Perfect; but the draft said nothing of the
Portuguese. Fox would not enter into any league
against the King of Portugal; but Puebla had assured
Fernando that the English would agree to take a
neutral course. Yet, nothing in the articles bound
the English to abstain from war. More curious
were the articles touching France. Fernando's purpose in the treaty was to act on Paris from the line
of Normandie and Maine; but in the draft of treaty
there was not a word implying that the English
would attack his enemies in the rear. A "show of
war" would only serve his foes. On turning back
to Puebla's letter, he observed a statement that the
English agents, holding a mass-book in their hands,
had sworn on oath, that Henry, when the marriage
was concluded, would be ready to make war against
the French. Fernando wished to have that oath
recorded in the draft. "If Henry does not like," he
wrote, "to put into the treaty all that he has
promised, let the marriage treaty be concluded
without it; but cause him to sign and swear a
separate treaty, he and his servants, to this effect,
that, after the alliance and marriage of our children
shall have been concluded, he will bind himself, if
asked by us, within (a blank number of) days, to
call upon the King of France to give us back our
provinces of Rossillon and Cerdaña, which he now
keeps from us; and if within (a blank number of)
days after that demand the King of France has not

restored to us those provinces, he will at our request make war upon the King of France." If Henry should agree to sign this separate article Fernando said the treaty might proceed. His motive, he again repeated to his agent, was to get Rossillon and Cerdaña from the French.

7. When Puebla read these orders he was much perplexed. He wished to serve two masters, and obtain from both his meed of praise and pay. "I dare not mention some of these conditions," he replied. He begged for time, and his arrear of pay. If time were given him, all would yet be well. What need was there for haste, when the commissioners would not sit again till Easter in the ensuing year? By nature Henry was averse to war; by policy he was averse to a renewal of the fierce and bloody war with France. The hope which had disturbed so many Kings, of wearing both the French and English crowns, was gone from him for ever. What he had to gain lay nearer home, and Henry's thoughts were given to the immediate duty in his front. He had to soothe the partisans of York. He had to reconcile the Welsh to English rule. He had to plant an English government on Irish soil. He had to manage and conciliate the Scots. These things would give him unity and strength. His policy was peace at home, not war abroad; peace, order, growth and piety, within the round and compass of his isles; not rapine, slaughter, and confusion on his neighbour's soil. What chance had Puebla of persuading one who held this policy of peace to draw the sword? But while the cripple's words

were tossing on the seas, events were doing for
him what he never could have done without their
help.

———

BOOK THE FOURTH.

BRETON WAR.

CHAPTER I.

Bretagne.

1488.

1. THE day on which the articles fixing Catharine's dower were signed by Puebla, Henry sent his Hail, all hail! to Catharine's parents on their victories against the Moors. These Moors were Saracens in blood, and Henry, with his fancies kindled by the prowess of Sir Gawaine, wrote about Fernando smiting enemies of the Christian faith, as that poetic champion smote his Saracens of the South; but having paid his compliment, he turned to other things; the union of his states, the building of his palace, the improvement of his coinage, the repression of his barons, and the settlement of his Irish towns. All details of the marriage could be left to Bishop Fox and Father Christopher. At Easter, when they were to meet again, his boy would be a little man—two years and seven months old. What Henry needed he had gained; a pledge of peace by sea and land,

an entry into the fraternity of reigning kings, and a
return to regular course of trade. When Puebla
came to London, no one but the Pope and King of
France had recognised the Tudor prince. That
mission turned the scale; and of the greater princes
who denied his title, Max, the fugitive from Flanders,
stood alone. His wisdom was to watch and wait.
Some years must pass before his son would be of
age to marry. If the Princess could be got to
England, as the young Archduchess had been got to
France, his objects would be gained. He saw how
much the French were gaining from the fact of
Marguerite being in Paris; but he dared not press
this point too soon in Spain.

2. But he was not to watch and wait in peace.
Events were coming on him which he could not
meet alone. He, too, was forced to look for allies;
and in place of waiting for the Spanish princess to
be flung into his lap, he had to send in search of
her, though well aware that by this sending into
Spain, he would be throwing his master suit into
Fernando's hands.

3. A warlike fury had arisen among his people;
and Henry was not strong enough to ride the
tempest and divert the flash. On every side, his
peers and citizens were raging at the French, for
what was called their selfish dealing with the duchy
of Bretagne. For Charles, who had been lately
battering at the walls of Nantes, was occupying
every post that he could seize, and threatening to
annex the province to his crown. Of all the feudal
duchies into which the Frankish kingdom had been

split, the duchy of Bretagne alone retained her
semi-sovereign state; but with the growth of royal
power in France, a time was coming when the duchy
of Bretagne would have to follow in the wake of
Normandie, Provence, and Maine.   By force, if
Charles could win by force,—by fraud, if he must
stoop to fraud,—he was resolved on reuniting her
to France. His pretext mattered little; yet, the pretext he had published was defensible in law; his
right as feudal lord to follow up a rebel into any
part of his domain. His cousin Louis, Duke of
Orleans, son of the poet, and first prince of the
blood, had risen against the regent, Madame Anne,
and having failed to drive her out, had fled to
Rennes, where he was joyously received by Francois
the Second, Duke of Bretagne, as an enemy of
Charles. Duke Francois was a worn and feeble man,
without a son to bear his name, and ruled by
favourites and women. Orleans soon became his
master. Charles had asked the Duke to send his
cousin Orleans back to Paris, and on this command
being disobeyed, the French had poured their troops
into his wild and lonely dales. These troops had
occupied some towns before the Bretons, roused to
action by their imminent danger, could despatch
ambassadors to Max, to Henry, and to Alain d'Albret,
begging for immediate help in ships and men.

4. Friendship for Duke Francois, who had sheltered him in exile, urged the King of England to
assist the Bretons in repelling Charles; the more
so, as a King of France who held the Breton ports,
would be a dangerous foe to England in a time of

war. But Charles had also been his friend, and
Henry was a man of peace. He hoped that matters might be smoothed at Rennes and Paris; for
the King of France professed to have no ends in
view beyond the seizure of his rebel on the Duke's
estate. Charles swore he had no eye on the estate
itself. If Louis could be reconciled to Charles,
there seemed good reason to believe the French
might turn aside. Affairs were not going well with
them. If they had carried Vitré and St. Aubin,
they had failed before the walls of Nantes. A bare
and hilly district, with impenetrable woods, deep
rivers, and innumerable castles, was the kind of ob-
stacle which hinders and disgusts a soldiery like
the French. Though sweeping everything before
them in the open field, the French were tiring of a
hard, inglorious task, where men were starved to
death in lonely woods, and drowned in fording
nameless streams. Charles spoke of peace, and
begged his English ally to employ some man of
trust who could arrange the terms between Duke
Francois and himself.

5. Father Christopher had been going to and
fro; at first in secret and alone; but afterwards in
public form and with a fitting train. He had been
charged to see the King of France, and if he found
that sovereign in pacific mood, he was to go from
Nantes to Rennes and sound the ducal court. A
holy man, he seemed the proper agent for a work
of peace. A priest, his cloth was likely to impress
the Duke; an aged man, his beard was likely to
impress the King.

6. Charles, seventeen years of age, was small in person, weak of eye, and flat of face; a mean and ugly lad, with head too big and neck too short, with lanky legs and crooked knees, and mind as dwarfed and twisted as his bodily frame. He had been trained to lie and cheat, as ordinary boys are taught to speak the truth and pay their honest debts. But higher learning he had none. "He needs no grammar," said his father, who detested books; "he knows enough if he has learned to hide his thoughts." The youth had learnt this art of hiding thought, for he could fawn and yield when he was lifting up his hand to strike. A boy of seventeen years misled the aged and experienced priest; for Father Christopher, in all his dealings with the world, had never met a lad like Charles.

7. Having wormed from Father Christopher the secret that on finding grounds for hope he was to make for Rennes, the King took care that he should find a reasonable hope. It suited Charles that Father Christopher should go to Rennes; because he knew that Orleans would dictate the Duke's reply; and he was certain that his cousin Orleans would not yield. The odium of rejecting terms would lie at Rennes; the English priest would form a bad opinion of the ducal court; and Henry, vexed at the rejection of his offers, would conclude that France was acting in her lawful right. Charles told the Father he was all for peace; he had no hidden purpose in his mind; he loved the Duke, who was his kinsman, and the duchy, which was part of France. He only wanted Orleans to sub-

mit. At Rennes the monk had met a franker mood
than in the royal camp near Nantes. What message had he brought? The Duke had sent for
help and not advice; for General Brooke, not
Father Christopher; and he was vexed to find a
messenger of peace had been with Charles. "The
Duke," said Orleans, speaking for the helpless man,
"having been a kind host and parent to the English King in other days, expected from him soldiers
to defend his rights, not monks to talk of articles
of peace. Let Henry, if he can, forget the past.
Yet in his wisdom he must see how much he has
to risk in future, if this duchy is annexed, and all
her harbours fall into an enemy's grasp." Duke
Francois, moping in his chair, allowed the prince to
speak, and Father Christopher quitted Rennes in
rage against the ducal cause. Near Nantes, by
which he passed on his return, the King received
him with a doleful face. They had not listened to
his words of peace! He begged the father to report
the language he had heard; his ally ought to know
the men, with whom they had to deal. Charles
wanted nothing for himself. He only asked for
law and justice. Louis was his heir, and being in
arms against him, could not claim protection at a
vassal's court. The thing was now in Henry's
hands, to deal with as his wisdom should suggest.
That Henry might be free to speak and act, said
Charles, the French would raise the siege of Nantes
and re-ascend the Loire. Christopher was enjoined
to add, from Charles, that rebels would not listen
to advice, however sound, unless the friendly argu-

ment were backed by force. That force the King
of France was ready to apply, in aid of any course
his English ally should propose.

8. Though wary as to phrases, Henry was no
less deceived than Christopher; for Charles withdrew his troops from Nantes and crossed his frontiers, so that Henry might appear to act in perfect
liberty. A second embassy was therefore sent to
Rennes; a stronger tone was taken with the Duke;
and Henry was induced to pledge his word for
Charles. Being pressed on every side, the Duke
gave way; a truce was made between the parties;
and the English ruler was appointed arbiter of the
dispute. The King was in his glory as a friend of
peace. Father Christopher came merrily back, and
Henry had the happiness of countersigning articles
by which the French and Bretons were to keep
the peace for eighteen months. Thus, truce was
made on every side, and Henry the Pacificator rode
to Windsor with his Queen to spend the summer
days. But he was rudely wakened from his dream.
Before his ink was dry, the French were set in
motion. Breaking through the Breton lines, they
captured Ancenis, Chateaubriand, and Fougères, and
pushed their vanguard rapidly towards Rennes.
Amazed by this return, the Bretons ran to meet
them with a mongrel army and divided chiefs.
Twelve hundred lancers sent by Max, four hundred
archers under Rivers, showed themselves in front,
and fought against the French like men; but every
leader in the Breton army had some separate purpose of his own to serve. D'Albret hoped to see

Orleans captured.   Orleans wished to hear that D'Albret had been killed.   The Bretons were dispersed.   By help of D'Albret, Orleans was a prisoner. Rivers fell among his archers, who were cut to pieces.   Rennes was occupied.   Duke Francois crept into his bed and died; and as he left no son, his duchy fell to Anne, his eldest girl.   But Charles was now her master, and the little Duchess had to sign an article that she would never marry, save with the consent of Charles.

As salt on fire, the news of this astounding act of treachery and invasion fell on English towns and shires, already burning to renew the fight; and Henry, seeing that "a show of war" at least must now be made, began to arm in haste, and seek what allies he might find against the French.

CHAPTER II.

Embassy to Spain.

1488-9.

1. AN agent who could sail for Spain, procure an audience of the King, and get him to adopt the articles which Fox and Daubeney had signed, was wanted. Father Christopher was busy with the work at Rennes; and Savage, who as priest and doctor of the canon law was like an English Puebla, seemed the fittest man. He was adroit and nameless. If he failed, he could be disavowed. A mate was found for him in Nanfan, one of the King's body-guard, an English counterpart of Sepulveda. But as neither Savage nor Nanfan spoke Castillian, Ruy Machado, one of Henry's foreign heralds, was to help them with his tongue and pen. The day they left, Nanfan, riding near the King, was told to kneel, and Henry laid a sword across his back. The embassies were now of equal rank. A Spanish doctor and a Spanish knight were balanced by an English doctor and an English knight. "They do not know me yet in Spain."

2. Puebla and Sepulveda took their leave of King and Queen, and travelling to the coast with Savage, Nanfan, and Machado, sailed with them for Bilbao in two Spanish ships. They hoped to make

that harbour in a week; but winter blew them into
Plymouth, where they lost ten days, and afterwards
into Falmouth, where they lost nine more.   Their
vessels, squat in build, with heavy hamper and a
flowing sail, were rudely handled by the crews.
Fair breezes set them free from Falmouth roads;
but as they rolled past Ushant into the Bay of
Biscay, these breezes freshened into gusts and
squalls.   All day and night they drove before the
gale, and in the storm they parted company.   The
English were amused to hear the Spaniards shout-
ing to their saints for help.   The sailors' saint was
San Vicente, on whose shrine they swore to light
innumerable dips of wax.   "By God's grace, and by
the prayers and pilgrimages promised to the good
saints, they were comforted and saved."   A sailor
sighted land; a hill in the Asturias; and drifting
up the coast, they made the port of Laredo, in Old
Castille.   The greeting which the pious English
heard on landing was a vesper-bell.

3. By short and early stages they ascended
from the sea line to the ridges leading into central
Spain.   A road no better than a trail ran up through
oak and chestnut woods; now climbing over rocky
ground, here lost in snow, there floundering into
ooze and swamp.   In three days, cold and hungry,
they arrived in Burgos, city of the Cid.   De Castro
took them in, and cheered them up with food and
wine.   All three were lodging with Diego's uncle,
when Puebla, who had made Bilbao, came up to
join them.   Feasts and junkets were provided by
the traders, who remembered Cheape and Wap-

ping; and the men of Burgos sent them flesh of
roebucks, capons, conies, spices, and confectionary,
with a skin of wine.   When the mayor and judges
heard of their arrival, they despatched an officer to
the tavern where their servants lodged, to tell the
host he was to make no charge.   At length a message from Fernando came.   The King and Queen
were at Medina del Campo, where the Queen had
built a castle of defence among the ruins of a
Roman camp, and thither Henry's agents for the
peace and match were asked to ride.   In spite of
trouble in the Pyrenees, affairs were going on well.
Their last assaults upon the Moors, delivered on
the eastern line, had given them Vera, Velez Blanco,
Huescar, and some other towns; and they were
wintering in Medina as a post from which they
could observe the French.

4. One mile from Burgos the ambassadors took
their leave of Castro, and their personal woes began.
From Burgos to Valladolid, the road ran through
a string of villages, with neither inn nor convent,
and in which the food was scant, the lodging bad,
the custom of the country rude.   Valladolid, when
they came to it, was empty, for the court had gone
away in anger at the people having raised their
voice against the new and holy office, which the
Queen had planted in a house adjoining that in
which she lodged.   Savage and Nanfan were conducted to a fine, but empty house, the residence
of Ruy de Portillo, a wealthy merchant, who had
been arrested on suspicion of heresy, and flung
into a dismal vault.   The Queen and her inqui-

sitors had stript his house of everything; his chair
and stool, his bed and bench, his food and wine;
not having left enough, as Savage found, to feed
a rat. Some beds and chairs were fetched from
magazines; the Mayor sent in some lard and sweet-
meats, with a couple of skins of wine; so that the
English ate and drank, and made them merry in
the ruined heretic's house. They were not yet
aware how many houses had been lately emptied
in the Spanish towns.

5. On drawing near Medina, they were met by
three processions: first, by the Bishop of Malaga,
Secretary Alvarez, and other gentlemen; next, by
the Bishop of Palencia, the Bishop of Segovia, the
Grand Commander of Leon, and a train of knights
and priests; and at the city gates, by the Duke de
Alboquerque, the Count de Haro, the Constable of
Castille, and hosts of bishops, counts, and knights,
who led them to their lodgings in the town. Medina was a Moorish town, with massy walls and
gates, and narrow streets and houses built on granite
shafts, with open squares, and fountains nestling in
the shade of trees. One side of the great square
was occupied by a pile which had been church, and
mosque, and church in turn; a strong and gloomy
pile, inscribed to Antolin, a saint of high repute in
Spain, although unrecognised by Rome. The Queen
had made this church collegiate; had adorned the
angle with a belfry; had supplied a chime of bells,
with two bronze men to fling the midnight cadence
far and wide. On coming to their lodgings, Savage
saw that care was taken to impress them with the

wealth of Spain. Their rooms were hung with tapestry, their beds were bright with coverlets, and everything about was snug and warm.

6. Three days elapsed before they were received. At seven o'clock at night, a crowd of officers came into the square with lighted torches, to convey them to the royal palace, called Castillo de la Mota, for an audience of the King and Queen. This castle stood a mile beyond the city wall. A wide and windy plain was broken and commanded by a mount, on which, in ancient times, the Romans had erected a colossal camp. Vast fragments of this stronghold still remained; huge gateways, roadside temples, solid towers, and far-extending walls. Among these ruins Juan had commenced, and Isabel completed, a feudal castle, with a tower which swept the corn-fields, dusty roads, and many a distant town. The air was damp, the water bad, the site unhealthy; but the Queen had found her parliament in Toledo an unpleasant neighbour, and proposed to make this Castle on the Mount her ordinary home. The district of Medina was the country of her youth, the stronghold of her cause. Arevalo was near. Segovia, Valladolid, and Avila were the outworks and defences of Medina. From her Castle on the Mount her husband and herself had dated the commission of her first inquisitors. In the lofty turret of her castle she was safe, and in the lofty turret of her castle she proposed to live and die.

CHAPTER III.

Catharine Pledged.

1489.

1. WITHIN this Castle of the Mount a comedy
had been prepared. The King and Queen were
dressed in cloth of gold, with puff of silk and
edge of fur, and belts about their waists ablaze
with precious stones. Mendoza, who was next the
Queen, and on the same seat with her, sat superb
in his attire; nor were the lords and ladies in
attendance far behind the King and Queen. Fernando's usual dress was that of any Moorish prince;
a cap, a scimitar, a breast-plate, and a flowing
robe; but in this evening pageant at Medina, he
was decked in stiff brocade and cloth of gold.
The Queen, who commonly affected poor attire—
the gown and fillet of a nun—was richer than her
lord. Machado, with a herald's eye for clothes
and jewels, priced the dress she wore that night as
worth the whole of Catalina's dower—two hundred
thousand crowns of gold.

2. On kissing hands, the English agents made
a Latin speech, and then the Bishop of Ciudad
Rodrigo was commanded to reply in phrases which
should sound polite, and yet mean nothing to the
point. Before he spoke the word, Fernando wished

to learn how far these agents were empowered to
go. A weak old man, with neither lungs nor teeth,
the Bishop of Ciudad Rodrigo rose, and mumbled
something to the guests, which Savage tried to
catch, but could not. When the priest had done,
the English agents bowed and took their leave,
suspecting they had heard as much as they were
meant to hear; but it was long past midnight when
with torch and guard they left the Castle on the
Mount.

3. The family at Medina were the King and
Queen; Don Juan, Prince of the Asturias; Doña
Isabel, Doña Juana, Doña Maria, and that baby
Catalina, whom the English agents were to see.
Don Juan was eleven years old, a pallid and ascetic
boy, with sweet and suffering face, and tastes which
rather fitted him for the trade of minstrel than for
that of king. Although a child, he liked to be alone,
to ponder over books, to sit in church and cloister,
and to trifle with the strings of his guitar. He
studied Latin, and he played on pipe and reed.
His tutor was Diego de Deza, secretary and successor of the Grand Inquisitor of Spain. Like all
the members of his house, he entered a religious
order, wore a penitential sack beneath his silk and
gold, and thought no man was safe unless he wore
a monkish hood. His sister Isabel, the "child of
sin," now eighteen years of age, was frail in health
and weak in mind. Her lungs were hurt; her temper
was desponding; and the Queen had fears about her
life. A girl of feeble frame, and yet more feeble
will, she was the slave of a confessor who had power

to bind and loose, to save and damn her soul.
Juana, close on ten years old, was deemed the
beauty of her house. Her mother called her Suegra
(mother-in-law), from her personal resemblance to
the beautiful and wicked Queen. She was so bright
and quick, so full of flash and fire, that it was hard
for any one to guide her steps. Her tutor, Fray
Andreas, a Franciscan, had the task of curbing her
unruly flights; but Fray Andreas found this task
beyond his strength. A something of her uncle,
Enrique the Liberal, seemed to live again in her.
Maria, seven years old, was yet too young for any
one to say what she would live to be in after days;
and Catalina was an infant three years old.

4. A second audience being arranged, the English
agents asked to see Don Juan and his sisters; but
Fernando, who had set his spies to listen and inquire, contrived to put them off from day to day.
Don Juan they might see, and Doña Isabel they
might see; but for the younger children they must
wait awhile. At last he yielded to their earnest
wish. A time was fixed when they were introduced
with much ado, and saw the baby Catalina richly
dressed with seven young maidens waiting on her.
All the family were present. Don Juan sat on the
ground beside his father; Doña Isabel danced with
a young Portuguese. Maria also danced. Fernando
gave a bull-fight at Medina; first, that brutal sport
in which the horse is ripped and gored to death,
and then the bull is fired and stabbed; and afterwards that Moorish game in which a troop of dogs
is chased in festive war. The Queen was in her

box, and held the baby Catalina in her arms to see the horses gored and ripped, the bulls tormented and despatched. Mendoza sat beside her in the royal stand. "Well, it was beautiful to see the Queen hold up her daughter, the Infanta Catharine, Princess of Wales," Machado wrote; at which time she was three years old. The fight being done, the King and Queen retired into their castle, where the ladies danced with knight and picador, and Isabel's iron men beat out the midnight chimes before the English agents marched with torch and banner through the city gates.

5. Amidst those frolics of the bull-ring and the dance, Fernando kept an eye on Rennes and Brest, which Charles was threatening to attack. Against that danger he must be prepared; for he had projects of his own, as yet untold, which Charles would cross if he were master of that duchy. When he learnt from spies how far the English agents were empowered to yield, he signed, in presence of Savage and Nanfan, that "Project of Medina del Campo," which was dated March 28, 1489.

6. The Kings agreed that Arthur, Prince of Wales, should marry Catalina when he came of age; and that the Kings of Spain and England should assist each other in defence of their estates. It was agreed between them that if either Spain or England were at war with France, the other should attack the French; and neither kingdom should conclude a separate peace, unless the King of France had first restored the provinces he held. Rossillon and Cerdaña were noted as the Spanish provinces

held by France; Guienne and Normandie were
noted as the English provinces held by France. If
France should give Rossillon and Cerdaña to the
Spaniards, they might sign a separate peace; if
France should give Guienne and Normandie to the
English, they might sign a separate peace.   By this
arrangement of his terms Fernando thought he had
outwitted and deceived the English; for if Henry
and Fernando were to march on France from opposite points—the English landing on her coasts,
the Spaniards pouring through the Pyrenees—the
French would be compelled to buy off either one
or other of their foes.   Which would they buy?
No doubt, the cheaper of the two.   Fernando was
this cheaper of the two.   To give up Perpignan
and Salsas was a trifle; but to give up Rouen and
Bordeaux would be to mangle France.   If, therefore, after two or three defeats, the French should
try to square accounts with either, they were sure
to square accounts with Spain.   Rossillon and Cerdaña cost them nothing and were not their own.
Guienne and Normandie were necessary parts of
France.   Fernando thought the treaty so arranged
that he could get his duchies at a trifling cost, and
leave his English ally to the burthen of a war.
Before a shot was fired, he fancied he had won his
prize.   But he forgot that Henry, whom he hoped
to cheat, might have his own reserves and purposes.
That Prince had no intention to observe the articles.
He meant to use them, as Fernando meant to use
them, for the purpose of controlling friends and
foes.   The Spanish girl was only three years and

four months old; her lover ten months younger than herself.

7. Of this alliance Catharine was the price. Fernando was to send his child to England at his own expense, with store of plate and jewels, such as might beseem her royal birth. One point the gamesters had to leave in doubt—how far the cups and ornaments were to be treated as her property. Were they to be her own—her own apart from public dower, her own to hold and keep, her own to use and wear; her own to give and sell? Savage had understood they were to be so. Puebla, on the other side, declared that Fox had counted them as portions of the dowry, reckoning them at fifty thousand crowns. No hint of such agreement had been given to Savage. Fox was not a man to overlook a sum of fifty thousand crowns, nor was it like the King to take a woman's ornaments in payment of a public debt. Would it be possible for Catharine's cups and trinkets to be taken from her? If not, how could they be inserted in the treasurer's accounts? Unless they were received as public property, they could not stand as dowry. Dowry was a public matter, and a counter-part of settlements on the other side. A lady who became Princess of Wales in England was entitled to her settlements by law; but personal ornaments and plate were not esteemed a portion of those settlements. Fernando stood on what was called the Bishop's word. As Savage could not yield, it was agreed that Fox should say and swear, if such a bargain had been made or not.

CHAPTER IV.

Duchess Anne.

1489.

1. ERE Savage could return from Spain with
news that articles of peace were sealed, the English
King was forced to arm. He had been hoping that
the French, since they had taken Orleans prisoner,
would retire on Tours and Blois; but week was
following week, and not a sign was shown of their
intention to retire. Instead of falling back, they
were advancing to the front. St. Malo fell. Guincamp was occupied. Dinan was surprised. Some
remnants of the English volunteers were holding
out at several points, and striving to avenge their
leader's death; but they were pressed by heavy
odds, and calling on their countrymen for help.
The English garrisons in Jersey heard by every
boat that towns and forts were falling to the French.
The capital was lost, and Brest and Vannes were
menaced from the sea. The town of Nantes seemed
safe; but there were parties in the council-room,
where Alain d'Albret had a voice above the power
of Duchess Anne.

2. With slow and halting steps the King was
dragged along this road of war. At first his "show"
was all; but he was borne along the rolling tide.

The clergy and the nobles in his council were as hot for fighting as the archers at his gate. To learn what men were saying in the shires, he called a Council of his realm, which Council was so strong in favour of the duchy, and so ready to supply him with the means of acting, that he found himself constrained to move. He sent ambassadors to Max. Once more, his almoner went to Paris, and was welcomed with a laughing eye and lying lip by Charles. Recruiting agents marched through every shire. A Parliament was summoned for an early day; yet Henry paused at every step, and caught at every pretext for delay. He spoke to Puebla in a dubious tone. He felt, he said, how much he owed to France; how many of his friends would fall from him the moment he deserted Charles; yet he would fight, if, after all his efforts, he should fail to bring about a general peace.

3. When Parliament met, all doubts of what the country wanted were dispelled. The country wanted war, and Henry could not hold his country back. Supplies were granted for the war; a hundred thousand pounds a-year; a tax for three years next to come. Some trouble rose about the share of clerk and layman; for the commons wished to lay two-thirds of the amount on Church and Abbey; while the monks and prelates held that Church and Abbey were not liable to the tax. At length the several shares were fixed; a fourth part by the clergy and the other three parts by the laity. The commons could not stand against the upper house, and in that upper chamber Morton reigned supreme.

Some bills were passed in favour of the troops. A
person serving in Bretagne was to enjoy the benefit
of his public spirit. He could make a will without
a fine; by his attorney he could plead his absence
as a bar to suits; and he could claim protection
from the courts of law.

4. While Parliament was sitting, several knights
and gentlemen, Sir Richard Edgecombe of the royal
household with them, sailed for Morlaix. Edgecombe
gained the town; but all the rest fell back, and
spread reports through England that the French
were masters of the land. These stories whet the
English appetite for war. In no long time, ten
thousand men were under arms; a fleet was riding
off the southern coast; and every ear was listening
for an order to embark.

5. Three thousand men were sent to Calais and
adjoining ports; three thousand to the fleets in
Portsmouth and the Down; four thousand to the
menaced Breton towns. As Max had not yet come
to terms, some companies of English marched from
Calais to assist him, and the world soon heard
what sort of war-dogs Henry held in leash. The
English plumes were always seen in front, and in a
desperate charge, some English pikemen cut a line
of steel from which a regiment of Flemings had
recoiled. Maréchal de Querdes, the French commander, stormed against these new assailants, but
Daubeney proved a stubborn foe, and by his timely
succour Max was able to recover St. Omers. Max
held his old opinion of the English prince, whom
he regarded as a rebel and assassin; but this rebel

and assassin was the only man in Europe who could
help him to regain his towns. He signed a treaty
with the prosperous monarch; hoping to renounce
his friendship at an early date. Imperial agents
came to London, which they made a centre of intrigues against the French. All hearts were soon
on fire. Even Henry caught the martial glow; and
when, in early spring, the court left London for the
ports of embarkation, he inspired his army to go
forward and protect the youthful Duchess from the
rage of Charles.

6. A child with full blue eye, pink cheek, and
tender mouth, the Duchess was a shy and pious
thing, whom Fra Bartolommeo might have painted
for a young Madonna. She was followed by a host
of lovers, hardly one of whom bestowed a thought
upon her charms of person and her gifts of mind.
As yet she was too young for love, though writers
of romantic history, like Abbé Irail, fancy she had
given away her heart at ten. If she had not yet
learned to love, it could not be for want of practice
in that science. At her cradle there were sighs and
hopes; her father, being without a son. As Bretagne
passed to female heirs, the man who married Duchess
Anne would be the Duke.

7. The Sire de Leon, eldest son of Viscount de
Rohan, was her earliest swain, and almost in her
cradle Anne was pledged to marry him. Henry of
Richmond, while at Begar Abbey, had bestowed his
thoughts on Anne: but Henry was a man in years
when she was nestling in her nurse's arms; and long
before she reached her teens, his fortunes led him

13*

to Elizabeth of York. A little later he suggested
Edward, third Duke of Buckingham and Constable
of England, as a fitting match for Anne, and tried
to make this marriage with an English subject a
condition of his helping to expel the French. The
Duke was young and winning, but the Duchess was
a semi-sovereign lady, and her councillors could
hardly be expected to consent. Another lover was
the Archduke, Philip the Fair, a son of Max, and
heir of the imperial crown; but Philip was too
young to act alone, and no one thought the offer
which was made for him would stand. A fifth was
Charles d'Egmont, Duke of Gueldres, one of the
many paupers of imperial stock who hung about
the Kaiser's court. The claim of d'Egmont, who
had lived in Max's household, was supported by
those friends of Duchess Anne who looked on Philip
as a prince beyond their reach. A sixth aspirant
to her hand was Alain D'Albret, father of Jean,
king-consort of Navarre. His mother was a Bre-
tonne; his half-sister was the Countess of Laval;
and this intriguing woman was the governess of
Duchess Anne. Each lover had his faction in the court
of Rennes. De Rieux supported Leon, as the match
already made. Comminges took the part of D'Albret.
Edgecombe stood for Buckingham. Orange was for
Gueldres. D'Albret, a man of forty-nine, with
eight children by a former wife was ready to
settle all his lands and monies on his offspring by
the Duchess. Anne would never listen to his suit.
"A convent if you like," she said, "but D'Albret—
never!"

8. Orleans had fluttered these pretenders to her smiles. When Anne first saw the man who was to be her second husband he was twenty-three years old. If Charles should die and leave no heir, Orleans would be king. That Louis fell in love with Anne is not to be supposed, although as heir of France he saw his great advantage in the match. He thought of the advantage, not the woman; and was only eager that her husband should be king of France. D'Albret, on finding Orleans in his way, had crossed that prince at every turn, and made the Duchess suffer by his passions. In the battle of St. Aubin, where they should have joined their forces, D'Albret would not act with Orleans, and the English archers had been cut to pieces through the wish of these excited men to bring each other to a shameful end. When Orleans was removed by Charles, D'Albret imagined he had won his game. But while these fools were plotting in their tents, a still more dazzling lover came upon the scene. This man was Maximilian of the golden locks and condor nose.

CHAPTER V.

Anne's Lovers.

1489.

1. In Max—a man of thirty, bronzed and hand-some, with the light of an imperial crown about his face—the courts of Europe recognised their chief. He was a soldier and a student, like the princes of his line; a man of books and pictures, and a patron of the singer's and the graver's art; and yet so poor he often had to pawn his books and sell his pictures to prevent a mutiny of his troops. Like all the princes of his house, he dreamt of marrying duchies, provinces, and kingdoms. Marie, only child of Charles the Bold, had given him Flanders and Bourgogne in trustship for his son. A second wife, who had a similar fortune, would be welcome; and Bretagne, though hardly to be named with Flanders and Bourgogne, was still the amplest dower of any princess then alive. A marrying man, he kept an eye on every court in Europe where the males were sickly, and the sceptres could descend through female heirs. If Isabel of Spain had lost her son, he would have wooed her eldest girl, the "child of sin," oblivious of his mother's passions and his cousin's wrongs. In search of provinces to marry, he was led in thought to Rennes. No sooner was he heard

than he was answered; for a council wrangling over such poor claims as those of D'Albret, Buckingham, and Gueldres, was elated at the coming of a prince who could impose his will on France, and raise his wife to an imperial throne.

2. Fernando tried to keep on terms with all these rivals, who were fighting for his duchies in the Pyrenees as much as if they had been storming Salsas in his name. In London he professed to think the most of Buckingham. At Ghent and Frankfurt he was happy to support the claims of Max. At Nantes, which D'Albret held, his agents were instructed to support the Navarrese. The shrewdest of his ministers, Francisco de Rojas, was despatched to Rennes, where he was told to watch events, and turn them to account in dealing with the court of Charles. Fernando had a purpose of his own to serve. Of all the men who had been named for Duchess Anne, not one was to his mind. No English, French, or Austrian husband suited Spain; for Spain had no desire to see an English, French, or Austrian prince at Rennes, and master of the ports from Nantes to Brest. Nor were the candidates of equal weight. Fernando looked on Leon as a fool, on D'Egmont as a dupe, on Philip as a child. As yet, he had not heard of Max. Buckingham was only strong in Henry's grace. D'Albret was of greater weight, from his connexion with the duchy; but, the father of Jean, King-consort of Navarre, was in the last degree obnoxious to the Spanish court. D'Albret in Rennes would strengthen Jean and Catharine in Pamplona, out of

which Fernando had a mind to drive them when
his time should come.   No; D'Albret must not wed
the Duchess Anne.

3. The matter needed to be touched with skilful
hands, for Henry was a jealous prince, and England
had a gallant fleet at sea.   Fernando opened the
affair by offering to support the Duke of Buckingham if Henry were inclined to press his suit; but
he submitted whether Buckingham was the fittest
man for Henry to propose.   Was not his object to
secure the Duchess on her throne?   If so, what did
he think of D'Albret?   D'Albret was a soldier of
repute.   The town of Nantes was in his hands.
Madame Laval was on his side; De Rieux was also
on his side.   If D'Albret and De Rieux were driven
into the arms of France, the duchy might be lost
for ever.   As a friend of Anne, the King should
weigh these points, and let Fernando know his
thoughts.   What they had most to fear were French
"fine words."   They must beware of Charles, and
of his sister, Madame Anne.   Let every one be
armed.   If Henry were not ready in the spring,
the French would burst into the duchy and surprise the
forts. Let Max and Henry take the field, and Spain
would follow in their wake.   If Henry thought that
Max would be a better match, Fernando would
support his choice.   Spain simply wished to please
the English prince, and find a firm support for
Duchess Anne.   These words were framed to cloak
two secret schemes.   Fernando meant to let his
allies fight, and afterwards secure the duchy for
his son.

4. In spring an English force, eight thousand strong, was ready to embark. Lord Willoughby de Brooke was to command these troops, but their confederates showed no signs of life. Fernando was too busy with his war against the Moors to think of Charles; and Max, who had returned to Ghent an older, not a wiser man, could hardly spare a lance from his unruly towns. The Pope, incited by the French, was working to prevent a war. His eyes were bent on Naples, and the King of France announced his readiness to avenge the Holy See. Fernando was a kinsman of the King of Naples; nay, the Pope suspected him, as the eventual heir, of stirring up his cousin to reject the Papal yoke. A war to weaken France and strengthen Spain was greatly to be feared by Rome. The French were friends, the Spaniards foes. In Paris, said the Papal legate, every one was busy with the Pope's affairs. The Prince of Salerno was providing maps of Naples; Madame Anne was sending for Maréchal de Querdes; and Charles was studying plans of a campaign. But all this ardour in the cause of Rome had been suddenly arrested by the din of coming war. If English regiments landed on his coasts, the King of France could hardly send a man across the Alps. The Pope must interfere. A Papal chamberlain, Perseo Malvezzi, left for London with a moneybox, a parcel of indulgences, a cap of state, a consecrated sword, and a request that Henry would turn his arms against the Moslems rather than against the French.

5. Though Henry met Malvezzi with a cheerful

smile, and gave him leave to shake his money-box
and sell his indults and indulgences in church, he
was obliged to hold with him a language hostile to
the French.   He took the consecrated sword and
cap with joy, and caused a solemn service to be
held in honour of these Papal gifts; but he replied
to Innocent, that while he wished to satisfy the Pope,
he was obliged to help the Duchess Anne.   He had
no wish to fight the French, and every wish to
fight the Turks; but Charles was ravaging a district
near the English coasts.   If any crusade was prepared
against the infidel, he should be ready to embark;
but for the moment Charles of France was the offender,
and his course of violence must be stayed.   A holy
man was gone to Paris in the name of peace.   If
Charles would listen to his almoner all would soon
be well; if not, he must defend the orphan girl with
all his strength.

6. Malvezzi brought from Rome a promise of
the Cardinal's hat for Morton, and in turn this pluralist stood beside the Papal chamberlain in council,
church, and market-place.   The primate had a gift
for raising money, and his genius for extortion was
a by-word in the town.   His chief device was known
as Morton's Fork.   When sending out collectors, he
instructed them to set aside excuses.   "If a man
lives sparely, say he must have saved and can afford
to pay; if lavishly, declare he must be rich and can
afford to pay."   But Morton could not make the
people, who had given a war-tax eagerly, subscribe
their money for indulgences and crusades.   Folk
were mad against the French, and in the push and

clang of warfare, Morton's voice was drowned by that of Brooke. Impose another tax! The King would nail a money-box to his door, and ask his peers and ladies to subscribe; but he could do no more, he told the Papal chamberlain, without exciting hatred of the Holy See. When peace was made with France, he could accede to Innocent's wish, and lay a crusade-tax. He added, with his touch of humour, that the Pope should write to Charles and other kings, exhorting them to grant a tax, in order that the burthen of defending Holy Church might not be borne by him alone.

7. Malvezzi came to London fired with golden dreams. In Rome these islands were supposed to be a mine of gold and silver, much of which Malvezzi hoped to sweep into the papal chests. On landing he was hurt by hearing fife and drum, and still more hurt by learning that a war-tax had been laid. He thought the Pope as worthy of assistance as the Breton Duchess. If the English could afford to fight the French, they could afford to pay for the salvation of their souls. He showed his bag of papers, and inquired how much his holy wares would fetch. "Not more than twenty thousand ducats," some one answered. "Twenty thousand ducats!" He had counted, in his fancy, many times that sum, and he was fit to cry with rage. "If I had only heard of this in time," he wrote to Innocent, "I should not have published the bull till you had heard about the case. For such a sum it was not wise to lay yourself under obligation to the King of England. Since the bull is out, I cannot call it back; but I refuse to hear these tales, and try to show

that they are false." Malvezzi found the King a
servant of the Pope, and fancied all the English
peers and knights were like the King; but he was
slowly undeceived by his attempt to sell these holy
wares. In six months after his arrival, he had sold no
more than twenty-seven dispensations, and received
no more than forty-nine pounds in English money.
Even the twenty thousand ducats he had flouted
seemed a long way off. But he had still the King
and court; the opening of his box would be the test.
This box was hung by Henry to a door at court,
where every one could see it, and his peers and
knights, his dames and abigails, were asked to drop
their gifts into a coffer which the King himself would
open with a royal show. The gifts were understood
as peace-offerings, and the sum subscribed would
represent the feeling of the court in favour of the
policy of Rome. A day was fixed for this august
affair. Malvezzi was invited to receive the courtly
gift in presence of the chiefest dignitaries of Church
and State. The King and Queen, the King's mother,
the Queen's mother, Archbishop Morton, and a press
of prelates, dukes, earls, marquises, and knights, were
present. The ambassadors of foreign powers were
asked to witness the imposing scene, and note how
lavish of her money England could be when the
object—only half concealed—was to divert her from
a war with France. Malvezzi took the box, and, lifting up the lid, displayed the royal sum—eleven
pounds and eleven shillings in the current coin!
"Our hearts sank within our breasts," Malvezzi wrote
to Innocent; "for in so great a company we expected
to have found much more!"

CHAPTER VI.

Charles and Anne.

1489-90.

1. THE English troops embarked with Willoughby
de Brooke, and, having thrown themselves on shore,
pushed up into the country, making straight for
Guincamp, as the strongest fortress near the sea.   In
haste the French let down the grille and closed the
posterns; but on seeing Brooke prepare to storm
the town, the garrison retired and the inhabitants
drew back their gates.   Brooke entered in the midst
of pealing bells and kindling fires, hailed everywhere
as a deliverer of the country from a loathsome yoke.
Four days he lodged at Guincamp, where he spent
Palm Sunday, and received a message from the
Duchess, praying him to march at once for her relief
towards Rennes.   The fort of Moncontour was in
his way; but when the French who held that fort
perceived his banners in the distance, they destroyed
a portion of the wall and fled.   At Moncontour Brooke
celebrated Easter with imposing rites, while one of
his columns, which had wheeled upon St. Brieu,
moved forward on the fort of Chanson, and compelled the garrison to yield.   Meantime an English
fleet had doubled Bec du Raz and thrown some
troops on shore near Vannes.   The towns of Vannes

and Hennebon were held by strong French garrisons;
yet on a menace of assault a portion of the walls
was tumbled down, the garrison fled, and the vic-
torious English entered through the breach.

2. Rohan, commanding for the French, was forced
to stand on his defence, avoid a general action, and
secure his lines of passage to Anjou and Maine.
He found this task too much. At Brest the people
rose upon his troops, and held them prisoners in
the citadel.   The Duchess was at Rennes, where
Edgecombe, as an officer of the English household,
ruled her court.   No day passed by without some
Breton noble who had hitherto held aloof from
parties, riding to the English camp and giving his
adhesion to the Duchess Anne. If Spain and Austria
had been equally alert, the French could not have
kept a foothold in the duchy; but Fernando only
sent two thousand men from Spain, and Max had
not supplied another lance from either Ghent or
Worms.

3. Instead of Max assisting Henry, Henry was
compelled to succour Max.   Aware that Max was
entering into leagues against him, and was seeking
to engage the hand of Duchess Anne, Charles sent
an order to his general in the north, Maréchal de
Querdes, to cross the frontier with an army, occupy
the town of Ypres, and advance into the country,
on pretence of helping the inhabitants to defend
their local rights against the Austrian prince. The
town of Dixmunde blocked his way.   De Querdes
required the garrison to yield; they answered by a
challenge to assault. A siege was laid, and guns

were mounted for attack.   De Querdes himself returned to Ypres, where his main array was lodged,
in order when the fort was carried to advance on
Bruges.   But Daubeney, watching from his lair these
movements of the French, drew out of Calais, Guisnes,
and Hamme, a thousand pikes and bows.   A thousand men were brought unseen from England, when
Daubeney sailed for Nieuport in the Sands, pushed
through the narrow streets in silence, crossed the
level country, entered Dixmunde by the eastern gate,
and, picking up a few stout fellows, sallied from the
town against the French.   A bloody fight ensued;
the camp was stormed; eight thousand French were
slain; the guns were captured, and the siege was
raised.   His work being done, Daubeney marched
to Nieuport in the Sands, embarked his men, and
sailed for Calais, leaving his sick and wounded in
the hospitals of Nieuport with an English guard.

4. De Querdes, disturbed in his repose at Ypres,
took the field with a superior force, and marched
on Nieuport to avenge his honour, but the English
garrison received him with such ardour that he had
to draw his men away, before Daubeney could ar-
rive by sea.   The English lay too near at Guisnes
and Calais, and Maréchal de Querdes fell back, exclaiming that it never would be well in France
while Calais lay in English hands.   "To drive these
English out of Calais I would fry seven years in
hell," the Maréchal cried.   The French now saw
they could not fight three enemies at once; and,
since the easiest terms could be arranged with
Max—who hated both his allies—Charles despatched

an agent with instructions to propose a separate
peace.   Within a month of the affair at Nieuport,
Max was base enough to sign a treaty with the
French, by which he undertook to act in concert
with the French at Rennes, and made a pact with
Charles, that all the English troops then fighting in
the duchy should be driven away.   Max urged De
Rieux and D'Albret to insist upon this measure
with the Duchess Anne, who was at length induced
by them to beg her only friends to leave.   She
signed a treaty with the French, by which she
bound herself to send her English and her Spanish
troops on board their ships.

5. A change was taking place in Paris.   Louis,
now restored to grace, advised his cousin Chàrles
to give up Marguerite and to marry Anne.   In losing Marguerite, Charles would lose Franche Comté
and Artois, two wealthy provinces on his frontier;
but, as Louis thought, of less importance to his
kingdom than Bretagne; a duchy that would round
off France by sea and give him the command of
all her ports.   His sister, Madame Anne, held
firmly to her former view.   To send back Marguerite would offend the Kaiser and provoke a war
with princes who invested France from Lille to
Dole.   Artois and Franche Comté would be lost;
rich provinces, which her enemies might be able to
defend against her arms.   What would her brother
gain by wedding Duchess Anne?   A poor and barren country in their rear, which Nature must herself
restore to France.   Madame was right.   In fact, a
union of Charles and Marguerite was seen to be so

much the better policy for France, that serious statesmen paid no heed to rumours that the royal imp might some day break his word, renounce his bride, and challenge Germany to mortal strife. But Charles was a fantastic youth, as weak in head as he was false in heart. To puzzle and surprise his neighbours was his boyish pride, and in this project of his cousin Louis there was every charm to take his flighty soul. There was a secret to conceal, there was a treaty to discard, there was an ally to mislead, there was a neighbour to offend. A girl whom he had courted, and who thought herself his consort, was to be dismissed and outraged, while a girl whom he had injured, and who called herself another man's wife, was to be wooed and carried off. Force, fraud, and frolic, were combined to captivate the mind of Charles.

6. But Charles was not yet clear that he must lose the duchy if he failed to wed the Duchess. Louis thought so; but his cousin Louis was a bookworm, not a knight in mail. Could he contrive to win and hold the duchy by his arms? He loved the blare and smoke of war, and chose to rule by might where he could easily have ruled by right. Could he expel the leaguers and destroy the league? Already he had signed a separate peace with Max. If he could square accounts with either Spain or England, he might hope to hold his ground. He knew the price of peace with Spain. Was he prepared to pay that price? Not yet. Rossillon was the gateway into France, and while he held it she was covered from attack. Was there no cheaper

way? He thought there was, and threw out feelers to provoke reply. In Rome, in London, and elsewhere, his agents whispered that a treaty could be got by France on other terms than the restoration of Perpignan. He listened for the answer out of Spain. In England it was easy to intrigue for peace; the war being pressed in England by a turbulent people, and opposed by a sagacious prince. Believing that those turbulent folk would listen to the Pope when they would hardly give an ear to Henry, Charles persuaded Innocent, whom he deceived as he had cheated Father Christopher, to send his legate, Lionel, Bishop of Concordia, as a messenger of peace to London. Lionel was in Paris on that business of the Pope's dispute with Naples. Innocent was told that Charles could send no troops across the Alps while war with Henry raged. The pontiff therefore had an interest of his own to serve. The Bishop of Concordia, whose auspicious name was held to be an augury of his success, was ordered to cross the sea, and urge his son, the King of England, to arrange his quarrel with his son, the King of France.

CHAPTER VII.

A Year of Intrigue.

1490-1.

1. FERNANDO, sitting in his tent before Granada, turned these bruits in Paris, Rome, and London, to his own account. Could Duchess Anne be forced to wed his son, the swart and sickly boy of twelve? If not, how could he put such pressure on the French, as would induce the King to buy him off, as he had done with Max? At once he fell to work. A sharp and angry message was despatched to Rome. The Bishop of Badajoz, his minister at the Papal court, was told to wait on Innocent, and let him know, in language strong as he could use, that Spain resented very much his meddling in affairs beyond the Alps. Of course the Pope's intentions had been good. Spain raised no word against a priest proposing peace; but Innocent's time and agents had been badly chosen, even for the ends he had in view. The holy father must be told that peace between France and England was of no importance. War would still disturb the world, though Charles and Henry should be brought by Innocent's means to sheathe their swords. Rome's first concern, the Pontiff must be told, should be to bring about a peace between Castille and France.

14*

If Spain were satisfied the English would at once
retire. But Innocent must also understand the
terms of peace. Rossillon and Cerdaña must return to Spain. This cession of the districts in dispute stood first and last. All other points were
open to debate: but France could never be at rest
until these counties were restored.

2. In London he had need to take another
tone. Since war began, the English council had
been pressing him to change the articles. When
Henry signed the draft prepared by Fox, he fancied
he was buying Catharine with a word; no thought
of war with France was in his mind; and he supposed the clause about his claim to Normandie had
no more meaning than Fernando's claim to be the
Duke of Athens. But as war had broken out, and
Henry was afield in company with a man who had
a separate end to serve, the English council asked
to have that clause amended, so that neither Spain
nor England could retire unless her ally were included in the terms of peace. Fernando could not
yield so much. This clause was nearly all that
he had gained by his adroitness at Medina, and to
give it up was to abandon for the moment every
chance of winning back his duchies in the Pyrenees.
Yet he could hardly justify the draft; and still less
could he own his motives for declining to revise it
as the English council wished.

3. The ground was loose beneath his feet, and
Puebla was instructed how to feel his way. Fernando hoped that England might be led, by her
desire to mend the articles, into carrying out his

larger scheme. Aware that every man in London
would object to Juan marrying Duchess Anne, and
bringing Spanish fleets into the Channel, Puebla
was to choose his words—to hint at dark intrigues
—to mystify the council—and to get the English
sovereign to suggest a Spanish match. He was to
throw out hints that foreign courts were talking of
the King of France and Duchess Anne. He was
to watch the King, and notice how he took the
rumour. Puebla was to urge how much the English
would be injured by a union of the duchy and the
kingdom, which would follow on a union of the
King with Duchess Anne. He was to add that
Spain, although she was not menaced so directly,
had her coasts, her commerce, and her allies to
consider. It was well for Spain and England to
repress this growing and aggressive power of France.
Could they not see their way to act in common,
and engage their honour to oppose all candidates
except their own? If Henry chose to name a
suitor, Puebla was empowered to say that Spain
would back his suit. Would Henry do the same for
Spain? A common interest ought to lead them to
a common action. After what the Kings had done,
the Duchess could not criticise a lover of their
choice. If Henry listened to these words—but
made no further sign of his intention—Puebla
might proceed to hint that people had begun to
speak of Juan, Prince of the Asturias, as a proper
mate for Anne; but that his parents would not
hear of sending him—their only son, the heir of
more than twenty crowns—to live in a provincial

town, the husband of a subject of the Kings of
France. He was to speak of them, however, as of
princes who were open to advice. If they were
shown that no one else could carry Anne against
the French, they might be brought to sacrifice their
son. If Henry were to put Don Juan forward as a
rival to the King of France, they would not hold
him back. Should Henry listen, Puebla was to add,
that if the English council bought out Juan as a
candidate, they might amend the articles in any
sense they pleased.

4. At Rennes, the Spanish agent, Rojas, played
a bolder game. This able minister induced the
Prince of Orange to adopt Don Juan as a candidate, and got the Duchess to confess that she
would like to have the Spanish Prince. Aware that
Anne preferred the suit of Max,—a lover who could
make her Queen and Empress, Rojas whispered in
the court of Rennes that Max was trifling with the
Bretons, that he never dreamt of marrying Anne,
and only made his show of courtship to distract
the French. Fernando told him to assert that Max,
instead of raising her to the imperial throne, was
minded to bestow her on his creature D'Egmont.
Should the Duchess think of Juan, Rojas was to
say that Spain could get the Austrians to consent.
He was to act with seeming fairness, telling her the
choice was wholly in her hands, and that the King,
his master, would sustain her acts. If she selected
Juan, he would answer for the Austrian prince; if
she selected Max, he would support that Austrian
prince. The choice must be her own.

5. Anne took the Spanish agent at his word, and being urged by Rieux, she fixed her maiden eyes on Max. Espousals were arranged in secret, and the Prince of Orange, standing at the altar for his lord, received the Duchess in his name. The rite was done before the Spanish ministers could protest; and afterwards they thought it prudent to refrain. They spoke of the affair like men who had been badly used. They thought the Duchess should have taken counsel with her friends, the Kings of Spain and England. Spain and England would have put no veto on her choice. So said the ministers. Fernando held his tongue; but sent an order to recall his troops and ships from Brest.

6. Though Henry had been urged by Parliament to cross the sea, he shrank from taking part in active war. As Morton knew his secret wishes, he was labouring with his clergy in behalf of peace. He sent to Rome, where he had many friends, and stirred the sacred college to go on. A cardinal was coming into England on a mission which concerned the Church even more than war with France: the doings of those Bible-men whom Pecock's Repressor had been utterly unable to repress. Malvezzi's failure had alarmed the Roman court. Were English bishops, as alleged, a set of proud and shameless pluralists? Were English friars, as stated, a fraternity of idle, dissolute and ignorant rogues? Were English people, as asserted, falling from the Catholic Church? If so, the pontiff ought to hear the truth, and Adriano de Castello,

Cardinal of Corneto, was proceeding into England
to inquire.   Castello might be made an instrument
of peace.   Connected with the highest families in
the state, a man of generous tastes and easy man-
ners, he dispensed his income like a prince.   The
Roman court was lavish, and, excepting Borgia,
hardly any Cardinal in Rome had spent his revenues more freely than Castello.   Thus a mission
to a country rich in stalls and mitres suited him,
and those who could dispose of stalls and mitres
could rely on his support.   He bore a cardinal's
hat to Morton, and in no long time the Roman
cardinal came to see through Morton's eyes.   A
stall in London, and the rectory of St. Dunstan's in
the East, expressed a part of Morton's gratitude;
and Adriano de Castello, while pursuing his more
spiritual labours, urged the pontiff to assist that
party in the English council which was striving to
avert a general war.

7. But long before the Pope could interfere, the
passions of all parties were inflamed by an event in
Nantes. So soon as D'Albret learned that Max and
Anne were plighted to each other, he renounced his
duty, wrote to Charles, threw down his arms, and
yielded up his fortress to the French.   This act of
treachery, by which the Bretons lost their second
city, fired the English people into frenzy.   Morton
was no longer heard. Castello was no longer heard.
From Kent to Cumberland the country was aflame,
and Henry was compelled to take a leading part.
Swift messengers were sent to Spain and Germany,
requesting them to arm at once and throw their

forces into France. Isabel answered fairly; but her troops, she wrote, were tented round Granada, where they could not leave a single fort unwatched. She was erecting Santa Fé, a fortress near the Caliph's city; in a little while that fortress would be built and armed; and when the Moorish capital was masked, she might have men to spare for distant points. The English must be patient with her. Max was more alert in words. He undertook to put ten thousand men afield; he would be ready in six months to march; and Henry was advised by him to act in concert with his troops, although their blows should be directed on the opposite sides of France. The Duchess Anne, as Max's consort, took the style of Queen of the Romans. Yet the Last of the Ritters was content with writing notes and brandishing his sword. A winter and a spring slipt past, but Max's lancers never came in sight. Men lost all patience in these long delays, and Henry was so strongly urged by peers and commons to go forward swiftly, that he had to push preparations for attacking France, though he might have to enter on the war alone.

CHAPTER VIII.

The Duchess Married.

1491-2.

1. AT length the King of France perceived that he must choose between the ladies and their portions. Marguerite or Anne—Franche Comté or Bretagne; which would he have? Not caring for the ladies, he referred the business into wiser hands. Orleans .told him he should marry Anne. As Charles assented, all the rest was detail; but the details were not easy to arrange. The King was pledged to marry Marguerite. The Duchess had assumed the name and rank of Max's consort. If the King could cast off Marguerite, how could he wed the wife of Max? A King of France is potent, but the marriage made at Rennes could only be unmade in Rome. Such things required much art and secresy; but Orleans was a bold intriguer; and a troop of able priests were sent by him to Rome and Rennes. These agents were to hint that Anne was not a lawful wife. She was a ward, who could not wed without the license of her feudal lord. This doubt being raised, the Bretons wondered whether Anne was married to the Austrian prince or not. The girl herself was

troubled in her mind. In Rome, another game
was played. The nuptial rites could hardly be
denied; but France, as champion of the Papacy,
was powerful in the Roman court. Much coin was
spent, and many promises were made. What hin-
dered Charles, these agents asked, from marching
to the Pope's assistance? Nothing but the Breton
war. If that affair could be arranged, the chivalry
of France would stream across the Alps. In Borgia,
then the leading cardinal, Orleans found the man
he needed in his scheme for marrying Duchess
Anne to Charles. In secret all the necessary breves
were drawn; in silence they were sent to France;
in secresy and silence they were lodged in readiness
at Tours.

2. Dunois, a favourite of the Duchess, spoke to
her of Charles, whom he described as young and
dashing—as a prince who loved her with a virgin
heart. He spoke to her of Max, a man growing
fat and old, as being a coward, who had married
her by proxy, and had never had the pluck to
show his face. The heart of Max, he said, was
with his offspring by a former wife; the children
who would be his heirs; the son who would in-
herit his imperial crown. If Anne should marry
Max, her children would be younger sons. But if
she married Charles, her state would be the first
in France; her son and grandson would be Kings.
Anne, piqued by Max's absence, listened to her
favourite's words. Dunois knew all the secrets of
his friends in Paris. He could tell her when her
vow to Max was cancelled by the Roman court,

and when her license to accept the King of France was sealed.   At length she yielded to his arts.

3. The King of France might now have ridden down to Rennes and married her in open day, but such a course had no attractions for an imp like Charles.   To please the King, there must be mystery, deceit, and outrage.   So a mock proposal for a truce—a mock arrangement for a peace—was made.   The French agreed to let the "Queen of the Romans" go to join her German husband. They undertook to pay her certain pensions, and to rule her duchy by a separate code, administered by a native judge.   And then they let her go. With few but trusty servants, Anne set out to join her Austrian lord, whom she had never seen, and never wished to see.   Near Tours the King of France was waiting to receive her as a guest.   A bishop was at hand.   The Roman breves were read. The youth and maiden started for the halls erected by Pierre de Brosser, barber of St. Louis, where the Bishop of Albi, who was in their secret, read the service and 'declared them man and wife.   No love was made by either boy or girl.   The bridegroom got his duchy, and the bride obtained her rank of Queen; but their espousals were so much a business and a bargain, that the lady was compelled to bind herself, in case the King should die without heirs male, to marry his successor on the throne!   In brief, the Duchess married France.

4. Before he knew how much he had been tricked by Charles and Louis, Henry wrote a letter to the Pope, explaining how he had been labouring

in the cause of peace. In urging Charles to let his
cause be judged by reason, he had done his best.
The French had seemed to yield, and even signed
a treaty; but while their ministers were signing articles of peace, their troops were cannonading towns.
They had usurped and occupied the duchy. Nor
was Charles content with having wronged him in
the Duchy. He was stirring up the Scots to cross
his border lines, and bribing Irish kernes to rise
against the English rule. Since nothing just and
fair could now be hoped from France, the King,
though much against his will, might have to enter
on a war. If peace could be secured by giving
way, he was prepared to yield; but this impor-
tunate craving of the French for what was not their
own, could never be appeased, and must in honour
be opposed. This craving threatened every one in
turn. He told the Pope that Italy was not safe;
nay, injury might fall on Rome herself. To stem
this torrent, England was preparing all her strength;
though nothing was so hateful to the King as Christian armies shedding Christian blood. "We promise
your Holiness," he said, "that just as we have always been devoted to you in the past, we shall be
devoted to you in the time to come. To our ut-
most, we shall always guard the freedom of the
Church . . . and we implore you to support our
rights and acts."

5. At Santa Fé these nuptials of the King and
Duchess seemed to open out a new and splendid
prospect for the reigning house. As yet, this house
was barely recognised by foreign courts. In France

and Germany the Excellenta was regarded as the
lawful ruler of Castille, and while the French and
Austrians were united in the pledge of Charles and
Marguerite, Fernando saw no hope of gaining ground
with them. The King of France had spurned his
offers, and he had not dared to tempt the German
prince. But now those courts were finally es-
tranged. No prince had ever suffered and forgiven
such wrongs as Charles had heaped on Max. That
Max would fight, Fernando felt assured; that even
after fighting he would hate and loathe the French,
he also felt assured. All allies would be welcome,
and an ally such as Spain would be the moment
she had won Granada, might be strong enough to
make her terms. Why not accept the union thrown
away by France? A close alliance with the Empire
would enhance his glory and protect his dynasty.
Why should not Juan marry Marguerite? Nay,
more, why should not Juana marry Philip? Philip
would in time be Emperor. At once Fernando
offered help to Max, and entered into articles with
England for a joint attack on France. Rossillon,
he could see, was in his grasp. What else might come
of his alliance with the Austrian court was left for
time to show.

6. Amidst his bridal junkets, Charles was told
that three great kingdoms were in league against
him, and preparing to invade his realm. A fleet
was carrying troops to Calais; Henry was among
his warriors; and an army such as France had not
encountered since the day of Azincour was sallying
from the lines of Guisnes. These English were

the first afield; twenty-five thousand foot and six-
teen hundred horse. If they should fight as troops
who bore the banner of St. George had always
fought, no force that France might raise in haste
could beat them back. Charles saw that he must
buy them off; and Henry was in mood to treat
for peace. The English monarch had displayed
his power; his people had been breathed by march
and skirmish; he was tented on the enemy's soil;
and his immediate objects had been gained. Pope
Innocent was dead, and Cardinal Borgia reigned
in Rome. He had to learn how matters stood
in Italy; and Charles proposed to pay him seven
hundred and forty-five thousand crowns of gold,
in yearly sums of fifty thousand francs, for peace.
That money tempted him to parley. Henry had
no thought of conquering Normandie and Maine;
and having gained his point, he signed a separate
truce, and left his allies to arrange their own
affairs.

7. But neither of these allies suffered from the
wrath of Charles. Fernando pressed his foes so
warmly in the duchies, that the King began to
parley, and his parley ended in a cession of Cerdaña and Rossillon to the crown of Aragon. Nor
was the flighty youth more fortunate in his war with
Max. In sending Marguerite home, Charles lost his
legal right to Artois and Franche Comté. Fancy-
ing he could keep by force what he might have to
cede in law, he had refused to yield these provinces; but he was roused from such a dream by
roar of guns; and after many feints and tricks, he

was compelled to render up to Germany his frontier
towns. Men, money, provinces, had all been thrown
away by Charles. The comedy of his marriage
was become a tragic farce. On every side he piled
up loss on loss. A yearly tribute had been pledged
to England; Rossillon and Cerdaña had been given
to Spain; Artois and Franche Comté had returned
to Austrian keeping. France was isolated in the
world. The Germans had become her mortal enemies. What had France to show for all these
losses? Charles was now at liberty to cross the Alps
and plunge his country into endless woes.

BOOK THE FIFTH.

CATHARINE AT GRANADA.

CHAPTER I.

Fall of the Caliphate.

[1492.

1. FERNANDO was on guard within his tent before the Moorish lines; the scene before him taxing
all his strength, and drawing out his military skill.
The Moors still fought like lions; yet the day for
which he had been toiling more than twenty years
was nigh. In looking back on every step by which
he had secured a point, Fernando felt the pride of
one who has been left to fight and win alone.

2. Those knights and friars who swarmed around
his tent and choked his court, so far from being
the whole of Spain, were not even types and servants of the whole of Spain. Some warriors of the
highest order were encamped around his tent; such
warriors as Ponce de Leon and Gonsalvo de Cordova; but his ranks were filled by denizens of every
clime and followers of every creed. From far and
near the men of broken fortunes flocked to Spain,
as kites come fluttering towards a field of blood.

Not many came like Rivers and his English troopers,
out of pious zeal. They fought for pay, and pil-
laged every farm they passed. No blessing of a
liberated people rested on their heads. Some natives were a little better than these strangers; yet
the best of even these natives were but samples of
two classes in a country rich in races, creeds, and
callings; an unlettered gentry, who could ride and
stab, and make a profitable trade of war; a brutal
peasantry, who could push a pike and grovel in the
dust before a monk. If blue in blood and rich in
quarterings, many of those gentry wanted bread,
and looked in hunger and despair to feeding on
the more industrious Moor. When Don Alonzo de
Gusman, Knight of St. Santiago, and a distant
cousin of the King, grew sick of waiting in the
court for place and pay, he seized a pike, enlisted
in the rank and file, and turned his point against
the Moors. "I am of gentle blood," he said, in his
unconscious humour, "and I claim the dress of
Santiago for the deeds I am about to do." Alonzo
added, with a touch that made all Spanish knights
his kin; "I scorn to work, and yet I dread being
poor." Too proud to labour, he was not too proud
to beg. When hunger pinched him, he was not
afraid to steal. The throng of knights who lay
about Fernando's tent were faithful copies of this
knight of Santiago.

3. Lettered and industrious men had no such
feeling as inspired these lean and noble knights.
To drive the Caliphs out of Spain appeared the
settled purpose of Fernando's war, and with those

Caliphs all the Arabic schools of science, art, and trade. How could a man who loved his country join in such a crusade? Every one engaged in either art or industry was looking to those schools for light. A Moor was better taught and better fed than almost any Goth in Spain. A chemist, farmer, chronicler, he read more books, and books of a more liberal kind. He was a higher judge of courtesy. If two Castillian nobles had a quarrel, they preferred to state it in Granada, with the Caliph for an umpire, rather than submit their points of honour to a native prince. A Spanish cavalier who wished to gain renown in war, repaired to the Alhambra, where he entered as a student in the Moorish school of arms. Ponce de Leon and Gonsalvo de Cordova had formed themselves on Moorish models. A Castillian smith who wrought and tempered swords employed a Moorish artist in his forge. An Aragonese builder who had public work to do, applied to Moorish architects for help. A Spanish silversmith copied arabesques and damascenes. Moors had founded the great workshops of Toledo and Zaragoza; and the finest blades of Spain were stamped with Moorish marks. When Zaragoza wished to build a tower that should excel the campaniles of Venice and Bologna, she employed Ballabar and Monferriz, famous Moorish builders, to construct for her that splendid pile.

4. All Spaniards borrowed from the Moors, as Russians borrowed from the Tartars of Kazan. A gentleman of Toledo looked to Moorish sources for the fashion of his coat, the plumage of his hat, the

15*

science which preserved his health, the story which
beguiled his pain, the music which enchanted him
to sleep. He hung a Moorish hanjar on his thigh,
and strapped a Moorish saddle to his steed. A poet
visited Granada for the subject of his muse, and
found among the pomegranates and vines an atmo-
sphere of song. A writer who would sell his
romance, had to choose a Moorish knight as hero
of his tale. Maza and Sarife were the popular
idols. If a man grew famous for his valour, wisdom, and success, he was considered worthy to
have been a Moor. The greatest name in ballad
lore was that of Dias, who was known to common
people only by his Moorish rank of Seid or Cid.
Gonsalvo, the most perfect knight in Spain, the
Bayard of his country, plumed himself on being, at
every point, a Moorish gentleman. The arms he
wore were Moorish work. The songs he sang were
Moorish verse. He was so perfect in the Moorish
speech and style, that he could pass in the Alhambra for a Moor. The King and Queen were no
less ready than their subjects to obey this general
rule. Fernando wore the same red velvet cloak as
Abd-allah, and Isabel donned the same mantilla as
Zoraya. In a Moorish house, the rooms were
brighter, cooler, healthier, than in any Spanish
house. In building, husbandry, and literature, the
Goths had everything to learn from their more brilliant neighbours of the south. What church in
Gothic Spain was equal to the Mosque of Cordova?
What tower was equal to the Tower of Seville?
Where, in Gothic Spain, was garden like the Gene-

ralife? The Alhambra was the finest palace in the west; the libraries of Granada were the richest in the world.

5. No one felt sure that if the Moors were driven from Spain, the Jews would not be forced to follow them. A Goth could hardly see in what a Jew was different to a Moor. They had the same dark eyes, lithe frames, and swarthy skins. They had the same quick senses, and the same capacities of speech. Each turned his back on Catholic worship; each retired into his synagogue and mosque; and it was hard to say in what a synagogue differed from a mosque. If Jew and Moor were gone, what schools of learning, poetry, and science, would remain? In art and industry the Jews were equal to the Moors; in song and science, they were more than equal to the Moors. Ince de Gali was a worthy peer of Ballabar. Zacuto had no rival in astronomy and mathematics. Alonzo de Zamora, Pablo de Heridia, and Pedro de Cartagena, ranked among the leading writers of the age. Abravanel was a master in philosophy as well as in finance. To drive away these Moors and Jews from Spain was to deprive the country of her excellence in all the arts; yet every one suspected that the King and Queen, incited by their friars, were bent on driving every Moor and Jew from Spain.

6. Fernando pushed his trenches to the city walls, destroyed the water ducts, and intercepted the supplies of corn. At length the Caliph yielded to his fate; but even then he yielded more to guile than force. Gonsalvo stole by night into the city,

every lane and court of which were as familiar to
his sight as the arcades of Cordova, and with his
Moorish garb and accent passed in safety through
the gates and streets. A Moor in spirit, he was
able to address the Caliph in the only language he
would deign to hear. The war was represented as
a sort of tournament in which the Moorish and
Castillian knights had jousted for Granada. The
Castillian knights had won the prize; but nothing
else was changed. Abd-allah still remained a King.
His capital was lost; but in the mountains of the
Alpujarras he had still an independent kingdom
left. That kingdom was secured to him for ever.
He was free to march, and free to take with him
his harem and his wealth. If any citizen of Granada
wished to quit the city he was free to go; but
nothing in a citizen's life would be affected by the
change of rulers. Every one would be protected
in his person, in his property, and in his creed.
The Spanish knights had won their prize, but they
were knights and gentlemen, and treaties made
with knights and gentlemen are sacred things. A
contract was arranged between "the Moors" and
"the Castillian knights." Not knowing those with
whom he had to deal, the Caliph yielded, with a
sigh, and the Sultana covered him with her im-
mortal scorn: "Yes, sigh for what is lost like a
woman, since thou couldst not defend it like a
man!"

7. No stroke of fortune ever stirred men's minds
more deeply than Fernando's victories against the
Moors. Not forty years had passed since Constanti-

nople fell before an Asiatic horde. A Moslem host
was storming up the Danube, overflowing Greece,
disturbing Sicily and Venice, and extending every
year their frontiers towards the west. Vienna was
not safe by land, Palermo was not safe by sea. All
Europe was amazed by this advance. A holy war
was preached; a sacred fund was raised; and
princes were enjoined to imitate the virtues of St.
Louis and the Lion Heart. A Holy League was
formed. Yet nothing had been done to stop the
Moslem hosts. What cared a King of France about
the safety of Belgrade? Why should a Kaiser send
his pikes to Cyprus? Innocent and Alexander tried
to rouse the faithful; but the money paid into their
hands was spent on other things than ships and
guns. So far from fighting for the Cross, the French
had made a treaty with the Turks. All simple
Christians, therefore, heard with throbbing pulse
and flashing eye of the assault of Baza, of the blaz-
ing tents of Santa Fé, and of the final sorties of
the Moors; a sense of danger quickening their delight in this great feat of arms.

8. Rome gave the signal for rejoicing when
Granada fell; for in no other city was this victory
of Spain so welcome as in Rome. As King of Sicily, Fernando had a motive for repelling the Mo-
hammedans, not shared by any ruler in the west,
and Sicily, his sea-girt island, was an outwork of
the Papal States. A pasha in Palermo would have
been an awkward neighbour to a Pope in Rome.
The downfall of Granada, therefore, was a triumph
for the Church, and Rome, in honour of that great

event, proclaimed a festival of the Cross.   In London, where the Saracens were chiefly known from song and legend, their defeat was judged more soberly than in Rome; yet even in London, Cardinal Morton told the people at St. Paul's that while the Church, unhappily, was losing ground elsewhere, that high and mighty captain, Don Fernando, King of Spain, and father of the young Princess of Wales, had won a kingdom for the Cross; for which high victory of the faith all Christian men and women were enjoined by him to thank Almighty God.

CHAPTER IL

Granada.

1492-3.

1. WHEN Savage left the baby Catalina clapping hands at dog and bull in the arena, she had been carried from the Castle on the Mount to Jaen, where Isabel fixed her court and kept her children, while Fernando rode afield and spent his fiery days in camp.   When Baza fell, and the great siege began, Isabel had broken up her house, and with her boy and girls had ridden into the field, and never left her troops till they had won the highest turrets of the Moor.   Her tent was pitched before the city wall; the Moors came out; the camp was set on fire; and Catharine lay among the burning sheets

and poles. She saw that camp of canvas grow
into a camp of stone. Her window gave upon a
lovely landscape; and she looked across that landscape to a massive tower from which the crescent
glittered like a moon. She saw the crimson walls
of the Alhambra, topped with cypresses and hung
with vines; and hailed the fairy palace on the
mountain side. She was a girl of seven when
Christopher Columbus came to Santa Fé and begged
her mother's leave to add an empire to her states.
When the observant friars were sent into Granada,
where they ravaged through the mosques, and
smeared the marble floors and golden shafts with
wash and dirt, she rode from Santa Fé into the
wrecked, yet lovely and mysterious palace of the
Moor.

2. Her home was ravishing. The city at her
feet sprang proudly from a nest of groves and vineyards, over which the towers and shafts of the Alhambra shot into the air, and showed in lines of
light against the brown and sunburnt hills. Around
her lay a hundred slopes of orchard, planted walk,
and cypress grove. A balmy air flowed down into
her chambers and arcades. A flood of sunshine
bathed the pavement of her garden all the year,
yet snow was always in her sight on the sierra tops.
"Granada," sang the native poets—and Granada
was a school of poets, male and female—"is a
palace for the eye, a place of contemplation for the
soul; she is a watch-tower on the hills; a place of
beauty and a place of strength; high walls secure
her from a foe, and rivers intersect her houses,

mills, and markets, and supply her baths with an
abundant stream of purest water; down her mea-
dows, and among her cypresses, these rivers flow
like streams of gold between her emerald banks;
the soil is rich enough to bring forth everything
that feeds the body and enchants the mind." Art,
trade, and learning, found a refuge in Granada.
Though the pearl of earthly beauty, she was held
to be more famous for her men and women than
her graceful towers, her shady groves, and smiling
fields. A home of scholars, heroes, and physicians,
her especial pride was a poetic crown. "The seat
of science, empire, and religion, God has blessed
her most," the Caliphs said, "in making her the
birthplace of a school of poets, male and female,
whose productions are the dowry of mankind."
Within her walls were born those female singers,
Nazhim, Zeynab, and Hamdah; women whom the
Moors respected as the Miriams of their race.

3. Catalina saw this city harried and opprest,
and many of those poets, artists, and physicians,
driven away. Against the letter and the spirit of
her treaty with the Moors, her mother sent inquisitors into house and mosque. In vain the citizens
appealed to "the Castillian knights." In vain they
cited article and text, which guaranteed the freedom
of their mosques and houses. Isabel was stiff. She
had a duty to fulfil. Her pledge had long ago
been given to the Dominicans that she would pluck
out heresy from the soil of Spain. Granada was a
part of Spain. The honour of Castillian knight-
hood was not sacred in her eyes, though she had

gladly pledged that honour when she had a Caliph
to deceive. Her spies went up and down the city,
seeking whom they could betray. Their victims
were the rich, the noble, the renowned in name.
Some left their homes; some put away their riches;
some defied her officers. It was a dangerous thing
to stir the passion of a quick and ardent race,
accustomed to the use of arms, and fired with an
idea that their losses had been caused by civic feud
and personal weakness rather than by national
decline. Fernando tried to curb his consort's zeal.
A man of worldly mind, he cared for unity of rule
far more than unity of faith. He saw that it was
idle to denounce, and dangerous to excite, the
people of his conquered lands.

4. But no such worldly wisdom saved the Jews.
Though rich in art and skill, the Jews were few in
numbers, and were noted by inquisitors as Friends
of Light. Three months of grace were offered to
the Jews, in which they were to make a final choice
—baptism or banishment. If they accepted Christian rites, they could remain; but under pain of
death should they relapse into their ancient ways.
Of this relapse the Fathers of St. Dominic were to
be the judges. Some were weak enough to yield;
and every one desired a respite from the fatal word
of Isabel. Rabbi Aboab threw himself before the
Queen. He begged for mercy, if he dared not ask
for justice, at her hands. His people, he could
truly urge, were old inhabitants of the soil; yea,
older than the local nobles and the reigning house.
They had committed no offence. They were not

subject to an Inquisition founded to protect the
faithful from corruptions of the faith. Aboab spoke
in vain. Abravanel at last repaired to court. The
King and Queen received him like a prince, and
listened to his tale. "I come to offer ransom from
my people," said Abravanel. A man as wise as he
was rich, he spoke the language likely to arrest
Fernando's ear. Six hundred thousand crowns in
gold he offered, if this great iniquity might only pass
away.

5. While Abravanel was speaking, Torquemada
rushed into the royal closet, holding out a crucifix.
"Behold Him!" cried the friar; "He whom Judas
sold for thirty pieces! Would you sell Him too?"
Abravanel fell upon his face. "Look on us, O
King," he cried; "have mercy on thy people. Take
from us all we have, but do not drive us from the
land we love. O let us live and die where we
were born." Fernando wanted coin; six hundred
thousand crowns were much; but Isabel was seated
nigh; and with her icy breath she froze Fernando's
melting soul. She would not yield a jot; her pledge
was given; and she would keep that pledge, if she
unpeopled half her realm. Abravanel gazed in
wonder at the woman's face. A mute and stony
face, it frowned on him and on his suit. He turned
to prelate, count, and monk, and begged them if
they had the hearts of men to intercede with Isabel.
But no one dared to whisper mercy in her ear. At
last the Hebrew rose, and going to his brethren in
their porches, said with firmness, "If they leave us
life, we live; if they choose to kill us, we shall die;

but they shall never force us to transgress our holy law."

6. The poor and aged Hebrews thought of the long road and of the unknown journey's end. "Come," said Abravanel, "let us quit these lands, and seek a place elsewhere." A month flew past, and men with horns strode up and down the city, crying out, "Begone, ye Jews, begone! A month is past. In two months more, all ye who lag behind are lost." Each month these men with horns strode up and down the city, calling on the Jews to fly from coming wrath. In families they broke up house and home; but who would buy the things they had to leave behind? They were compelled to go, and could not carry with them produce, workshop, implement of trade. An artist had to quit his study and a scholar had to lose his books. Zacuto left his globes and astrolabes behind. No one would buy the things for which he had no use, and few would give a price for things of daily need. A house was sold for a donkey, a vineyard for a piece of cloth. But loss of house and land was not the worst. A Jew has a peculiar reverence for the field in which his father sleeps; and feels his deepest pang when taking farewell of his family grave. The record of one scene remains. The Hebrews of Segovia, who had flourished under Enrique the Liberal, received the edict of expulsion with amazement, and delayed their flight in some vague hope that such a monstrous act would never be enforced. When they were undeceived, their misery became supreme. Without a tear, they broke

up house and farm, and having left and lost them all, they went into the grave-yard, where their fathers slept their final sleep on earth. In groups they fell upon their knees, and spent three days and nights in fervent prayer. At last they rose and girded up their loins for flight. "In one day," says Abravanel, "three hundred thousand young and old were ready for the march. With God for leader we set out."

7. They sailed to Italy, to Germany, to Africa, to Anadol. Some found a home in Genoa and Florence, but the fathers who had driven them out of Spain pursued them into Italy, and roused the passions of a bigoted mob against them. Some found refuge in Navarra, and others sought protection from the King of Portugal. One body of these fugitives went to Rome, where they were suffered, under pontiffs far less bigoted than the Queen of Spain, to live and die in peace. Still more took ship for Smyrna, Alexandria, and Stamboul, and carried to those Moslem ports their enterprise and wealth. The royal poet, Bajazet, who watched the doings of Fernando with a curious eye, exclaimed, on hearing of this increase to his towns, "You call Fernando wise, yet he has made his country poor, to make mine rich!"

NOTES AND DOCUMENTS.

FIRST BOOK.

CHAP. I.—1. *Anales de la Corona de Aragon*, compuestos por Geronymo Zurita (Zaragoza, 1610), lib. XX. cap. 65.

2. *Coleccion de documentos ineditos para La Historia de España*, por D. Miguel Salvá y D. Pedro Sainz de Baranda, XVIII. 271; *Historia de los Reyes Catolicos, Don Fernando y Doña Isabel*, por Andres Bernaldez (Granada 1856) c. 75, 76. The best portrait known to me of Don Juan is in the Adoration picture by Miguel Zitoz; a picture which has recently been transferred from the Ministry of Public Works in Madrid to the National Collection. It is not yet hung and numbered; but a photograph has been taken of it by M. Laurent for his series, in which it bears the number 533.

3. *Historia critica de la Inquisicion*, por Juan Antonio Llorente (Madrid, 1822), c. 5. art. 1; *Bibliotheca Hispana Vetus*, auctore Nicolao Antonio (Matriti, 1788), I. 132; *Bibliotheca Lusitana*, por Diego Barbosa Machado (Lisboa, 1741), I. 76; Yanguas y Miranda, *Diccionario de Historia y Antiguedades de Navarra*, lib. I. c. 4; Stirling, *Annals of the Artists of Spain*, III. 84-6.

4. *Tropheos y Antiguedades de la imperial Ciudad de Zaragoza* (Barcelona 1639), 170-6; *Zaragoza en el Bolsillo: breve reseña historica de la capital de Aragon*, por D. Romualdo P. Altafaj (Zaragoza, 1869), 93; My Note-book. All descriptions of country, town, and site in this work are from my own notes, taken on the spot, in connexion with local records and existing remains.

5. *Geschichte der Juden von der ältesten Zeit bis auf die
Gegenwart* von H. Graetz (Leipsic, 1864), VIII. 301, 334;
History of the Jews in Spain and Portugal, by E. H. Lindo
(London, 1848), 249, 264; *Die Juden in Navarra, den Basken-
ländern und auf den Balearen* von M. Kayserling (Berlin,
1861), 104-5; *Geschichte der Juden in Portugal* von M. Kayserling (Berlin, 1867), 120.

6. *Etudes Historiques, Politiques et Littéraires, sur les
Juifs d'Espagne*, par D. José Amador de Los Rios (Paris,
1861), 295-416; *History of Spanish Literature*, by George
Ticknor (London, 1863), I. 241, 371, 372; Llorente, *Inquisicion*, c. VII. art. 2; Graetz, *Geschichte der Juden*, VIII. 234.

7. *La España Sagrada*, por el Padre Enrique Florez
(Madrid, 1747), XXX. 426; *El Templo del Pilar*, por D.
Gerardo M. de la Cerda (Zaragoza, 1872), cap. 2; *Troph.
Zarag.* 170-6; Altafaj, *Zaragoza*, 33-56.

CAHP. II.—1. Zurita, *Anales*, lib. XX. c. 49.

2. *Vida del Glorioso P. y Patriarcha Santo Domingo de
Guzman, fundador de el Orden de Predicatores*, escrita por
Fray Francisco de Possadas, Madrid, 1721; *De Guzman
Stirpe S. Dominic*, edita a Fr. Ant. Bremond (Roma, 1740);
Il Perfetto Leggendario, ovvero Vite de Santi (Roma, 1841),
VIII. 35-48; *Lives of the Fathers, Martyrs, and other principal
Saints*, by the Rev. Alban Butler (Dublin, 1833), II. 190-204.

3. *Histoire des Hommes illustres de l'Ordre de St. Dominique*, par le Rev. Père A. Touron (Paris, 1743-9), I. 1,
127, 441, II. 58, III. 543; *Memorie dei piu insigni Pittori, Scul-
tori, e Architetti Domenicani*, del P. Vincenzo Marchese
(Genova, 1869), I. 59, 234, II. 12; *Histoire du Christianisme*,
par l'Abbé Fleury (Paris, 1837), VI. 450; *Histoire des Républiques Italiennes du Moyen Age*, par M. Simonde de Sismondi (Bruxelles, 1838), VI. 236-7.

4. *Historia de la insigne Ciudad de Segovia*, par Diego de
Colmenares (Segovia, 1637), 437; Antonio, *Bibl. Hisp. Vet.*
II. 340-1; Los Rios, *Etudes sur les Juifs*, 143-56. There is
a powerful likeness of Torquemada in the Adoration picture by Zitoz.

5. *Anales Ecclesiasticos y Seculares de la Ciudad de Sevilla*, por Diego Ortiz de Zuñiga (Sevilla, 1747), III. 389-98;

Diccionario Geografico-Estadistico-Historico de España, por Pascual Madoz (Madrid, 1846), III. 165-71, XIV. 292-434.

6. My Note-book; *Historia de Sevilla*, por Alonso Morgado (Sevilla, 1587), lib. II. c. 16; Madoz, *Dicc. Esp.* III. 165, XIV. 292; Bernaldez, *Reyes Catolicos.* c. 44.

7. *Cosas Memorables de España*, por Lucio Marineo (Alcala, 1539), lib. XIX.; *Tribulacoens de Ysrael*, por Samuel Usque 191-3; Llorente, *Inquisicion*, c. VI. art. 2; Los Rios, *Etudes sur les Juifs*, 150. The political character of the Inquisition may be considered as established. Comp. Guizot, *Cours d'Histoire Moderne*, V. lec. II.; Los Rios, *Etudes Historiques sur les Juifs*, 127-56; Adolfo de Castro, *History of Religious Intolerance in Spain*, 14-21; Ticknor, *History of Spanish Literature*, I. 428, 429, III. 235; Dyer, *History of Modern Europe*, I. 188; and Lacordaire, *Mémoire pour le Rétablissement de l'Ordre des Frères Prêcheurs*, c. VI. On the other side, however, see Buckle, *History of Civilization*, II. 18-20.

8. *Historia de las Grandezas de la Ciudad de Avila*, por Fray Luis Ariz (Alcala, 1607) par. I, p. 46; Antonio, *Bibl. Hisp. Vet.* II. 340; Llorente, *Inquisicion*, c. VIII. art. 6; Zurita, *Anales*, lib. XX. c. 65; Touron, *Ordre de St. Dominique*, III. 544-56; Graetz, *Geschichte der Juden*, VIII. 307-19.

CHAP. III.—1. Zurita, *Anales de Aragon*, lib. XX. c. 49; Madoz, *Diccionario de España*, II. 392-415; Castro, *Hist. Rel. Int.* 15.

2. My Note-book; Eugenio Tapia, *Historia de la Civilizacion Española*, II. 302; Altafaj, *Zaragoza en el Bolsillo*, 90; Cerdá, *El Templo del Pilar*, c. 3.

3. Zurita, *Anales*, lib. XX. c. 56-65.

4. Llorente, *Inquisicion*, c. V. art. 1, c. VI. art. 2; Touron, *Ordre de St. Dominique*, III. 558; Kayserling, *Die Juden in Navarra*, 105.

5. *Fueros y observancias del Reyno de Aragon*, 1. 7. 10; Llorente, *Inquisicion*, c. VI. art. 2.

6. Llorente *Inquisicion*, c. VI. art. 2; Graetz, *Geschichte der Juden*, VIII. 334.

7. *Elementi della Storia de' Summi Pontefici da San*

Pietro, raccolti dal Canonico Giuseppe de Novaes (Roma, 1821), VI. 53; Llorente, *Inquisicion*, c. V. X.

CHAP. IV.—1. *Historia general de España*, por el Padre Juan de Mariana (Madrid 1782), II. 491; Zurita, *Anales*, lib. XX. c. 65.
2. Llorente, *Inquisicion*, c. VI. art. 2; Kayserling, *Die Juden in Navarra*, 90-110.
3. Madoz, *Diccionario de España*, XVI. 556-646; Zurita, *Anales*, lib. XX. c. 65; Touron, *Ordre de St. Dominique*, III. 558.
4. My Note-book; Altafaj, *Zaragoza*, 41; Llorente, *Inquisicion*, c. VI. art. 3; Zurita, *Anales*, lib. XX. c. 65.
5. Castro, *Hist. Rel. Int.* 15-17; Bernaldez, *Reyes Catolicos*, c. 77; Zurita, *Anales*, lib. XX. c. 65.
6. Carvajal, *Documentos ineditos*, XVIII. 271-2; *Commentarius brevis et jocundus Itineris atque peregrinationis pietatis et religionis causa susceptæ, ab illustri et magnifico domino, Domino Leone libero Barone de Rozmital* (Olmutz, 1577), 109.
7. Vergaras, *Petition to the Council*, cited by De Castro, 74-5; Kayserling, *Juden in Navarra*, 72-90; Kayserling, *Die Juden in Portugal*, 85-119; Graetz, *Geschichte der Juden*, VIII. 234, 326, 334.

CHAP. V.—1. *Historia de Cataluña y de la Corona de Aragon*, por Victor Ballaguer (Barcelona, 1860), I. VIII. c. 28; Haro, *Nob. Gen. de los Reyes*, 3, 4; Bernaldez, *Reyes Catolicos*, c. 8; *Report of English Commissioners*, printed in *Memorials of King Henry the Seventh*, edited by James Gairdner (London, 1858), 277-8. Portraits of Fernando are not rare. One picture hangs at Windsor Castle; there is a fine bust of him at Granada; a good likeness of him taken at the time described in my text occurs in the Adoration picture by Miguel Zitoz.
2. Ticknor, *Hist. Span. Lit.* I. 335; Graetz, *Geschichte der Juden*, VIII. 233; Lindo, *Hist. Jews in Sp.* 242; Altafaj, *Zaragoza*, 33-44, 108-10.
3. *Elogio de la Reina Catolica, Doña Isabel*, por D. Diego Clemencin (tom. VL "Memorias de la Real Academia de la Historia"), 91-105; Fernando and Isabel to Guevara

and Puebla, Jan. 1490; *A Hand-book for Travellers in Spain*, by Richard Ford (London, 1855), 922.

4. Marineo, *Cosas Memorables de España*, lib. XVII.; Zurita, *Anales*, lib. XVI. c. 54, lib. XVII. c. 11, 24; Ballaguer, *Hist. Catal.* lib. VIII. c. 28.

5. *Vidas de Españoles Celebres*, por Manuel Josef Quintana, (Paris, 1849), 71-101; Ballaguer, *Hist. Catal.* lib. VIII. c. 18-25; Marineo, *Cosas Mem. de España*, lib. XVIII.

6. *Compendio de los cinco tomas de las Anales de Navarra*, por el Padre Pablo M. de Elizondo (Pamplona, 1732), lib. IV. c. 1.

7. *Cronica del Rey D. Enrique el Quarto*, por Diego Enriquez de Castillo (Madrid, 1787), 158; Clemencin, *Elogio*, VI. 56-9; Zurita, *Anales*, lib. XVII. c. 25, lib. XVIII. 16, 21, 26.

CHAP. VI.—1. *Opus Epistolarum Petri Martyris* (Amstel. 1570); Antonio, *Bib. Hisp. Vet.* II. 348; Marineo, *Cosas Mem. de España*, lib. XIX; Bernaldez, *Reyes Catolicos*, c. 9. There is an old portrait of Isabel at Windsor, and a bust of her at Granada. The safest likeness of her is in the Adoration picture by Zitoz.

2. Berni, *Creacion Antiguedad y Privilegios de los titulos de Castilla* (Val. 1769) 66-8; Ticknor, *Hist. Span. Lit.* I. 172; Zurita, *Anales*, lib. XX. c. 49; Mariana, *Historia de España*, II. 517.

3. Zurita, *Anales*, lib. XX. c. 49; Graetz, *Geschichte der Juden*, VIII. 240; Ticknor, *Hist. Span. Lit.* I. 420; Colmenares, *Historia de Segovia*, 379; Castro, *Hist. Rel. Int.* IV. 20; Haro, *Nob. Gen. de los Reyes*, 4.

4. *Il Perfetto Leggendario*, ovvero *Vite de Santi*, v. 247-252, VII. 35-44; Altafaj, *Zaragoza*, 108-9; Colmenares, *Hist. Seg.* 431; Madoz, *Dic. Esp.* III. 167, XIV. 823; Morgado, *Hist. de Sev.* lib. III. c. 1; *Historia de la Ciudad de Toledo*, por A. M. Gamera (Toledo, 1862), 791.

5. Informacion de lo que pero Sarmiento corregidor de Medina dixo lo qual no sevio con la turbacion del tiempo que entonces corria Año de 1507. Arch. Gen. de Simancas, Est. leg. 1, 2⁰, 192. Gomez Manrique, a con-

temporary poet, addressed the following stern language
to Isabel in person.

> "Al mayor de los mayores
> Con sacrificios plazibles
> La sangre de los nocibles
> Crueles y robadores.
> Esto le sacrificad,
> Con gran deliberacion;
> Pero, señora, guardad
> *No se mezcle crueldad*
> Con la tal ejecucion.
> El regar de los Salterios
> Y el dezir de las horas
> Dejad á las regadoras
> Que están en los monasterios."
>
> Castillo, *Cancionero General.*
> 1520.

6. Samuel Usque, *Tribulacoens de Ysrael* 188, 192;
Graetz, *Geschichte der Juden*, VIII. 233-5; Llorente, *Inquisicion*, c. VI. art. 2.

7. *Quadro Elementar das Relações Politicas de Portugal*,
pelo Visconde de Santarem, I. 371; Clemencin, *Elogio*, VI.
491-4.

CHAP. VII.—1. My Note-book; Carvajal, *Documentos
ineditos*, XVIII. 248-9; Haro, *Nob. Gen. de los Reyes* 344.

2. Shassek, *Commentarius brevis*, 74; Castillo, *Cronica
del Rey Don Enrique el Quarto*, 4-7; Berni, *Titulos de Castilla* 65; Adolfo de Castro, *Hist. Rel. Int.* 6.

3. Colmenares, *Historia de Segovia*, 333; M'Crie, *History of the Reformation in Spain*, 44, 61; *Flores de Miraflores*
(Burgos, 1657); Ticknor, *Hist. Span. Lit.* I. 374, 403; Kayserling, *Die Juden in Navarra*, 121; Graetz, *Geschichte der
Juden*, VIII. 233, 237.

4. Los Rios, *Études sur les Juifs*, 117-126; *Bibliotheca
Hispana Nova*, auctore Nicolao Antonio (Matriti, 1783), I.
132; *Bibliotheca Hispana Vetus*, II. 348.

5. Graetz, *Geschichte der Juden*, VIII. 239, 327; Ticknor,

Hist. Span. Lit. Ap. A. III. 390-402; Colmenares, *Hist. de Segovia*, 363.

6. Castillo, *Cronica del Rey Enrique*, 15, 60, 66; Fernando and Isabel to Puebla, Bergenroth's *Cal. Span. Pap.* I. art. 22; Gairdner, *Mem. Hen. Sev.* 274; Clemencin, *Elogio*, VI. 76; Anderson, *Royal Genealogies*, 718.

7. Castillo, *Cronica del Rey Enrique*, 62, 229; Zurita, *Anales*, lib. XVI. c. 14, lib. XVIII. c. 31, lib. XX. c. 49; Anderson, *Royal Genealogies*, 718.

8. My Note-book; *Historia de las Grandezas de Avila*, por Luis Ariz (Alcala, 1607); Berni, *Titulos de Castilla* 118-165.

CHAP. VIII.—1. *Historia de los Reyes Catolicos Don Fernando y Doña Isabel*, por Andres Bernaldez, c. VII; Padre Pablo, *Anales de Navarra*, lib. IV. c. 1, s. 3; Santarem, *Quadro Elementar*, I. 369.

2. Zurita, *Anales*, lib. XVIII. c. 21, 26; Castro, *Hist. Rel. Int.* 11, 12.

3. Castillo, *Cronica del Rey Enrique*, 234; Bernaldez, *Reyes Catolicos*, c. VII; Gamero, *Historia de Toledo*, 779-91; Clemencin, *Elogio*, VI. 91-115; Anderson, *Royal Genealogies*, 718.

4. Colmenares, *Historia de Segovia*, 399-416; Zurita, *Anales*, lib. XIX. c. 13, 18.

5. Santarem, *Quadro Elementar*, I. 369, 380; Zurita, *Anales*, lib. XIX. c. 23, 30; Castro, *Hist. Rel. Int.* 13, 14.

6. Tratado de paz entre el Rei e Rainha de Castilla e el Rei de Portugal, Sep. 4, 1478; Clemencin, *Elogio*, VI. 491; *Chronique des Faits et gestes admirables de Maximilian I.*, translatée par Octave Delepierre (Bruxelles, 1839), 1, 2.

7. Santarem, *Quadro Elementar*, I. 381-83.

8. Memoir of the Privy Council of Castille, printed in Bergenroth's *Cal. Span. Pap.* II. 396-7; Clemencin, *Elogio*, VI. 91-3.

CHAP. IX.—1. Bernaldez, *Reyes Catolicos*, cap. 77, 78; Carvajal, *Documentos ineditos*, XVIII. 272.

2. *Chronica de los muy altos y esclarecidos Reyes Catho-*

licos Don Fernando y Doña Isabel por Fernando del Pulgar (1567), parte III. c. 53; *Opus Epist. Pet. Mart.* Ep. XXIV.

3. Pulgar, *Reyes Católicos*, lib. III. c. 53; Yanguas y Miranda, *Diccionario*, lib. I. c. 2; Los Rios, *Etudes sur les Juifs*, 151.

4. *Historia de la Ciudad de Compluto, vulgarmente Alcala de Santjuste y aora de Henares*, por el Doctor Miguel de Portilla y Esquivel, primera parte, c. VIII, XIII.

5. My Note-book; Portilla y Esquivel, *Hist. Comp.* c. XV, XIX, XXIII, XXXVI; Madoz, *Diccionario de España*, I. 364-376.

6. My Note-book; Portilla y Esquivel, *Hist. Comp.* par. L

CHAP. X.—1. Marineo, *Cosas Memorables*, 114; Kayserling, *Die Juden in Navarra*, 104-5; Lanuza, *Historias Ecclesiasticas y Seculares de Aragon*, I. 553.

2. Doge and Senate to Hieronimo Zorzi, Sept. 15, 1485; Fernando to his agent in France, Add. Mss. 28,572. f. 1.; Excerpts from Sanuto, II. 262.

3. Fernando and Isabel to the Serene and Mighty Prince, Nov. 5, 1485. Fernando's first letter to the King of England runs:—

"Serenissimo et potentissimo Principi Dei gratia Anglie &c. Regi consanguineo et amico nostro carissimo Ferdinandus dei gratia Rex Castelle, Aragonum, Segionis, Sicilie &c. salutes et prosperos ad vota successus cerciores facti sumus a Columbo vice admiralo marium Regni Francie et prefecto classis cristianissimi Regis Francorum nuper in mari oceano juxta Lusitaniam interceptas fuisse quatuor venetorum triremes intraque eas multa subditorum nostrorum merces et bona. Quo facinore contra omnia que inter suum Regem et nos amicitie consanguinitatis et foederis jura sunt perpetrato aiunt eum ad dividendam predam in aliquem portum vel stationem regni serenitatis vestre divertisse. Rogamus igitur eamdem pro bona et equa justitie culta ipsum Columbum ubicumque eum intra ditionem suam esse deprehenderit detineri jubeat rogatque ut bona ipsa et merces omnes integre restituat dilecto et fideli nostro harum exhibitori que hac tantum de causa sua et aliorum mercatorum nomine in istam provinciam proficiscitur. Quod profecto ultraque est justum accipiemus precipui officii loco a serenitate vestra; cui nos ad ea que ipsi mutua grata erunt et ad meritorum vicissitudinem paratissimos offerimus. Et Deus vos tueatur serenissime et potentissime Rex consanguinee et amice noster carissime. Datum Complute v Novembris anno salutis millesimo quadringentesimo lxxx quinto.

"Yo el Rey,

"L. GONÇALES, Secret."

4. Llorente, *Inquisicion*, c. VI. art. 4; Yanguas y Miranda, *Dicc. Hist.* lib. I. c. 2; Kayserling, *Die Juden in Navarra*, 104.

5. Altafaj, *Zaragoza*, 41; Llorente, *Inquisicion*, c. VII. art. 3; Madoz, *Dic. de Esp.* XVI. 570; Zurita, *Anales*, lib. XX. c. 64, 65. I found in the Primate's palace at Alcala a collection of papers, which belong to the province of Toledo, and have never been examined by historical writers. Many of them are processes against suspected Jews. There is a collection of processes against priests for abuse of the confessional; and another collection, also considerable, of processes against nuns for breach of vows.

6. Pulgar, *Reyes Catholicos*, lib. III. c. 53; Zurita, *Anales*, XX. 64; Portilla y Esquivel, *Historia de Compluto*, primera parte, XXXVI. 36; Mariana, *Hist. Esp.* II. 490.

SECOND BOOK.

CHAP. I.—1. Mendoza, *Cronica del Gran Cardenal*, 23.

2. Carvajal, *Documentos ineditos*, XVIII. 272; Clemencin, *Elogio*, VI. ib. 13; Madoz, *Diccionario de España*, VI. 175, 183; *Vida de Don Diego Hurtado de Mendoza*, prefixed to "Guerra de Granada" (Valencia 1776) V. VI.; Lopez de Vega, *Aranco Domado*, Acto 3.

3. Mendoza, *Cron. del Gran Card.* 153, 180.

4. Portilla y Esquivel, *Hist. Comp.* segunde part. XIX.

5. Pulgar, *Reyes Catholicos*, lib. III. c. 53; Portilla y Esquivel, *Hist. Comp.* pri. part. XXXVI.

6. Aleson, *Anales de Navarra*, v. 11; Mendoza, *Cron. del Gran Card.* 181.

7. Portilla y Esquivel, *Hist. Comp.* pri. part. CXXXVI.

CHAP. II.—1. Florez, *España Sagrada*, XXX.; Altafaj, *Zaragoza*, 109; Carvajal, *Documentos ineditos*, XVIII. 272; Touron, *Histoire des Hommes illustres de l'Ordre de St. Dominique*, III. 558-9.

2. Gayangos, *History of the Mohammedan Dynasties of Spain*, I. 18, 20, 43.

3. Madoz, *Diccionario de España*, VIII. 467-564; Mendoza, *Guerra de Granada*, 7-9.

4. Gayangos, *Moh. Dyn. of Spain*, II. 369, 374.

5. Conde, *Dominacion de los Arabes*, III. 217; Gayangos, *Moh. Dyn. of Spain*, II. 369, 376; Mariana, *Historia de España*, II. 493; Pulgar, *Reyes Catholicos*, III. c. 48.

6. Gayangos, *Moh. Dyn. of Spain*, II. 378.

7. Carvajal, *Doc. ined.* XVIII. 272.

8. Gayangos, *Moh. Dyn.* II. 378; *Anales de el Reyno de Galicia* (Santiago, 1746), vol. I.; *Historia del Apostol de Jesus Christo* (Santiago), por M. C. Ferrer (Madrid, 1610); *España Sagrada*, Segunda Edicion, por el R. P. M. Fray Henrique Florez, III. 39-131.

CHAP. III.—1. Gayangos, *Moh. Dyn. of Spain*, I. 48; Bernaldez, *Reyes Catolicos*, c. 83.

2. Carvajal, *Documentos ineditos*, XVIII. 273; Gayangos, *Moh. Dyn. of Spain*, II. 38.

3. *Histoire de l'Empire Ottoman, depuis son origine jusqu'à nos jours*, par J. De Hammer (Paris, 1836), IV. 20, 21.

4. De Hammer, *Hist. Emp. Ott.* IV. 21; Los Rios, *Etudes sur les Juifs*, 166.

5. Gayangos, *Moh. Dyn. of Spain*, II. 380.

6. Gayangos, *Moh. Dyn. of Sp.* II. 381; *Opus Epist. Pet. Mart.* Ep. 62.

7. Bernaldez, *Reyes Catholicos*, c. 87; Gayangos, *Moh. Dyn. of Spain*, II. 381.

CHAP. IV.—1. Carvajal, *Documentos ineditos*, XVIII. 274.

2. Yanguas y Miranda, *Dicc. de Hist.* lib. I. c. 4; Zurita,

Anales, lib. XX. c. 72; Llorente, *Inquisicion*, c. VI. art. 7; Kayserling, *Die Juden in Navarra*, 104.

3. Ballaguer, *Historia de Cataluña*, lib. VIII. c. 28, 29; Zurita, *Anales*, lib. XX. c. 72; Morgado, *Historia de Sevilla*, lib. II. c. 16.

4. *Historia del derecho Español*, por Juan Sempere (Madrid, 1847), lib. IV. c. 1-3; Zurita, *Anales*, lib. III. c. 62; *Manual Historico y Descriptivo de Valladolid* (Val. 1861), 40; Mariana, *Historia de España*, XI. 499-501.

5. Zurita, *Anales*, lib. XX. c. 21, 72; Pulgar, *Reyes Catholicos*, partie III. c. 95; *Manual de Valladolid*, 40; *Coronaciones de los Serenissimos Reyes de Aragon*, escritas por Geronimo de Blancas (Zaragoza, 1641) lib. III. c. 18.

CHAP. V.—1. *Précis Historique sur la Reine Catholique Doña Isabel*, par Don Diego Clemencin, note 58; Mariana, *Hist. Esp.* II. 392, 466; *Privy Purse Expenses of Elizabeth of York*, edited by Harris Nicolas, pref. XXII.

2. Padre Pablo, *Anales de Navarra*, lib. IV. c. 3.

3. *Histoire des Français*, par Simonde de Sismondi (Paris, 1821-44), XIV. 391, 613; *Die Juden in Navarra*, 105; Yanguas y Miranda, *Dicc. Nav.* I. c. 11, 117.

4. Clemencin, *Précis Historique*, note 58; *Histoire des Républiques Italiennes du Moyen Age*, par Simonde de Sismondi (Bruxelles, 1839), VI. 162. ·

5. Santarem, *Quadro Elementar*, I. 388.

CHAP. VI.—1. *Musée des Archives Nationales, Documents Originaux de l'Histoire de France, exposés dans l'Hôtel Soubise*, publié par la Direction Générale des Archives Nationales (Paris, 1872), 292, 294.

2. *La Couronne Margaritique* (Lyon, 1549); Fernando and Isabel to Fray Bernard Boyl, Dec. 6, 1486. The sovereigns write:—

"Potestes Ferdinandi et Elizabeth, regis et regine Castelle, Legionis, Aragonum, etc., pro Bernardo Boyl, priore anacoritorum coenobii Beate Marie de Monteserrato, et Johanne de Merimon, milite, tractandi et concludendi de et super fœderibus et conventionibus nuper initis cum Carolo rege Francie, nec non de et super matrimonio Infantis Elizabeth primogenite filie, jam pubis, dictorum regis et regine Hispaniarum cum ipso Carolo Francorum rege, ac demum de et super quibuscunque causis controversiis et questionibus que pendunt, sunt vel esse possunt inter regem et reginam Hispaniarum et ipsorum regna, ex una parte, et Carolum regem Francie ejusque regna, ex altera parte, pretextu oppignorationis Commitatuum Rossellionis et Ceritanie.

"Actum in civitate Salamantina die sexto Decembris, anno MCCCCLXXXVI.

"YO EL REY.   YO LA REYNA."

3. Isabel to Boyl, July 29, 1487; Fernando and Isabel to Boyl, July 29, 1487. These letters (Archivo General de la Corona de Aragon Reg. vol. 3686, fol. XCIII.) run:—

29 *Julio*, 1487.

LA REYNA,—(Lo que vos padre Fray Boyl haves de dezir de mi parte al Rey de Francia y a Madama de Bevjv (Beaujeu) stando juntos, y enderezando las nuevas al uno o al otro o a ambos segund que vierdes que cumple juxta la materia y esto ante las personas debraxo nombradas, o de aquellos dellos que alli stuvieren es lo siguiente.)

Que yo tuve siempre tan buena voluntat a essa paz que attendie do lo que en los tiempos passados en ello fize, quise agora procurar este negocio como ella ha visto, pareciendome que para poner el sello en todo, solo esto me quedava por fazer, en lo qual es cierto que el Rey mi Señor e yo nos huvimos tambien y tan amigablemente con el Rey de Francia su hermano que toviendo tiempo de poder mucho crecer su necessidad si nos quisieramos juntar con sus enemigos que lo queriau y desseavau y aun lo procuravan bien affincadamente con hartos offrecimentos dignos de ser no solamente scuchados, mas aun acceptados, no solo non lo quisimos fazer en publico nin en secreto, ni fazer a ello demonstracion alguna, mas ni aun les quisimos responder, mas antes en senyal de limpia amistad enpeçamos a le fazer buenas obras como en la verdad lo ha seydo y por obra ha parecido, que si el contrario fizieramos ni el hoviera tan presto fecho lo que ha fecho en sus negocios, ni el Rey de los Romanos stuviera tan quedo como lo ha stado sperando lo que nosotros fariamos, y en conclusion sus fechos no stuvieran en el stado que stan, y dezilleys que bien se penzó, y aun algunos lo creyeron que ellos mostravan querer entender en esto. El fin agaora parece, y en la verdad el Rey mi Señor e yo algo dello pensamos, mas en que con tan sana voluntad entendiamos havernos con el y con su honra y stado creemos que de la misma manera nos havia de corresponder como era razon y por esso nos pareció era mejor entender en ello con buen amor y con limpios respectos no faziendo cosa engannosa nin mal fecha, ántes todo afin de le ayudar y valer y de tener su honra y fechos por propios nuestros, y aun por esso mismo salimas luego al casamiento y dimos tanta prissa a ellos porque si el otra cosa fiziesse lo que no se devia crèer, havriamos enteramente complido con lo que deviamos a Dios a buena y leal amistad principalmente, antel qual y antel mundo seriamos descargados, y que pues a ellos parece que por agora non se entienda en la platica deste negocio, esso mismo parece a nosotros. Pero dezisles eis que les rogamos e yo la Reyna les Ruego que en lo de Rosselon den forma se complio lo que el Rey su padre dexó mandado tornando nos aquellos nuestros Condados, e si nosotros en alguna cosa fueremos obligados, siendo por justicia deserminado lo compliremos enteramente e faziendolo assi fara como quien es, descargará los animos de su padre guardará la buena paz y alianzas antiguas de nuestra casa, y de la suya y quitarse han los inconvenientes males y danyos que del contrario seguir se podrian. E no queremos que esta fabla sea delante otras personas algunas, salvo de Mossen de Benjn del almirante, del arzobispo de lordens, de Mossen de Sagre, et de Joan Frances, o de aquellos dellos que alli se fallaren. Fecha en el Real de Malaga a XXVIIII de Julio del Año Mil CCCCLXXXVII.

Yo la Reyna.

29 *Julio*, 1487.

EL REY Y LA REYNA,—Devoto padre fray Boyl vimos vuestra carta y entendimos lo que Mossen Marimon nos dixo sobre lo que allá se ha platicado, y todo bien considerado nos parece que esse negocio va en dilaciones, y pues al tiempo que esta recibierdes sera ya passado el termino que con vos tomaron de las seys semanas, si fasta entonces no se hoviere tomado assiento en lo que llevastes deves os luego venir sin attender mas porque no es cosa razonable que steys mas allá procurando de vuestra parte cosa que a ellos stuvier mas honesto de procurar.

E si por agora les parece que no hay opportunidad para entender en ello, bien es que por el presente se dexe. Porende venid vos luego y no mireys de sperar otra letra ni mandamiento mestro.   Del Real de Malaga a XXVIII dias de Julio del año mil CCCCLXXXVII.

Yo el Rey,   Yo la Reyna.

4. Puebla to Fernando and Isabel, July 15, 1488.

5. *Das Kloster, Weltlich und Geistlich*, von J. Scheible (Stuttgart, 1846), b. IV. 4-52; *Chronique de Maximilian I.* par Octave Delepierre (Bruxelles, 1839), 369, 383; *Der letzte Ritter* von Anastasius Grün (Leipzig, 1845); *Œuvres complètes de Bernard de Fontenelle* (Paris, 1818), i. d. 4; *Documents Originaux de l'Histoire de France*, 270-93.

6. Puebla to Fernando and Isabel, July 15, 1488; Bergenroth, *Cal. Span. Pap.* 1, 22; Fernando and Isabel to Puebla, Dec. 17, 1488; *Historia Regis Henrici Septimi*, a *Bernardo Andrea Tholosate conscripta*, edited by James Gairdner (London, 1858), 25.

7. *Saxiola*, Aug. 8, 1483, Harl. MSS.; *Marie de Bourgogne*, par Oct. Delepierre (Bruxelles, 1851), 3.

CHAP. VII.—1. Commission to Rodrigo de Puebla, April 30, 1488; Puebla to Fernando and Isabel, July 21, 1488.

2. The Spanish merchants residing in London to Sancho de Londoño and the Sub-Prior of Santa Cruz, July 18, 1498.

3. Puebla to Fernando and Isabel, July 15, 1488.

4. Henry to Diego de Castro, Sept. 25, 1485; Jan. 31, 1488; Henry to Scover, July 25, 1488; Fabyan, *Chronicle*, 683; *Statutes of the Realm*, II. 4; The "Libel of English Policy," in Wright's *Political Songs*, II. 160.

5. Anderson, *Roy. Gen.* 709, 744.
6. Ticknor, *Hist. Sp. Lit.* L 362; Passport to Hubert and Staunton, Mar. 8, 1487; *Opus Epist. Pet. Mart.* lib. 1. Ep. 62; Mariana, *Historia de España,* II. 101.
7. Fernando and Isabel to Puebla, April 30, 1488.

THIRD BOOK.

CHAP. I.—1. *Letters and Papers illustrative of the Wars of the English in France during the Reign of Henry the Sixth,* edited by the Rev. Joseph Stevenson, 1861 (London); Puebla to Fernando and Isabel, June 16, 1500.

2. *Commentarius brevis et jocundus,* 48-52; Dugdale, *Baronage of England,* II. 241; *Statutes of the Realm,* II. 449; *Paston Letters,* V. CCCXVII.; *Registrum Abbatiæ Johannis Whethamstede, Abbatis Monasterii Sancti Albani,* edited by H. T. Riley (London, 1872), I. 187, 191, 359, 365, 425; *The Difference between an Absolute and Limited Monarchy,* by Sir John Fortescue (London, 1714), 85.

3. André, *Vita Hen. Sept.* 32, 33; *The Battle of Bosworth Field,* by William Hutton, edited by J. G. Nicholls (London, 1813), 181-271; Hall, *Tragical doings of King Richard III.* Fol XXXI-XXXVI.

4. *A Perfect Copy of all Summons of the Nobility to the Great Councils and Parliaments of this Realm,* by Sir William Dugdale (London, 1685), 476-7; *Parl. Hist.* II. 369, 414, 416, 417; *The Historic Peerage of England,* by Sir Harris Nicolas, ed. Courthope (London, 1857), 53, 459, 460.

5. *The Wright's Chaste Wife,* by Adam of Cobsam, Early English Text Society, 1865; *Religious Pieces in Prose and Verse,* by Richard Rolle, of Hampole, E. E. T. S. 1867; *Historia Monasterii S. Augustini Cantuariensis,* by Thomas of Elmham (London, 1583), Int. XVI.-XXIV.; *The Chronicle of England,* by John Capgrave (London, 1858), Int. IX.-XIII.; *Thomæ Walsingham Historia Anglicana* (London, 1863), II. Int. X.-XXI.

6. Wright, *Political Poems and Songs relating to English*

History, II. 258, 282; Fabyan, *Chronicle*, 1593; *Some Account of the Citizens of London and their Rulers*, *from* 1060 *to* 1867, by R. R. Orridge (London, 1867), 225.

7. *English Mathematical and Astronomical Writers from* 1086 *to* 1600, by A. De Morgan, in "Companion to the British Almanac" (London, 1837), 22-6; *A Catalogue of the Royal and Noble Authors of England, Scotland and Ireland*, by Horatio Walpole, Earl of Oxford (London, 1806), I. 200-224.

CHAP. II.—1. *Official Correspondence of Thomas Bekynton, Secretary of Henry the Sixth*, edited by George Williams (London, 1872), I. 155-8, 222; II. 270-311, 346-354; Wilkins, *Concilia Magnæ Britanniæ*, III. 471; *Reg. Alb. Mon. S. Alb.* I. 384; Puebla to Fernando and Isabel, June 13, 1496.

2. *Regist. Alb. Mon. S. Albani*, I. 169-172.

3. Shassek, *Comment. brev. et jocund.* 48-52; *History and Antiquities of the Cathedral Church of Canterbury*, by the Rev. J. Dart (London, 1726), 11, 12, 18; Dugdale, *Monasticon Anglicanum*, ed. Carey (London, 1830), I. 87.

4. Henry's Instructions to his Ambassador in Rome, Feb. 18, 1504; Halliwell, *Letters of the Kings of England*, I. 164; *History of the Mitred Parliamentary Abbeys and Conventual Churches*, by Brown Willis (London, 1718), I. 8, 25, 79, 106, II. 58.

5. *Rutland Papers* (edited by William Jerdan), 9; Williams, *Lives of English Cardinals*, II. 167; Gairdner, *Letters and Papers of Richard the Third and Henry the Seventh*, I. 95; Puebla to Fernando and Isabel, June 15, 1496. Rome considered England a fief of the Church, and Henry a vassal of the Pope. See note to Berg. *Cal. Sp. Pap.* I. 100.

6. Henry to Innocent, July 21, 1490. Henry writes:—
"Beatissime pater post humillimam commendacionem et devotissima pedum oscula beatissimorum et cetera. Cum illustrissima ac clarissima mater nostra Domina Margareta Richemondiae ac Derbey Comitessa, fragilem atque incertum humanae vitae cursum ac statum meditans: certum quoddam sit sibi electrra sepulchrum, quo

posteaquam furrit vita functa recondiatur: cupiatque ut
ecclesia ipsa qua sibi sepulchrum hujusmodi elegerit,
apostolicis quibusdam et favorabilibus decoratur indultis,
quae non ad suam tantum sed ad totius Christiani generis
salutem cedant! Instantissime nobiscum egit, ut penes
vestram sanctitatem intercedere diligenter vellemus, quo
tam anime ipsius matris nostrae quam animabus defunctorum pro quibus missæ furrint in dicta capella, qua
sibi sepulchrum elegerit, celebratae eas indulgentias et
illam peccatorum remissionem concedere dignatur, quam
consecuntur animae defunctorum; pro quibus in capella
beatae mariae de scala coeli'nuncupata, in ecclesia sive
extra ecclesiam monasterii sancti Anastasi cisterciensis
ordinis extra muros urbis missæ celebrantur. Quare cum
prefatae illustrissimae Dominae matris nostrae pius sit
zelus et Catholicus animus tam in sui ipsius, quam in defunctorum omnium animarum salutem: eandem vestram
sanctitatem ex animo rogamus votis suis ac desyderio et
sancto proposito velit nostro intuitu et precipua nostra
intercessione favorabiliter ac gratiose annuere. Sicuti La-
tinus ex oratore istic nostro venerabili pre domino David
Willelmo, cui hoc onus imposuimus eadem vestra sanctitas intelligerat. Faciet autem rem imprimis non medio-
criter nobis grata vestra sanctitas. Deinde saluti animarum plurimum consulet. Supêst ut vestra sanctitas felicissime valeat ad vota.

"Ex regiâ nostra grenuici die XXI Julii 1490.
"E. V. Sᵗⁱˢ.
"Devotissimus atque obsequentissimus filius Dei gra.
Rex Angliae et Franc: ac dñ's Hyb'niae.

"HENRICUS R."

"Sanctissimo Clementissimoque domino nostro Papae."

CHAP. III.—1. Gairdner, *Memorials of Henry the Seventh*
(London, 1858), Pref. XXIII. XXIV; *The Baronage of England*, by William Dugdale (London, 1675), II, 233; Ayala
to Fernando and Isabel, July 25, 1498.

2. Giovanni di Giglis to Innocent, Aug. 17, 1487;
Halliwell, *Letters of the Kings of England*, I. 162.

3. André, *Vita Hen. Sept.* 10; News from London, April 1, 1499, cited by Brown from Sanudo's Diaries, 11, 304.

4. Julius the Second to Henry the Seventh, July 9, 1507; Henry the Seventh to Julius the Second, Sep. 8, 1507; Instruction of Louis the Twelfth in *Letters and Papers of Richard the Third and Henry the Seventh*, 11. 138; Giovanni di Giglis to Innocent, Jan. 28, 1489. Giglis writes:—

"Beatissime pater post humillimam commendationem et pedum oscula beatissimorum. Scripsi non multis ante diebus ad Sanctitatem vestram de adventu Domini persei Malvitij Sanctitatis vestre Cubicularij cum ense sacro et galero quem S. V. ad hunc inclitum regem per illum transmisit: et de honorifica ejusdem Domini persei receptione de qua ille latius ad Sanctitatem V. scripsit. Non potuisset certe honorificentior esse quam fuerit: cum nihil in ea praetermissum sit quod ad Sanctitatis V. decus atque honorem et ad muneris venerationem pertinere possit: posteaquam munus praesentatum fuit Regie Majestati post aliquot dies medio Domini Archiepiscopi Cantuariensi gratissimam audientiam a Majestate Regia consecuti sumus in qua juxta Sanctitatis V. instructiones quas dominus perseus attulit ab ipso Domino perseo sunt Mandata Sanctitatis V. Regi exposita astante domino Archiepiscopo prefato et domino Episcopo exoniense qui apud illum sunt summi et utroque etiam favente sed precipue Dominus Cantuariensis, qui in omnibus rebus Sanctitatis V. se praebet diligentissimum cum singulari (ut videtur) affectione, propter negotia regni que multa occurrunt et ardua non habuimus ad tunc responsum certum, gratum tamen et quale nos in optumam spem adduxit, ut Sanctitatis V. tempore congruo satisfacere possimus: que omnia latius a me aliis literis sunt scripta. Postmodum vero hiis festivitatibus natalis Domini, Dominus perseus et ego ad Regem accessimus illius visitandi gratiâ ubi rex ipse de Sanctitate V. ac devotione in eandem ac Beatissimam sedem illam multa affectuosissime et christianissime narravit. Inter cetera asserens se tantum Sanctitati V. obnoxium quantum christianus princeps esse possit, seque

cupere aliquando aliquid efficere posse in quo suam in eun-
dem optimum animum ostendere queat Sibi in animo nihil
esse majus quam ut paratis Christianis rebus se unum
prebere qui aliquid egregium contra infideles gerat ad
dei laudem et eterni Christi et fidei exaltationem. Hec
et hujusmodi multis verbis et affectuosissimis est pro-
sequutus. Interloquendum etiam subjunxit se in Regem
francorum ac statum suum nihil moliri neque ei quid-
quam noceri cupere. Sed coactum esse ad presens res
britannicas defendere, cum propter ingentia beneficia ab
defuncto Duce in calamitatibus suis suscepta que notis-
sima sunt tum pro tuitione regni sui. Ita enim res
britannice cum hiis anglicis connecte sunt ut ex casu brito-
num necesse sit hos periclitari. Misit oratores ad Regem
francorum pro pace qui si sortiatur effectum bene erit sin
minus statuit britanniam et duxissam illam pupillam pro
viribus defendere. Missi sunt etiam oratores ad Regem
Castelle pro confederatione hic tractata et pene conclusa
confirmanda in qua inter cetera actum est de matrimonio
contrahendo inter hujus meliti regis filium unicum et
unam ex filiabus presati regis Castelle. Missi sunt etiam
oratores ad Regem Romanorum et flandrenses pro rebus
illis componendis si fieri possit. Sin minus saltem amicitia cum utrisque fiat aut cum altero illorum qui equi-
oribus conditionibus acquiesceret: quo mercatura inter
hos et illos diu interdicta in solito cursu restituatur. Die
XIII hujus mensis institutum parliamentum initium capiet.
Cujus precipua cura erit de rebus bellicis providere et
precipue de pecunia in eo gerendo necessaria que res
non erit parve difficultatis. Nam non solum laycis honera
magna in hiis prestandis incumbent sed etiam clericis
quibus tres decimas imponendas agunt. Hiis peractis
agetur de negotio Sanctitatis V. Rex (ut dixi) si verbis
illius animus judicari possit, nobis bonam spem tribuit
Dominus Archiepiscopus Cantuariensis nobis non decrit.
Nos etiam si qua industria in nos est eam adhibebimus et
in solicitando nihil laboris aut diligentie pretermittemus.
Non possum pretermittere Beatissime pater quin de
domino Episcopo   regio oratore verbum
fatiam qui Sanctitati V. est deditissimus servitor et con-

tinuis literis suis ad Regem et alios datis fidelissimum atque optimum erga Sanctitatem V. animum suum pate-facere non desistit.

"Usque ad diem x Januarii superius scriptum et deinde nuntius qui recessurus putabatur husque in hunc diem remansit: interea pater Beatissime celebratum est parliamentum maxima frequentia: in que hactenus factum est de pecunia invenienda ad bellum si quod immineat gerendum. In qua re omnes consenserunt ut regi in triennium provideatur de centum milibus libris hujus monete que faciunt summam CCCC milium et quingen-torum ducatorum quod onus pro tribus partibus suppor-tabunt Layci: quartam autem partem clerus: quamvis id nondum conclusum sit quum aliqualis altercatio inter clerum et laycos fuit. Volebant enim layci ut nobis due partes imponerentur de tota summa ipsis aut una tantum. Tandem post aliquas deputationes et collocutiones prela-torum et principum ad hoc deventum est quod dixi et ita credo quod concludetur. Statuit autem Rex ad presens exercitum x mil. hominum congregare quorum pars in britanniam mittetur et ex biis jam quidem precesserunt, pars alia ad classem deputabitur, tertia autem ad presi-dium calisie et aliorum locorum que habet hic Serenis-simus rex ad confinia francie. Ita pro nunc decretum est. Cetera autem secundum quod in dies opus esse videbitur disponentur atque ordinebuntur. Dominus Sanctitatem V. ecclesie sue conservet incolumem.

"Londinum die XXVIII Januarii MCCCCLXXXIX.

humillima et dec^{ma} creatura

Jo. D   s Collector in Anglia."

"Extra.

"S^{mo} Domino Nostro Papae."

5. Giovanni di Giglis to Innocent, Jan. 28, 1488; Precum Liber, written by Father John, in the possession of E. H. Lawrence, Esq. of Abbey Farm Lodge; *Historical Me-morials of Westminster Abbey*, by A. P. Stanley (London, 1868), 162; *Annals of Windsor*, by R. R. Tighe and J. E. Davis (London, 1857), I. 422; *Fasti Ecclesiæ Anglicanæ* (Oxf. 1854), III. 372; Harl. MSS. 366; Patent Rolls, April 23, 1487.

6. Henry to Innocent, July 16, 1488; Henry to Julius the Second, May 20, 1507; Fernando and Isabel to Puebla, July 20, 1496; Giovanni di Giglis to Innocent, Dec. 6, 1485, Aug. 17, 1487; Londoño and Matienzo to Fernando and Isabel, July 18, 1498.

CHAP. IV.—1. Royal MSS. XVI.; *Privy Purse Expenses of Elizabeth of York*, Pref. XXXI.; André, *Vit. Hen. Sept.* 37-42; Hall, *The Polity Governance, of Henry the Seventh*, fol. I.
2. *Patent Rolls*, Mar. 5, 1486; *Fœdera*, XII. 329; *Lelandi Collectanea*, IV. 249.
3. *A Collection of all the Wills now known to be extant of the Kings and Queens of England*, by J. Nichols (London, 1780), 356-403; *Lives of the Princesses of England*, by Mary Ann Everett Green (London, 1849), III. 395-436, IV. 1-47; Gairdner, *Letters and Papers*, I. XXIII.; Fisher, *Funeral Sermon on Lady Margaret*, 109; Anstey, *Munimenta Academica Oxon.* I. 364; Fuller, *History of the University of Cambridge*, 90.
4. *The Antiquarian Repertory*, chiefly compiled by Francis Grose (London, 1807), I. 353; *Patent Rolls*, June 12, 1488.
5. Fabyan, *Chronicle*, 683; *Priv. Pur. Exp. Eliz. York*, LXI.; *Lelandi Collectanea*, IV. 207; Hall, *Henry the Seventh*, fol. V.
6. Prologue to Caxton's edition of *La Mort d'Arthur*, 1485; *King Arthur*, edited for the Ballad Society by J. F. Furnival, Pref. V.; *The most Ancient and famous History of the renowned Prince Arthur, King of Britain*, 1634; *The Scholemaster*, by Roger Ascham (London, 1570), 81; Pearson, *Early and Middle Ages of England*, 58.

CHAP. V.—1. Henry to Innocent, July 21, 1490; Tighe, *Annals of Windsor*, I. 408; Stanley, *Mem. of Westminster*, 161-4; Butler, *Lives of Saints*, II. 1126.
2. Henry's Instructions to his Ambassador in Rome, Feb. 18, 1504; *Historical Memoirs of English, Irish, and Scotch Catholics*, by Charles Butler, I. 45-51.
3. *Rotulorum Parliamentorum*, VI. 268-70; *Statutes of the Realm* (1816), II, 299.

4. Anderson, *Royal Genealogies*, 738; André, *Vit. Hen. Sept.* 9; *Statutes at Large*, 11, 299.

5. Giglis to Innocent, Oct. 5, 1488; Henry to Innocent, Nov. 10, 1488; *Fast. Eccl. Angl.* I. 270, 340, 567, 632, II. 40, 51, 61, 236, III. 26, 468; Campbell, *Lives of the Lord Chancellors*, I. 355-62; Cassan, *Lives of the Bishops of Winchester*, 324-51.

6. Cott. MSS. fol. II. cited by Collier, *Ecclesiastical History of Great Britain*. III. 400; *Revised Statutes* (London, 1870), 112, 116, 191, 271; Burnett, *History of the Reformation*, ed. Pocock (Oxford, 1865), I. 61-2; Coke, *Institutes*, part II. c. V. 39; *The History of Church Laws in England from 602 to 1850*, by Edward Muscutt (London, 1851), 28-32; *The Ecclesiastical Law*, by Richard Burn, ed. by Robert Phillimore (London, 1842), II. 32, 34.

7. *Statutes*, I. Hen. 7. c. 2.

CHAP. VI.—1. Puebla to Fernando and Isabel, July 15, 1488.

2. The Spanish Merchants to Londoño, July 18, 1498.

3. *Fast. Eccl. Angl.* II. 378, III. 373; *Vita Hen. Sept.* 33; Edward the Fourth to Pope Sixtus, Feb. 25, 1476; Willis, *Hist. Parl. Mit. Abb.* I. 132.

4. Henry to Cadagua, Nov. 14, 1485; the same to Dolaiciola, Jan. 20, 1486; the same to Pardo, Mar. 8, 1486; the same to Puddessey, Mar. 10, 1487; Commission to John Weston and others, March 10, 1488.

5. Commission to Puebla, April 30, 1488; Commission to Puebla and Sepulveda, April 30, 1488.

CHAP. VII.—1. Puebla to Fernando and Isabel, July 15; Breton to Sancho de Londoño, July 18, 1498.

2. Henry to Scover, July 25; Sub-Prior of Santa Cruz to Fernando and Isabel, July 18, 1498.

3. Henry to Fernando and Isabel, July 2, 1488.

4. *The Repressor of over-much Blaming of the Clergy*, by Reginald Pecock, edited by C. Babington (London, 1860), 6, 54, 86, 102, 176, 275, 452, 477, 561; Shakespeare, *Second Part of Henry VI*. act. IV. s. 7; Henry to Fernando and Isabel, July 2, 1488.

5. *Histoire de Bruges*, (Bruges, 1850), 150-166; Grün, *Der letzte Ritter*, 79-98; *Geschichte der Hofnarren*, von Karl F. Flögel (Leipzig, 1789), 190; Doran, *History of Court Fools*, 326-7; Menzel, *Geschichte der Deutschen*, c. 189.

6. Commission to Fox and Daubeney, July 6, 1488; *Fast. Eccl. Angl.* I. 376; *Historic Peerage*, 145; Jerdan, *Rutland Papers*, 8.

7. Puebla's Memorandum, July 5, 1488.

CHAP. VIII.—1. Bergenroth, *Cal. Span. Pap.* I. 22.
2. Puebla to Fernando and Isabel, July 15, 1488.
3. Fernando and Isabel to Puebla, Berg. Cal. I. art. 22.
4. Puebla's Memorandum, July 6, 1488.
5. Puebla to Fernando and Isabel, July 15, 1488.

CHAP. IX.—1. Indenture between Puebla and Sepulveda, ambassadors of Fernando and Isabel on one part, and Richard, Bishop of Exeter, and Giles Daubeney of Daubeney, Commissioners of Henry the Seventh on the other part, July 7, 1488.
2. *Robertus Blondelli de Reductione Normanniæ*, edited by the Rev. Joseph Stevenson (London, 1863); Martin, *Histoire de France*, VII. 398-497, VIII. 1-237; Ballaguer, *Historia de Cataluña*, lib. VIII. c. 22, 26.
3. Puebla to Fernando and Isabel, July 15, 1488; Indenture, July 7, 1488.
4. Memorandum drawn up by Puebla and Fox, July 6, 1488; Indenture of Articles, July 7, 1488.
5. Bergenroth, *Cal. Span. Papers*, I. art. 22; Puebla to Fernando and Isabel, Oct. 11, 1488.
6. Bergenroth, *Cal. Span. Pap.* I. 22.
7. Puebla to Fernando and Isabel, Oct. 30, Dec. 11, 1488.

FOURTH BOOK.

CHAP. I.—1. Henry to Fernando and Isabel, July 5, 1488; *Patent Rolls*, April 8, 17, May 16, 25, Aug. 5, 1488; *Documents Originaux de l'Histoire de France*, 292.

2. Commission to Thomas Savage and Richard Nanfan, Dec. 11, 1488.

3. *Histoire Ecclésiastique et Civile de Bretagne*, par Dom. P. H. Morice, continuée par Dom. Ch. Taillandier (Guincamp, 1835), X. 102; *Annales Bretons*, Morice, Ap. XIV. 421.

4. *Documents Originaux de l'Histoire de France*, 296; Morice, *Hist. de Bret.* X. 103-7.

5. Florez to Innocent, May 16, 1488; *Histoire de Bretagne*, par Dom. Gui. Alexis Lobineau (Paris, 1707), I. 757, 783; Hall, *Henry the Seventh*, fol. XII., XIII.

6. *Storia d'Italia*, di Francesco Guicciardini (Milano, 1851), lib. II. c. 3; *Les Mémoires de Messire Phillipe de Commines* (Lyons, 1559), lib. VII; *Documents Originaux de l'Histoire de France*, 294-5.

7. Bacon, *Hist. Hen. Sev. Works*, VI. 69-70.

8. Lobineau, *Histoire de Bretagne*, I. 783; *Fœdera*, July 14, 1488; Morice, *Hist. Eccl. et Civ. de Bretagne*, X. 107-10.

CHAP. II.—1. Commissions to Savage and others, Dec. 11, 1488; *Journal de Ruy Machado*, printed in *Mem. Hen. Sev.* 157.

2. Carvajal, *Documentos ineditos*, XVIII. 274; *Journal de Machado*, 158-62.

3. My Note-book; *Journal de Machado*, 162-7; Gayangos, *Moh. Dyn. Sp.* II. 381-2.

4. *Journal de Machado*, 167; *Manual de Valladolid*, 41.

5. My Note-book; *Journal de Machado*, 169; Butler, *Lives of Saints*, II. 1121.

6. My Note-book; Madoz, *Dicc. Esp.* XI. 339; Ford, *Hand-book*, 563; Llorente, *Inquisicion*, c. V.

CHAP. III.—1. *Journal de Machado*, 170.

2. *Journal de Machado*, 170-1.

3. *Journal de Machado*, 173-4; Clemencin, *Elogio*, VI. II. 14; Fray Andreas to Archduchess Juana, Sep. 1. 1498.

4. *Journal de Machado*, 172-181.

5. Fernando and Isabel to Puebla, Dec. 17, 1488, Feb. 15, 1489; Puebla to Fernando, Oct. 11, Dec. 11, 21, 1488.

6. Treaty between England and Spain, March 27, 1489; Treaty of Peace, Sept. 20, 1490.

7. Zurita, *Anales*, IV. lib. 19, c. 12; Treaty, March 27, 1489.

CHAP. IV.—1. Morice, *Histoire Ecclésiastique et Civile de Bretagne*, X. 181; *Annales Bretons*, App. Morice, XIV. 424; Daru, *Histoire de Bretagne*, III. 135-144.
2. Giovanni de Giglis to Innocent, Jan. 28, 1489; *Fœdera*, Dec. 11, 1488; *Paston Letters*, Feb. 10, 1489.
3. Puebla to Fernando and Isabel, Dec. 21, 1488; *Statutes of the Realm*, II. 528.
4. Persio Malvezzi to Innocent, March 19, 1489; *Paston Letters*, V. 370; Flores to Innocent, Feb. 18, 1490.
5. Giglis to Innocent, June 28, 1489; Malvezzi to Innocent, March 19, 1489; Chieregato to Innocent, April 1, 1489; Sismondi, *Histoire de France*, XV. 99.
6. Morice, *Hist. Eccl. et Civ. de Bretagne*, X. 23. 26; *Histoire de la Réunion de la Bretagne*, par l'Abbé Irail (Paris, 1764), 66-7. In "Epîtres des Dames Illustres, traduits es Se Ovide, par le Rev. Père en Dieu Monseigneur l'Evesque d'Angoulême," a volume written and illuminated for Anne of Bretagne, there are two portraits of Anne; one as Queen of Charles the Eighth, the other as Queen of Louis the Twelfth. This precious work of art belongs to E. H. Lawrence, Esq. of Abbey Farm Lodge.
7. Puebla to Fernando and Isabel, Oct. 11, 1488; Fernando and Isabel to Puebla, Feb. 15, 1489; Anderson, *Royal Genealogies*, 621; Negociations of the English Ambassadors with Maximilian, in *Letters and Papers of Richard the Third and Henry the Seventh*, I. 218.
8. Daru, *Histoire de Bretagne*, III. 134-140; *Documents Originaux de l'Histoire de France*, 313. Portraits of Max are not uncommon. The portrait in the Römer Saal at Frankfort has been reproduced by Delepierre in his *Marie de Bourgogne*, p. 3.

CHAP. V.—1. Delepierre, *Chronique de Maximilian*, liv. IV.; *Der Weise Künig eine erzehlung von de Thaten Kaisers Maximilian der ersten* (Wien 1775); *Held und Ritters Tewrdanks* (Nürnberg, 1517); Argentré, *Histoire de Bretagne*, XIII. 41.

2. Puebla to Fernando and Isabel, Oct. 11, Dec. 11, 1488.

3. Fernando and Isabel to Puebla, Dec. 17, 1488.

4. Henry to Innocent, Jan. 2, 1489; Bishop of Concordia to Innocent, April 1, 1489; Malvezzi to Innocent, Mar. 19, May 9, 1489; Flores to Innocent, Feb. 18, 1490; Sismondi, *Républiques Italiennes*, tome VI. c. 7.

5. Giglis to Innocent, Jan. 28, 1489; Malvezzi to Innocent, May 9, 1489.

6. Malvezzi to Innocent, Mar. 19, 1489; Hook, *Archbishops of Canterbury*, v. 477; Campbell, *Lives of Lord Chancellors*, I. 361.

7. Malvezzi to Innocent, Mar. 19, May 9, 1489. (Venetian Calendar, under date.) Malvezzi writes:—"Beatissime Pater, post beatorum pedum oscula: Per benche per un' altra communa cum el Collectore Vostra Santita possa intendere el caso novamente de qua advenuto, niente di mancho per non lasòare cosa cognosca esser mio debito nei daro per la presente particulare aviso; Quella per piu mie hara inteso el denaro imposto da questo S. Re per tucta Lingilterra per aiutar la Bertagnia: et essendo ali di passati un gran Signore de existimatione et auctorita apresso de questo Sigr. Re cavalcato per cogliere denari nel suo dominio che e ne le parte boreale al recontro de la Scotia, certi soi subditi et del principali non volevano se mettesse tal graveza et a loro inussitata per li tempi passati: Per questo el dicto Signore destignato, non potendoli havere per via alcuna ne le mano, comincio a minacciar de voler loro fare et dire et in breve spatio radunate octocento persone deliberò per forza haberli. Questi tali Rebelli inteso questo, considerando che se venevano in sua potesta sarebono privati de vita, se messero per desperati et radunorno fra parenti et amici persone circa cinquecento, li quali aspectando dicto Signore infra breve tempe forono alemani, et lo primo morto fu el Signore. Li altri soi, vedutolo morto se dettero a fugire et cussi fu facto poco sangue non andando la cosa piu innanti. Imo retirandose li rebelli ale loro case et dolendose dopo el facto: mandarono de li a dui dì al S. Re per misericordia promettendo far quanto sua Maestà

vorra: La qual cosa non obstante ha deliberato questo S.
Re sì per mantener justitia como per dare exemplo ali
altri punirli et tucta via fa metter in ordine gente assai
cum proposito de andar in persona, et martedi o mercordi
deve andare; Non so che se fara: molti dicono che questa
cosa hara presto fine per esser quelli talli rebelli senza
capo alcuno et de poco auctorità: multi anchora dubitano
che qualche gran Signore non ce tenga mano et che habia
ad esser pegio che altri non existima; la qual cosa presto
se vedera: et quando sia me sforzaro darne subito pieno
aviso a Vostra Santità. Essendosi questa nova intesa in
Londra et seguente dì Monsr. R^mo. Cantuariense venne
qui per andare dal S. Re quale é lontano XX. miglia:
Andai una cum el Collector avisitar sua Signoria Re-
verendissima et dixece quanto per la communa letera V.
Santità intendera al quale habiamo obedito: et andati al
S. Re quale ce ha dicto pur quanto habiamo scripto comuna-
mente et bisognace obtemperarly non possendo fare altro:
Quando V^a Santità voglia in questo facciamo niente quella,
se degni commettere ce sia avisata la sua voluntà: che da
quella non ce parteremo. Nove sonno scripte per la comuna letera, per tanto non terrà V^a Santità a tedio: solo
avisando che bono foria quella se degnasse commettere
dui brevi al Sig. Re et a Mons. Cantuariense: li quali
avendo pigliata admiratione che essendo facti novi Cardi-
nali non ce sia stato assumpto el dicto Mons. Cantuariense,
maxime havendone supplicata V. Santità più volte et
havutane quasi speranza bona, considero essendo io
nel facto foria bono per V^a Santità scrivarli accio per-
severino in la bona dispositione et devotione verso quella
per la quale hucusque hanno facto quanto li sia stato pos-
sibile. Pretera habiamo operta la capsa che la Maestà del
Sig. Re volse havere in la sua corte; in la quale habiamo
trovate libre XI. et soldi XI., che ce ha facto mancare
lanimo per esser stati li Cl. S. Re, la Regina, la matre del
Re et de la Regina, con Duchi Conti et Marchessi et altri
Signori et oratori che credevanno havere molto più.
Habiamo havute dispense fin a lodierno dì XXVII. de le
quale habiamo havute libre de questa moneta XXXVIII.
che tucte le habiamo remesse al bancho: et de mano in

mano se mandarano le letere del cambio secondo el
tempo. Speramo per l'advenir far meglio de queste dispense per che già più dì se saputo per tucto, et tanto più
faremo quando havessemo le facultà che per una comuna,
fo avisato. Le nove habiamo souno scripte per la comuna,
altro non occurre preter humiliter et prostrate reccom-
mandarme ali piedi de Vª Beatitudine, quam Deus populo
Christiano incolumem conservet.
        "Londoniis, Die nona Maij MCCCCLXXXVIII.
            "E. V. Stª.
                "Servulus deditissimus,
                        "PERSEUS MALVITIUS."

    CHAP. VI.—1. Henry to Lord Oxford, April 22, 1489.
    2. Lobineau, *Histoire de Bretagne*, X. 181; *Annales
Bretons*, XIV. 425-7.
    3. Hall, *Henry the Seventh*, f. XVIII; Cotton MSS. Jul.
XI. 55.
    4. Treaty of Charles King of France and Max King of
the Romans, Frankfurt, July 22, 1489.
    5. Treaty of Charles and Max, July 22, 1489; Martin,
Histoire de France, VIII. 249.
    6. Fernando and Isabel to the Bishop of Badajos, their
Ambassador in Rome, May 6, 1490; Isabel to Puebla,
May 26, 1491; Flores to Innocent, July 28, Aug. 9, 12, 25,
Sept. 8, 1490; *Opus Epist. Pet. Mart.* lib. V. Ep. 120.

    CHAP. VII.—1. Fernando and Isabel to the Bishop of
Badajos, May 6, 1490.
    2. Henry's proposed additional clauses to the treaty
with Fernando and Isabel, September 20, 1490; Puebla to
Fernando, Aug. 25, 1498.
    3. Fernando and Isabel to Guevara and Puebla, Ber-
genroth's *Cal. Span. Pap.* I. 41.
    4. Fernando and Isabel to Rojas, July 4, 1490.
    5. Mosquera to Henry, Bergenroth, *Cal. Sp. Pap.* I. 57,
58; Morice, *Annales Bretons*, XIV. 427.
    6. Flores to Innocent, Feb. 18, 1490; Adriano Castello
to Innocent, Dec. 5, 1490; Henry to Innocent, April 21,
1491; *Patent Rolls*, Sept. 6, Nov. 17, 1490, June 29, 1492;

Fast. Eccl. Angl. I. 143, 466, II. 383; Pecock, *Repressor of over-much Blaming of the Clergy*, XXIV.; Lewis, *Life of Pecock*, 63-150.

7. Isabel to Puebla, May 26, 1491; Morice, *Annales Bretons*, XIV. 428; Lobineau, *Histoire de Bretagne*, I. 816-7, II. 1536-9.

CHAP. VIII.—1. Flores to Innocent, Sept. 8, 1490; Morice, *Annales Bretons*, XIV. 428.

2. Daru, *Histoire de Bretagne*, III. 175; Morice, *Annales Bretons*, XIV. 429-430.

3. *Le Trésor des Chartes*, par M. A. Teulet, Aug. 19, 1498.

4. Henry to Innocent, Dec. 8, 1491. Henry writes:—
"Beatissime pater, post humillimam commendacionem et devotissima pedum oscula beatissimorum. Cum superioribus annis galli primum in Ducatum Brittanie arma movissent: et bello gravi, ac forti manu premerent, ut ducatum ipsum sibi subderent; nos pro illo federe atque amicitia, quam cum ipso ducatu habebamus, oratores nostros ad ipsos gallos misimus, eis declarantes nos cum domina ducissa ac ducatu, Item et cum domino duce dum in humanis ageret suis se et esse confederatos, et ad eorum depensionem obstrictos: nec posse illi ducatui aliquam injuriam inferri quin esset nobiscum communis: atque idcirco eos rogatos fecimus: ut ab ipso bello vellent desistere: et omnem armorum vim ac copias militum revocare, si jus aliquod pretenderent, vel justam aliquam causam aliquod vendicandi haberent: non vi aut armis, sed jure et amicabili compositione rem suam vellent tractare: hi autem oratoribus nostris responderunt se se esse contentos, ut cause omnes quas haberent contra ipsam dominam ducissam ac ducatum compromiserentur, amicabiliterque tractarentur: pacemque tam cum ipsa domina ducissa quam nobiscum se esse composituros. Moxque ipsi galli superinde oratores suos ad nos misere, ut de pace inter nos et illos ac ducatum Britannie pariter fienda tractaretur. Post multa nos pacis amplectende cupidi; atque etiam prius nobiscum statuentes jus nostrum hoc prescriptum tempore negligere; et aliquod potius incom-

modum ac detrimentum pati et subire quam inimicias
cum illis fovere, tandem in quedam pacis capitula cum
ipsis gallis oratoribus convenimus: pro quorum quidem
capitulorum confirmatione, cum oratores nostros in gallia
misissemus: nil eorum que fuerant conventa nobiscum
approbare galli voluerunt: quin immo cum ipsi nova
quedam pacis capitula formassent, et oratores nostri ea
nostro nomine acceptare vellent, revocarunt illico quecumque ab eis fuerant oblata: quoniam nonnullis Brittanie proceribus illius ducatus regimen tenentibus, corruptis
et circumventis, non dubitabant sibi omnia pro voto suc-
cessura.   Sicuti dominus Episcopus Concordie vestre
Sanctitatis legatus si vera voluerit referre plane potuit
vestre Sanctitati affirmare: et ut paucis concludamus,
nobis pacem componere volentibus, nunquam nisi nostro
cum dedecore ad eam componendam voluerunt inclinare:
sed tandiu de pace nobis verba dedere et spem pacis
proposuere ut aliud animo volventes, continuato forti et
gravi bello, paulatim sibi universum illum ducatum usur-
parint et in potestatem suam redegerent: nec eo quidem
sint contenti: sed etiam tum nobis, tum vicinis et confederatis nostris reliquis, quecumque pernitiosa macchi-
nentur, et in dies magis ac magis interminentur. Et ne
omnia silentio pretereamus, scotos in primis suis literis
et nunciis sollicitarunt atque assidue sollicitant, ut contra
nos bellum moveant, et regnum nostrum invadant, pecu-
niasque et arma ac commeatus ad eos proinde misere:
Preterea et domicellos quosdam in dominio nostro hiber-
nie, nonnullosque hoc in regno nostro, multis pollicitatio-
nibus ad rebellionem contra nos sunt adhortati: ad hec
et nonnullos regni nostri fines hostiliter invasere, et pre-
dis atque incendiis sunt crassati. Quomodo autem in
flandria egerint, qua arte gandavum oppidum ab obbe-
dientia serenissimi Romanorum regis nostri confederati
retraxerint: Sclusasque occuparint: et alia item oppida
quam plurima in dies sollicitent, ut a serenissimo romanorum rege et ejus filio domino duce Burgundie herede
futuro, nostris confederatis deficiant, nemo est qui non
intelligat. Cum igitur que pacis sint omnia tentaverimus
et nil omnino quod justum honestumve esset assequi po-

tuerimus: nihil aliud pater sancte est nobis reliquum, nisi ut has tot injurias que nobis et amicis nostris quotidie inferruntur pro nostra et regni nostri dignitate repellamus et propulsemus bellumque in eos necessario sumamus: quandoquidem pro parte nostra nihil omnino intentatum reliquimus, quo pacem et amicitiam retineremus, ac de nostro potius aliquid dimitteremus, quam pacem in bellum essemus commutaturi, utpote qui nil magis abhorreamus quam cedes hominum, et christiani sanguinis effusionem. Non ferenda est profecto, Beatissime pater, non est ferenda tanta et tam insaciabilis aliem imperii cupiditas. Satis autem intelligimus quanta pernicies immineat vicinis omnibus populis et gentibus si hec tanta propagandi sitis non compescatur. Quod si tam insolens licentia nullis frenis cohibita, pro voto huc et illuc serperet; nescimus an fortassis in aliquos etiam Italie potentatus excurreret, et vestre quoque Sanctitati, ac sedi Apostolice cum sua pragmatica sanctione, quam nos semper damnavimus, aliquid inferret turbinis et nocumenti. . . . .

"Ex regia nostra grenuici Die VIII. Decembris, MCCCCLXXXJ.

"E. V. S^{tis.}

"Devotissimus atque obsequentissimus filius Dei gra'. Rex Anglie et Franc: ac D͠us hyb'nie.

"HENRICUS R."

Sanctissimo clementissimoque Domino nostro Pape.

5. Articles respecting a war with France, Nov. 22, 1491; Henry to Sforza, Jan. 10, 1492; Ballaguer, *Historia di Cataluña*, lib. VIII. c. 30.

6. André, *Vit. Hen. Sept.* 58-64; Novaes, *Storia de' Sommi Pontefici da San Pietro*, VI. 79; Sismondi, *Républiques Italiennes*, VI. 253; Henry to Alexander the Sixth, Dec. 12, 1492. Henry writes:—"Beatissime pater post humilem commendacionem et devotissima pedum oscula beatorum etc. Cum antea sepe felicis quondam recondationis S^{mo.} Domino notro Vestre Sanctitatis predecessori litteris nostris intimassemus nos ob certas quasdam legittimas causas, quas tum demonstravimus, bellum in gallos esse sumpturos: atque re ipsa id egerimus: non alienum esse duximus, ut qualis fuerit exitus, vestre Sanctitati

significaremus: arbitrantes illam grato animo esse accepturam quicquid a nobis superinde actum sit, atque etiam consilia nostra non improbaturam. Cum enim supra duos anteactos menses cum exercitu nostro personaliter trajecissemus, et ad hoc nostrum oppidum Callesium applicuissemus: Moxque occupatis quibusdam finitimis oppidis boloniam obsideremus oppidum munitissimum preter omnem expectationem oblate est nobis a gallis certa quedam pax cum hujusmodi conditionibus, ut a nemine Christiano Catholicoque principe satis recusari posse videretur: quare ipsam pacem acceptavimus: tum ut aliis negotiis intenderemus, tum etiam ut Christiani sanguinis effusionem quam semper abhorruimus pro viribus effugeremus sicuti latius ex oratoribus nostris istic existentibus, quibus fidem superinde haberi volumus, vestra Sanctitas latius intelliget, que felicissime valeat ad vota.

"Ex Callesio oppido nostro Die XII. Decembris, 1492.

    "E. V. Sûs.

"Devotissimus et obsequentissimus filius Dei gra'. Rex Anglie et franc': ac d'ñs hyb'nie.

                                    HENRICUS R."

"Sanctissimo clementissimoque Domino nostro Pape."

6. Dumont, *Corps Diplomatique*, III. 297, 300. Ballaguer, *Historia de Cataluña*, lib. VIII. c. 30.

7. Sismondi, *Républiques Italiennes*, VI. 267-71; Guicciardini, *Storia d'Italia*, lib. i. c. 1.

FIFTH BOOK.

CHAP. I.—1. Carvajal, *Documentos ineditos*, XVIII. 280; Ballaguer, *Historia de Cataluña*, lib. VIII. c. 30; Bernaldez, *Reyes Catolicos*, c. 100.

2. Giovio, *Vita Magni Gonsalvi* (in "Vitæ Illustrium Virorum"), lib. I. 212; *The Life and Acts of Don Alonzo Enriquez de Gusman*. Translated from an original manuscript in the National Library at Madrid, by C. R. Markham (London, 1862), 9, 10, 12, 17.

3. Gamero, *Historia de Toledo*, 893-932; Gayangos,

Moh. Dyn. Sp. I. 116-118, 140, 143, 151; Ford, *Handbook of Spain*, I. 56, II. 722, 798; Stirling, *Annals of the Artists of Spain*, III. 84-6; *Notice sur les armes defensive, et spécialement sur celles qui ont usitée en Espagne*, par Achille Jubinal (Paris, 1840); Áltafaj, *Zaragoza*, 112. The best way to see the superiority of Moorish work is to compare the Moorish and Spanish sections of a great museum.

4. Jones, *Palace of the Alhambra*, various plates; *An Architect's Note-book on Spain*, by Sir Digby Wyatt (London, 1872); Wolf, *Primavera*, I, 234; *Chronica del Cid*, c. 19; Giovio, *Vita Magni Gonsalvi*, lib. I. 211.

5. *Die religiöse Poesie der Juden in Spanien*, von Michael Sachs (Berlin, 1845), 180-213; Los Rios, *Etudes sur les Juifs d'Espagne*, 319-416; Ginsburg, *Cyc. Bibl. Lit.* I. 28, III. 725; Kayserling, *Juden in Portugal*, 85-119.

6. Capitulacion con Moros y Caballeros de Castilla (Archiv. Gen. Siman.), Estado leg. 1º; Giovio, *Vita Magni Gonsalvi*, lib. I. 211; Mendoza, *Cronica del Gran Cardenal*, 238; Bernaldez, *Reyes Catolicos*, c. 102.

7. Hammer, *Histoire de l'Empire Ottoman*, lib. XX.; Sismondi, *Hist. Rép. Ital.* VI. c. 4, 6, 7; Mendoza, *Guerra de Granada*, 9.

8. Bull of Innocent VIII. April 20, 1487; Bulls of Alexander VI. Feb. 16, 1493, August 5, 1495; Fernando to Elizabeth, December 4, 1489; Alexander VI. to Puebla, April 10, 1490.

CHAP. II.—1. *Coleccion de los Viages y descrubrimientos que hicieron por Mar los Españoles desde Fines del Siglo XV.* (Madrid, 1825), I. Int. 60; Usque, *Tribulacoens de Ysrael*, 193; Castro, *Hist. Rel. Int.* 24; Mariana, *Historia generale de España*, II. 470, 516; Carvajal, *Documentos ineditos*, XVIII. 274-9.

2. My Note-book; *Plans, Elevations, Sections, and Details of the Palace of the Alhambra*, by Jules Goury and Owen Jones (London, 1842), I. 16; Gayangos, *Moh. Dyn. of Spain*, I. 43, 44; also Notes to ch. II. p. 351; Mendoza, *Cronica del Gran Cardenal*, 238; Zurita, *Anales*, IV. c. 90.

3. Capitulacion con Moros y Caballeros de Castilla, La Real Vega de Granada, Dec. 30, 1492; Kayserling, *Die*

Juden in Navarre, 227; Graetz, *Geschichte der Juden*, VIII. 355-63; Lindo, 227, 248.

4. Bernaldez, *Reyes Catolicos*, c. 110, 112; Giovio, *Vita Magni Gonsalvi*, lib. I. 212.

5. Graetz, *Gesch. Jud.* VIII. 335, 358; Lindo, 377-84; Ginsburg, "Abravanel," in Kitto's *Cyclopædia of Biblical Literature*, I. 28.   The articles on Spanish Jews, by Dr. Ginsburg, are of special value.

6. Yanguas y Miranda, *Diccionario de Navarra*, 227; Colmenares, *Historia de Segovia*, c. XXXV.; Los Rios, *Etudes sur les Juifs*, 157-172; Ginsburg, "Sacculo," in *Cyc. Bibl. Lit.* III. 725.

7. Usque, *Tribulacoens de Ysrael*, 194-5; Los Rios, *Etudes sur les Juifs*, 173-194; Bernaldez, *Reyes Catolicos*, c. 113, 114.

END OF VOL. I.